I Dream of Demigods

by

Alexa Sullivan

The Law of Love, Book One

I Dream of Demigods

Cover Art by *The Wild Rose Press, Inc.*

The Wild Rose Press, Inc.
PO Box 708
Adams Basin, NY 14410-0708
Visit us at www.thewildrosepress.com

Publishing History
First Edition, 2023
Trade Paperback ISBN 978-1-5092-4583-3
Digital ISBN 978-1-5092-4584-0

The Law of Love, Book One
Published in the United States of America

Alex held my gaze. His eyes were mesmerizing pools of warm brown. "Listening and caring is just being decent. It shouldn't be shocking." He lifted a hand and smoothed my hair back from my face.

This wasn't normal boss behavior, but at some point I had forgotten Alex was my supervisor. The air felt warm and damp, and it smelled like the ocean again, the scent wild and comforting at the same time.

Alex's hand stilled against my temple.

Hardly breathing, I lifted my left hand and brushed my fingers against his.

He squeezed my hand.

I reached for his other hand, and either I stepped close or he pulled me in. Or maybe it happened at the same time. We were toe-to-toe now, inches away from full-body contact. My brain hazed over as I tilted my head up.

He angled his head down.

Our noses touched. Our mouths were an inch away from each other.

"This is probably about to be a bad idea."

His voice, low and husky, sent a pleasant tingle down my neck. "Terrible," I whispered.

I dove into his arms, and he pressed his mouth to mine.

Dedication

To my husband, Brad, who stole my soul the day we met.

Chapter One

I kicked off my Friday by setting my pants on fire. Again.

Honestly, I don't know what I was thinking when I tried the spell. I'd just gotten to work, and instead of doing what I was paid to do—work—I stood at my window, staring down at the brick-and-steel towers of various offices stacked like dominoes along the tidy grid of east Portland's streets.

Warm September sun glinted off windows and shone across the small city park a block from the Ainsley Barfield office.

I stood there daydreaming for several minutes before stuffing my long, wavy, brown hair into a messy bun. Reluctantly, I sat and tugged at the fraying cuff of my thin cardigan before logging in.

My email was a mess, as usual—technical questions from paralegals and legal assistants; an all-caps email from a cantankerous partner written in the heat of the last full moon, so I was ignoring it; and a long-running email chain with Arjun, the Firm's in-house programmer, who implemented new case-management software features as quickly as I could suggest them. The subject lines clamored for attention as three fresh messages rolled in.

Maybe my lack of coffee led to my poor judgment. After all, I'd only had a few sips when I searched the website for the National Association of Witches, NAW for short, and located a basic email organization spell. That really was the title. *Basic Email Organization Spell.*

I opened the PDF, mouthed the words a few times, and frowned at the diagrams before moving my right hand across my computer screen three times.

As I uttered the last line of the spell, heat seared my right leg. I gasped and shoved my chair back. A neon-blue flame danced on my shin, licking at the black rayon fabric of my pants—the ones I'd bought on sale only yesterday.

I yanked open the bottom drawer of my desk. Grabbing my spray bottle of holy water, I squirted my leg three times.

With a small hiss and a puff of noxious smoke, the flame winked out.

Groaning, I tossed the bottle back into the drawer and grabbed a can of lavender air freshener. I misted the area around my leg, and the acrid, mossy smell dissipated. Whew. Magic gone wrong smelled worse than a skunk.

I leaned down to examine my leg, and I winced. Tender, bright-pink skin showed through the jagged hole in my pants. Another potential scar to add to my collection, and another pair of pants ruined, unless I could get Tabitha to fix them. I should've known better.

Why'd I even bother?

If I'd had a hard copy of the spell, I would've crumpled it up, thrown it in the trash, and chucked the trash can out the window. Sadly, I only had the PDF, which I closed with an emphatic click of my mouse. Not as satisfying as flying garbage.

I dropped the air freshener back into the drawer and kicked it closed. Slumping in my chair, I stared at my inbox.

Shit. The spell had ruined my pants *and* scrambled my messages. Everything consisted of symbols and upside-down text. Also, since when did email come with gifs of dancing headless turkeys on the toolbar?

The turkeys were doing the can-can. Huh.

Gritting my teeth, I rebooted my computer. While I waited, I checked email on my phone instead. In his last email, Arjun had asked when I could be ready with the updated user guide for OpenFang. He was ready to release the new version anytime. I started to write him back, but a notification popped up on my phone.

All-IT Department Meeting. New Director.

Starting right now.

I sprang out of my chair. Dashing out of my office, I prayed no one would notice my damaged pants, especially not my new boss.

I raced down the hall toward the Belmont Room and yanked open the door. Most of the IT department staff already sat around the long mahogany conference table.

Tabitha waved me over.

"Hi, Rowan," Dave said as I passed him.

The sound of his voice made my teeth shiver, like the feeling of nails on a chalkboard. Last year, for six delusional months, I found that voice sexy. I'd believed all his smooth compliments and reassurances, and when I couldn't get hold of him for three days straight, or he disappeared for a "weekend with friends," I told myself I was just being insecure and jealous.

Technically, I *was* being insecure and jealous, but he was also sleeping with a paralegal behind my back, so I wasn't wrong.

I nodded. As a help-desk tech, Dave often forwarded

case-software questions to me. We had to work together, so I continued to be polite. That's all he was getting from me, though.

"Haven't had your coffee yet, huh?" He grinned, his fangs gleaming.

Haven't been dumped by Natasha yet, huh? I wanted to snap back. I clamped my lips closed, resisted the urge to give him the finger, and sat by Tabitha. I dropped into the antique wooden armchair and eyed her coffee mug, which was full to the brim with frothy milk. "Did you make a new one?"

"Sweetie, your leg." She gasped. "What happened this time?"

"Nothing. It's not that bad." I showed her my calf.

She waved her hand over my leg three times, whispering something in Latin.

The burn disappeared, and the hole in my pants repaired itself.

"Thanks." My face burned. I checked to my left and right, but no one else seemed to have noticed Tabitha's swift repair job.

She'd cleaned up my messes a hundred times—bloody noses, ink spurting from my office printer, a broken toilet.

I was thirty-one, and I needed full-time magical protection…from myself.

"Here, have a taste." She slid her mug toward me. "It's a lavender chai. I've been working on the spell."

We had an ordinary coffee machine in the break room, but Tabitha did spells to make it churn out all kinds of gourmet beverages.

I took a sip, savoring the cinnamon and lavender on my tongue. "Ooh, that's good."

"I'll make you one after this meeting is over." She glanced at the grandfather clock in the corner. "He's late."

"Hopefully not draining anyone dry." I still couldn't believe Karl, our previous IT director, had been taking vendor meetings just so he could suck the sales agents' blood. I mean, right there in his office with the glass magically frosted and the room sound-spelled. After months of this, an associate caught him escorting a bleary-eyed twenty-something down the back stairs, saw the blood seeping through the guy's shirt collar, and reported it.

The partnership fired Karl on the spot, leaving us without a director. Desperate to fill the position, they'd quickly hired a new director sight unseen—at least, unseen to the IT staff.

I imagined they'd vetted the new guy carefully, but I didn't know a thing about him.

Alexander Kouris. I'd tried stalking him on a professional networking site, but he was a technological ghost.

I yawned. The blackout shades were drawn as a courtesy to the vampires on our team, and with the low light from the crystal chandelier overhead, it felt like evening. "Wake me up when he gets here." I pillowed my head on my arms and closed my eyes, letting the quiet chatter in the room blur into white noise.

Tabitha shook my shoulder a moment later.

I popped up just as the conference room door opened.

The conversation stilled as a tall man strode into the room, a laptop tucked under his arm. He was clean-shaven, with curly black hair, dark-brown eyes, and a chiseled jaw. His pale-blue shirt and dove-gray pants popped against his brown skin. That tailored shirt clung to his shoulders and chest, hinting at sculpted muscles.

His broad smile revealed straight white teeth.

No fangs. Probably not a vampire then. Anyway, he looked too healthy.

"Hi, folks. I'm Alex. Sorry to keep you waiting."

Everyone's posture improved at the same time.

I smoothed my hands over my bun, trying to shove the flyaways back.

Alex's gaze snapped to mine, and my breath caught in my throat.

The corners of his eyes crinkled up and his lips pursed in a fleeting smile.

All right, fine, he was gorgeous. I couldn't let that sway my opinion of him. He was still our new boss, and who knew what kind of organizational changes he had in mind? Last year, a new partner took over the Supernatural Tax Law group and fired all the associates. Anything could happen.

Please don't fire me.

Alex took the empty seat at the head of the table and popped open his laptop. "It's nice to see you all." He spoke in a smooth baritone. "I'm Alex Kouris, and I suppose you've guessed I'm your new IT director. I know you weren't involved in the interview process, but I want to assure you that I've been vetted by the partnership, and I didn't, in fact, just crawl out from under a rock."

I laughed.

No one else did.

Dave smirked.

I slid down in my seat. Maybe I could hide under the

table.

"At least someone likes my terrible jokes." Again, Alex fixed me with those huge dark eyes.

I felt as if he was smiling only at me.

His gaze swept across the room. "I've been in IT for fifteen years, most recently as the chief technology officer of a tech startup. But I'm really here to find out about you. Could you please introduce yourselves and tell me what your role is here? I have an org chart, but this will help." He nodded to Eva, the gray-and-white werewolf on his left.

"I'm Eva, our network operations manager." She smiled, revealing a mouth full of sharp teeth. She sat on her haunches in one of the specially adapted larger chairs that were kept in all conference rooms.

Nearly all our werewolf staff chose to shift into their true forms at the office.

Eva had told me once it was stressful enough looking human during her commute or a trip to the grocery store.

"I wouldn't be able to do it at work eight or nine hours a day," she'd said. "Being human is…itchy."

She put one paw on the conference table for emphasis. "Right now, I'm developing some speed spells to test on our network. The partners are asking for a faster connection, which I plan to deliver by the end of the month."

My heart sank. Were we all going to talk about how we used magic in our jobs?

Arjun introduced himself next, then Tabitha. Both described the different spells they used to improve our firm's technology.

Why yes, we *were* going to talk about how we used

magic in our jobs. Great. Alex was going to wonder how the hell I'd gotten hired.

Tabitha finished her spiel about the word-processing training program she was developing for the paralegals, and everyone stared at me.

I spotted a huge hangnail on my left thumb and made a fist to hide it. "Uh, I'm Rowan. I'm the technical writer, so I do all the documentation for our in-house case-management software, plus I write user guides for basic tools like email and spreadsheets. Not super exciting, I know."

"You're selling yourself short." Tabitha placed a light hand on my shoulder and smiled at the group. "Her user guides are the best. I use them in my training classes all the time."

Alex nodded. "That's wonderful. And how do you use magic in your job, Rowan?"

Well, it was nice working here for the last few years. Bye, Tabitha's magical lattes. "I don't."

His smile wavered. "Not at all?"

"Rowan and magic go together like oil and water." Dave smirked. "You should ask her what happened to the coffee machine last year."

A couple of people snickered.

I gritted my teeth.

"*Dave.*" Tabitha's voice was taut as a wire.

"I'll look forward to getting to know you better, Rowan, and I'm really glad you're on the team." Alex frowned at Dave before turning to the next person.

Well, that was fun. At least Alex had shut down the jokes, but still. Too bad my legs weren't long enough to reach under the table and kick Dave in the shins.

When the introductions were finished, Alex folded

his hands and leaned forward. "Team building and employee morale are important to me. I hope you'll all join me later today in the Everett Room for happy hour from four to seven. I'd love to get to know each of you better. For those who can't make it, you're welcome to end your workday at four. Thanks, everyone."

Wow. Starting off right by offering free food, free booze, and a free hour off work. Not bad. I eyed the slope of Alex's broad shoulders. Maybe I'd actually show up to a work event.

Everyone burst into conversation as the meeting broke up.

Dave sauntered right over to talk to Alex.

Of course. Probably planned to blab about some programming topic to impress the new boss with his massive technical acumen.

"What do you think?" said Tabitha. "You want to hit up the happy hour for a bit tonight? Then do the usual?"

For our standing Friday night date, we theoretically practiced spell casting, but I was so terrible we usually ended up drinking wine and watching *Secrets of the Unseelie.*

"Do we have to? Forced group interaction makes me want to take a nap." I glanced at Alex again.

He nodded at Dave with a polite smile. The smile produced a dimple.

Hmm. On the other hand…

"Yes, but he's our new boss. We should probably make an appearance. Plus"—she leaned close and whispered—"he's cute."

"And?" I lifted one eyebrow.

"Just for an hour?" She widened her eyes and placed a hand on my arm. "I promise we'll get you home in time for plenty of *Unseelie*."

"I guess we could go for a bit." On the one hand, there would be awkward small talk with other co-workers, and I'd probably stuff my face with too many snacks. On the other hand, there would be curly-haired, dimple-faced Alex. "Why not?"

"Yay! Ready for that latte?"

"Definitely." As I followed Tabitha to the door, I peeked at Alex again.

He caught my eye and nodded.

Before I could stop myself, I waved. *Waved,* like I was a kid getting on the school bus. As soon as I realized what I'd done, I balled my hand into a fist at my side. My cheeks burned. Could I be more awkward? I didn't even know how to flirt anymore.

I mean, not that my new boss was flirting with me. It was a nod, not a blown kiss.

I followed Tabitha into the hallway, allowing the air conditioning to cool my flushed face and racing heart.

Chapter Two

At four p.m. that day, Tabitha and I headed up to the thirteenth floor. This was the showstopper floor—designed to impress clients—featuring full-length windows, a marble-topped reception desk, and an airy reception area with white brocade couches. The conference rooms boasted crystal chandeliers, Victorian furniture, and original art pieces, some of which had once been part of the oldest vampires' personal collections.

Tabitha and I strolled into the Everett Room and looked around.

So far, only Arjun and Dave had arrived. They stood together at a small round banquet table, deep in conversation. Dave fancied himself an expert on everything.

I rolled my eyes at Tabitha, and she steered me toward the spread on the other side of the room.

The linen-covered tables held several cheese platters, oysters and shrimp on ice, veggie and fruit trays, and a three-tier tower of cupcakes.

My mouth watered. Nice. Alex was winning points already with his catering choices.

At the end of one table sat an assortment of sodas, beer, and wine, along with three discreet black bottles with no labels. The Firm kept blood in stock for the vampires—donated, as far as I knew, from a local blood bank. All very hush-hush.

That's what made Karl's actions even more egregious. Hunting victims was out of style, at least in the corporate world.

I was used to the blood being present by now, although I tried not to look too hard at the bottles.

Tabitha and I swiped glasses of wine and loaded up small plates, then staked out a banquet table on the opposite side of the room from Arjun and Dave.

I gazed wistfully at the blackout curtains. When they were drawn, the room opened out onto a terrace overlooking east Portland. Couldn't have all the vampires on our staff getting sun poisoning at happy hour, though.

I piled a generous wedge of brie onto a cracker. "Where is everyone? I feel like we're at a wedding reception and the bride and groom are still taking pictures."

Tabitha laughed. "I'm sure everyone'll be up soon." She leaned toward me. "You know, I didn't see Alex wearing a wedding ring."

"Your point?" My words came out slightly garbled around the food.

"I mean, he's extremely attractive." One eyebrow flicked up as she picked up her wineglass.

I sighed. Obviously, I'd noticed Alex's appearance, but that didn't mean he'd noticed *me.* He also might not be into women. Maybe he had a boyfriend. Lucky man, if so. In any event, the Firm probably disapproved of bosses dating subordinates.

"It's just been a while since you've dated anyone. Several months."

"I know how long it's been." I swigged my wine.

The Willamette Valley boasted numerous wineries, and we always got the top-tier stuff at events.

I should delicately sip this sauvignon blanc, which was doubtless aged in a stainless-steel barrel and contained notes of fancy things like pears and cherries, but I was dealing with notes of stress and anxiety, so I swigged. "It worked out so well last time for me, too."

"Just because one person—"

I stared her down over the top of my glass. "I'm happy being single, Tabs. Give up the fight."

She frowned and stuffed a shrimp into her mouth.

I was letting her down, but she didn't get it. She had Paul, the kindest, sweetest man I'd ever met, who worshiped her and would do anything to make her happy, and—I knew because he'd taken me ring shopping—who planned to propose this November on her birthday.

Tabitha thought everyone just needed to find their Paul. She didn't realize Pauls were in short supply.

Most guys out there were Daves.

"Hi, ladies."

Speak of the devil. Dave sauntered toward us, goblet in hand. He'd been turned in the early nineties, at age twenty-five, and he kept his hair in the once-popular style of shaved underneath, long and floppy on the top. He even wore a striped collared shirt and baggy pants, like he was a nineties actor in some cheesy teen romantic comedy. It was all a bit much, but then Dave himself was a bit much.

"Goddess save us." Now Tabitha was the one chugging wine.

"What do you ladies think of our new fearless leader?" Dave leaned his elbows on our table. He met my gaze, his lips pursed.

Ah, what he really wanted to know was if I thought Alex was hot. I shrugged and dunked a shrimp into a ramekin of cocktail sauce. "Seems like a decent guy." Where was our new boss, anyway? It was almost four-fifteen.

"Didn't see a wedding ring." Dave's lips curled back to reveal his fangs, the hint of a rictus grin. He nudged me. "Huh? Huh?"

"Lovely," I muttered. Was *everyone* scrutinizing Alex's hand to determine if he might be available to wed me? "He's not a box of cereal, you know. I can't just pick him off the shelf and take him home."

Dave held up a finger as if to lecture me. "There's a dirty joke in there, because you said 'box,' but I strictly adhere to the Firm's anti-sexual-harassment policy and would never make such a joke."

I gritted my teeth.

"Funny." Tabitha glared. She'd never liked Dave, not even when I thought I was in love with him.

His eyes widened. "Hey, I didn't say a thing."

Tabitha's cheeks bloomed pink, and she flexed her right shoulder, winding up to do a spell.

I put a hand on her arm.

"Hey, folks!" Alex ambled in, trailed by a few other IT staff. A few curls of thick black hair brushed across his temple. He'd lost the suit jacket and the tie and rolled his sleeves up to reveal muscled forearms. The tattooed outline of a vine peeked out of the left sleeve, trailing down the inside of his forearm.

Yep. Still hot.

I hid a grin at the tattoo. The older, vampire partners wouldn't like that. So, Alex had a rebellious side. What other surprises hid beneath that calm, professional exterior?

Wouldn't I like to know...

Alex poured himself a glass of wine and strode over to our table. His wide, bright smile radiated like an Arizona sun. "How's everyone doing? Hope you're enjoying the food."

"It's great. Much better than a box of cereal." Dave's lips twitched.

The pink on Tabitha's cheeks deepened to red.

I tipped back my glass to get the last few drops of fancy sauvignon. The worst thing about Dave wasn't his terrible sense of humor, but that he found himself so clever. I'd admired his confidence when we first started dating, but later I'd realized it was just raw ego.

It was enough to make a girl want to dump cocktail sauce on his head.

"Do you mind if I take a picture of the three of you?" said Alex. "Carina asked me to get a few shots for the intranet."

"Of course." Tabitha set down her glass and threw her arm over my shoulder. "Hmm, no, you know what? Ro, you should be in the middle. Switch with me."

Squished next to Dave?

She gave me a strained smile, hinting that I should go with the flow.

I stepped between them, and Dave slid his arm around my shoulders. Oh, good, my nose was now at his armpit level. And the man needed a refresh on his old deodorant.

Alex patted his pocket a few times. "I guess I left my phone in my office. Sorry, folks. Just a minute. Uh, you don't have to hold the pose."

I wriggled away from Dave and picked up my

wineglass. I checked the grandfather clock in the corner and leaned toward Tabitha. "Forty minutes." And if Dave didn't mosey away now-ish, I'd leave in forty *seconds*. Alex's dimples be damned.

Tabitha tucked her left hand behind her back and mouthed something.

Uh-oh. What was she up to? Normally I'd be all for her doing a spell on Dave, but a workplace happy hour with our new boss might not be the time.

Alex stopped at the door and turned around, laughing. "Okay, new-person problems, I guess. I left my badge in my office, too. Can one of you let me onto our floor?" He ran a hand through his hair. Unlike Dave's gelled and sprayed mass of hair, Alex's hair looked sleek.

"I can—" began Dave.

"Ro has hers." Tabitha pointed to the lanyard around my neck.

As I followed Alex to the door, I glanced back at Tabitha.

She gave me a thumbs-up.

Sneaky. She must have nudged me into a different photo configuration to buy herself time to do a spell, relocating Alex's phone. Then she magically hid his badge, allowing me to escort him to his office. *Subtle, Tabs.*

Alex and I headed toward the elevators, and as we waited for one to arrive, I searched for something to say. "How are you liking it here so far?" Not brilliant, but it would get him talking, and then I wouldn't have to talk as much.

"So far, so good." He broke into another sparkling-white smile. "Everyone's been so welcoming."

Oh, I'd like to welcome him…to my bed. I clenched my jaw at the naughty thought. Again—boss, subordinate. Not a good combination. Seemingly good man, Rowan. Also not a good combination.

The elevator nearest us dinged, and the doors slid open.

Alex gestured for me to go first.

As the doors closed behind us, I caught a whiff of the ocean. Not the fake, sickly-sweet "water" scent you get with candles sometimes, but the real thing—fresh, crisp, briny. Was that his cologne? What kind could possibly smell that much like the Oregon coast? I inhaled again and considered asking him so I could buy a bottle and spray it all over my house.

Alex tipped his head at me. "You okay?"

"Great." I glanced down and pretended to brush dust off my pants. *I was just inhaling you, like a normal person.*

We got off the elevator, and I badged us in through the double doors.

Our floor had emptied out for the happy hour, and the air conditioning hummed loudly.

As I followed Alex to his office, he told me about the partner meetings he'd spent all day attending, and how his emails were piling up.

"The partners seem to have a lot of ideas," he said wryly. "Everything from improvements to the timekeeping system, to a better online research database. I think we're going to keep you very busy on the documentation side."

"Fine by me. It's job security."

Reaching his office first, Alex held the door for me. I breezed in and looked around while he rummaged through his desk. He had one of the large corner offices, with modern glass interior walls, along with the requisite blackout shades on the exterior windows in case you had to meet with a vampire.

I wandered to the window, raised the shades, and took in the view of the Willamette River.

The evening sun bounced off the water, turning it a shimmering glass-like gray. Several bridges crisscrossed it, connecting the east and west sides of Portland.

I loved how different they all were, the dramatic white towers and cables of the Salmon Crossing bridge contrasting with the steel trusses of the Larkspur.

"Beautiful view."

I jumped at his sudden closeness. Not a vampire, but whatever magic he possessed, he could sneak. When I turned toward him, I caught another hint of the ocean. What was he wearing?

He smiled and nodded toward the view. "Did you grow up here?"

A beam of early-evening sun shifted, casting a golden haze over the city below.

I watched the light play over the buildings. "Born and raised. You?"

"I grew up in Seattle, but I moved to California for college. Don't hate me too much." He winked. "Then I spent a little time traveling before I went to work."

"Where did you travel?" I wanted so badly to be one of those people who had backpacked through Europe or spent months working at a winery in Australia, but I'd never had the money. I was building up my savings, though, and someday I'd be one of those people.

I'd travel alone, obviously, since I was never going to meet anyone.

"All over the country. I love national parks. I've visited every one of them several times over." Alex's expression changed, and his mouth formed a flat line. "Hey, listen, Rowan, I wanted to talk to you about something."

My stomach clenched. Was he going to fire me already?

"I didn't think it was appropriate for Dave to make a joke about your magical abilities in today's meeting. I've already spoken to him, but I want to know if you're being harassed on a regular basis. By Dave or anyone else."

I let out a breath and my shoulders relaxed. "Oh, that. I'm kind of the running joke around here. A witch who can't do magic."

"Of course you can do magic."

"I don't think you understand." I snorted. "Every time I try, it backfires. I knock things over. Break windows. Once I blew up my toilet. This morning, I burned a hole in my pants and Tabitha had to fix it. I'm a walking disaster when it comes to spell casting."

His eyes widened.

I was secretly pleased he didn't know what to say.

He recovered nicely, nodding as if he'd figured it all out. "Maybe you just haven't worked with the right teachers."

"Trust me. I've had all the magical training you can get. Everyone says the same thing. My powers are there, but blocked, so they go haywire." I cleared my throat. My boss didn't need to hear my childhood sob story. "It's not a big deal, not anymore. People joke about it, but as long as they aren't filming me and uploading my failures to the internet, it's fine."

He leaned back, perching against the edge of his desk.

His bronze skin was smooth, his face almost pore-less. And those long eyelashes. It wasn't fair for a boss to be this handsome.

I shifted, hating the way my damp shirt clung to my underarms. Oh, gods, what if he noticed me pitting out? I clamped my arms to my sides, hoping to cover any stains. At least my short-sleeved blouse was dark blue.

Kindness warmed his eyes. "When did you first realize you were a witch, if I can ask?"

"When I was ten. I made my pet hamster levitate. He was very surprised." Poor Roger. Almost gave him a hamster heart attack.

Alex laughed. "I'll bet. So, you *used* to be able to do magic without issue?"

"Yeah. It's a long story." I cleared my throat.

"I don't mind long stories."

I played with a small piece of hair that had loosened from my bun. Should I tell Alex the truth? It certainly wouldn't be professional, but his empathetic and open expression drew me in, made me *want* to talk to him. I couldn't keep him longer, though, without being rude. I checked the wall clock. "I should let you get back to the happy-hour thing."

"You don't have to tell me. Only if you want to. And the happy hour will survive without me. Actually, I don't like crowds." He grimaced, producing adorable crinkles around his mouth. "I must admit, I worry. I hear Ainsley Barfield hosts a lot of events, and I'll be expected to make an appearance at most of them."

"They do. Mostly lawyer happy hours and professional conferences." I smiled. "I'm not an event person, either. I usually tap out after an hour and have to take a nap to recover."

He chuckled.

Maybe it was the wine, maybe it was the feeling that I'd met an old friend in Alex. The knot in my stomach went slack. "After the hamster levitation, I didn't tell anyone what I'd done. Not my older sister, certainly not my mom. I knew I had real power, though. I checked out library books on magic, and I just practiced."

"You're from a family of ordinaries?" His mouth opened. "You didn't have anyone to teach you?"

"My sister Megan was a witch too, but we didn't talk about it until years later." I braced against the sting of remembering Megan. "Our mom was a devout Catholic, so if she did have any magical talent, she must have squashed it a long time ago. We went to Mass every Sunday until I was in middle school."

"What changed?" His voice was soft and soothing.

"With my magical powers emerging, I knew the world was bigger than what I'd learned at church. The summer I turned thirteen, Megan left for college, and I decided I was done with religion. When my mom went to Mass, I stayed home and used the time to practice spells."

"And your mother was okay with this?"

"Oh, no." I gave a harsh laugh. "But she couldn't do anything about it unless she wanted to physically drag her thirteen-year-old daughter out of the house. She worked as a bookkeeper, too, so I was on my own a lot. Plenty of time to practice in secret. Anyway, I got pretty good at basic levitation spells. Just small stuff. Pencils, books, the hamster." I hesitated.

Thinking about this time in my life always reminded

me of one strange moment where I'd thought I could hear what little Roger was thinking. It had never happened again, and I'd never been sure if it was an extension of my magic, or I'd just imagined it. I'd never told anyone, not even Tabitha. It sounded a little wild, even for a witch—reading the minds of small rodents?

I shook my head. "One day that summer, I was performing a ritual to increase my power at the next full moon. My mom was supposed to be at work, but she came home early, not feeling well, and when she found out what I was doing, she lost it. You know, witchcraft is evil, et cetera."

His lips pursed, as if he knew what was coming. He lifted a hand, paused, then tucked it into his pocket.

Had he been about to touch my shoulder?

"And then?" His voice was soft as a gentle hug.

"She told me if she ever caught me consorting with the devil again, my punishment would be worse than Hell." I clenched my hands into fists, shifting away from the memory of deep shame. My mom had dumped the herbs and bowl into the garbage, vacuumed up the salt circle, and locked all the matches and lighters in the house in her dresser. "She stomped into my room and started screaming at me again, and…a dictionary flew off my bookshelf and clocked her in the head. Left a huge lump." I hadn't meant to do it. I really hadn't.

Alex nodded. "You made it happen?"

"Not on purpose, but I must have done it. She grounded me, called in a priest to come perform a minor exorcism, and then when I wouldn't agree to stop doing magic, she shipped me off to a girls' boarding school."

His eyes went round and sad. "Oh, no."

"The exorcism wasn't horror-movie stuff, but still."

I shrugged. "In some ways it was better for me to be away from her. At holidays I'd stay with my older sister instead of my mom, and that's when I found out Megan was a witch, too."

"I'm so sorry, Rowan."

I rubbed my arms. My skin had cooled in the air-conditioned office, and my shirt had partially dried under the arms. Goose bumps ran up my forearms. "That was probably more than you wanted to know, but you're shockingly easy to talk to."

"No, I asked. Thank you for sharing."

"You're not for real, right?" I shook my head. "You're just…so nice. No one's this nice."

Alex held my gaze. His eyes were mesmerizing pools of warm brown. "Listening and caring is just being decent. It shouldn't be shocking." He lifted a hand and smoothed my hair back from my face.

This wasn't normal boss behavior, but at some point, I'd forgotten Alex was my supervisor. The air felt warm and damp, and it smelled like the ocean again, the scent wild and comforting at the same time.

Alex's hand stilled against my temple.

Hardly breathing, I lifted my left hand and brushed my fingers against his.

He squeezed my hand.

I reached for his other hand, and either I stepped close, or he pulled me in. Or maybe it happened at the same time. We were toe-to-toe now, inches away from full-body contact. My brain hazed over as I tilted my head up.

He angled his head down.

Our noses touched. Our mouths were an inch away from each other.

"This is probably about to be a bad idea."

His voice, low and husky, sent a pleasant tingle down my neck. "Terrible," I whispered.

I dove into his arms, and he pressed his mouth to mine.

The kiss was like no other. His lips were full and soft, and he tasted like mint. The tip of his tongue slid into my mouth, testing.

I put a hand on the back of his head and drew him closer, wanting to taste his peppermint tongue. When I gently sucked on the end of his tongue, he moaned.

His hands slid down my back, settling on my hips, and where my shirt had hiked up, his hands brushed my bare skin. His touch was warm and electric.

And then *everything* was electric.

My veins burned throughout my body. Something sparked in my mouth as if a tiny firecracker had just gone off.

Alex sprang back.

I gasped and stumbled, coughing out a cloud of yellow smoke. Doubled over, I hacked several times. Smoke puffed out with each cough, clouding up the area around me with a filmy yellow haze.

My throat clogged, and something sharp scraped the back of my mouth. I coughed again, hard, and spit a jagged object onto the carpet.

Crouching, I stared.

The object was a six-sided crystal, about the width of my pointer finger and a couple inches long. It was deep blue, almost black. Despite having emerged from my mouth, it was totally dry.

What the…?

Alex veered into my peripheral vision. Squatting

next to me, he thrust a can of sparkling water at me. "Here."

I popped the tab and gulped, then held the chilled, sweating can to the side of my face. I still couldn't believe I'd coughed up a rock. That couldn't possibly be healthy. "Am I bleeding?" I opened my mouth for him to check.

He touched my jaw and gently tilted my head from side to side. "No. You're fine." His gaze strayed to the floor. "Wait, where did…"

"I coughed it up." My eyes watered. The smoke was clearing now, but this was too bizarre and humiliating. "Is this the start of a horror movie? Am I going to die in seven days?"

"Of course not." He frowned and waved his hand across the rock several times. "It's…it's some kind of magical object."

"How can you tell?"

"Scanning spell." His eyebrows shot up, and he picked up the crystal. "I don't know what this is, but I think I'd hang onto it." He dropped the rock into my hand, then helped me to my feet.

I stared at the crystal. It was translucent, and under the light, a deep sapphire blue. "So, do women normally hack up smoke and rocks when you kiss them?" My voice sounded scratchy, and my throat ached.

"Oh, all the time," he deadpanned. "Actually, no, that was a first. Maybe we should call someone…" He fumbled for his phone.

"Sure. They'll definitely believe me at urgent care when I tell them I spit up a crystal." I slid the unexpected object into my pants pocket. What was I going to do with this thing, exactly?

He was already punching a number into his phone. "I meant a healer."

I peeked over his shoulder. Ugh, he was dialing the national healer hotline. I tapped the button to end the call. "No." Healers charged even more than doctors, and our Witches Association insurance covered even less of the costs. "I'm not injured. I'm just confused. And a little disturbed."

"But what if it's the sign of a curse? They don't all manifest immediately." His brow scrunched, his dark eyes anxious. "You could go home tonight, be perfectly fine, and then get sick in the middle of the night." He didn't say *die*, but I knew he was thinking it.

I snorted. "Who would curse me? The only person I see outside of work is Tabitha." My stomach churned as the realization crept over me. Of course. This strange reaction came from my blocked magic, which must have backfired somehow when we kissed. Just like when I cast a spell. It was me; I was broken.

"I should probably get going. Thanks for the water." I took one last swig, then set the can on his desk.

"Wait." He touched my shoulder. "Are you okay? Shouldn't we talk about, uh, what just happened between us?"

"Nope. Not necessary." My cheeks flamed, and I booked it for the door. Goddess save me. I could never show my face at work again. I'd have to move to Mexico or Canada. No, those weren't far enough. Ecuador? Australia?

I didn't go back upstairs. I took the elevator down to the lobby and texted Tabitha, asking her to meet me downstairs with my purse, which I'd left in the Everett Room. While I waited, I lurked by the wall-mounted television and pretended to be captivated by a golf tournament.

For the first time, I contemplated keeping a secret from my best friend. I already knew how she'd react if I told her this story. First, when I admitted to kissing Alex, she'd squeal. Then when I told her about the yellow smoke and showed her the crystal, she'd go into Type-A panic mode, calling people for advice, conducting hours of research on the Association website. She'd probably drag me to a healer, too.

The person I wished I could talk to? Megan. She wouldn't have gone all red and screamy about Alex, and she would've examined the rock with her slight frown, her huge glasses sliding down her nose, and said, "Don't worry, we'll figure it out." My older sister had always known what to do.

My throat still ached, and now my heart ached too.

I slid the crystal from my pocket and held it in my palm. It weighed almost nothing. I tilted my hand back and forth. The overhead lights glinted off the planes and angles of the mysterious object.

Across the lobby, one of the elevators dinged, and the doors slid open.

"Hey, sorry!" Tabitha strode toward me. Her heels clacked on the tiled floor. "I've got your purse."

I clamped my hand shut. In my grip, the crystal pulsed like a tiny beating heart. Or maybe that was my own blood pounding through my veins.

"Everything okay?" She held out my purse. "Are you feeling sick? Was it the wine? Maybe the shrimp was bad."

"Everything's fine. I just reached my social-interaction limit." I arranged my lips into a smile and took my purse. On the pretense of hunting for my keys, I slipped the rock into a small inner pocket and zipped it tight. I looped my arm through Tabitha's. "Let's get out of here."

Chapter Three

I groaned and rubbed my eyes. Once again, nothing. I closed the article, "Weird and Dangerous Curses You've Never Heard Of—You Won't Believe Number Three," and checked the time on my phone. Shit. I needed to shower for work.

I'd been awake since four a.m. I'd spent most of the weekend researching what happened when I kissed Alex, with no luck. The Association website offered a magical symptom-checker called WebHealer, but my search for "Coughing up smoke and crystals after kissing someone" yielded zero hits. I found plenty of information on how to reverse curses that turned humans into javelinas, though.

For the hundredth time, the same ad popped up in the corner of my screen.

Can't find something? Try Olympus, Inc., the supernatural help hotline. Get an answer to your query from a certified god or goddess.

I hovered my mouse over the X to close the ad. I'd heard of the hotline before, but Tabitha had told me it was kind of a scam. You could hardly ever get through, and when you did, the information wasn't helpful.

On the other hand, the Association had done jack shit to shed light on my current problem.

I took out my phone and dialed the number.

After a few rings, a pre-recorded message in a

smooth female voice said, "Thank you for calling Olympus, Inc. Healers and healers' assistants should press One now. To speak to a member of our customer service team, press Two. For spell repair, press Three. For a *deus ex machina*, press Four. For all other inquiries, press Zero."

A *deus ex machina,* really? Huh. I guessed I was in the customer-service category. I tapped Two on my phone and waited…and waited…and waited.

Seventeen minutes of elevator music later, I gave up and threw my phone onto the couch. Tabitha was right. Totally useless. The only option left was a healer, and I wasn't shelling out two hundred bucks to find out I was sick with an incurable mystery ailment.

I struggled in and out of the shower and threw on mildly wrinkled pants and a clean blouse, then slipped my newly created crystal necklace over my head. Yesterday I'd wire wrapped the crystal and attached it to a chain. I used copper wire and a gold chain because anything silver would nullify the magic. At least, it would if this power worked the same as regular magic. I assumed the principle held.

I tucked the crystal beneath my blouse and patted it. Much more secure than keeping it in my purse.

I took the light-rail train into the city and disembarked a block from the building where our office was located. Late-September light winked off the windows, and the air smelled crisp and clean.

I stopped in the coffee shop on the first floor, ordering a twenty-ounce pumpkin spice latte I'd probably regret later.

The sixth floor was dead. Most people didn't arrive until eight-thirty, and it wasn't even eight. Usually,

Tabitha and I got here about the same time and hung out in the break room chatting over our coffees, but I needed to avoid small talk today. My best friend would know right away something was wrong.

Safe in my office, I switched on my computer and checked my email. A new message, sent at seven-thirty this morning, caught my eye. *Regarding Alex Kouris.*

The Firm would like to make all employees aware that Alex Kouris, IT Director, who began his tenure on Friday, possesses Stygian magic. Although this is the first time a Stygian has joined our staff, the Firm believes Mr. Kouris's powers pose no risk to others. He will have no face-to-face contact with clients, and he has signed an Agreement Not to Reap with regards to Firm employees.

As a reminder, the Firm prohibits all discrimination based on magical identity. We promote an environment of inclusiveness. If you have any further questions, please see HR.

I sat back in my chair and stared at the email.

A Stygian?

I picked up my coffee cup, and it shook in my hands. I set it back down.

No, no, no, this couldn't be.

My boss was a murderer.

I opened a new email message, typed in HR's address, and stared at my screen. Then I locked my computer and shoved my chair back. Springing to my feet, I marched out of my office and down the hall.

I passed the set of cubicles where Dave, Marin, and the other help-desk technicians sat. Just my luck, Dave was early today.

His wicked blue eyes sparkled. "Dude. Did you read

the email from HR?" He whistled. "This is gonna blow up."

"I read it." I strode past him.

"Sheesh, someone needs to get laid."

I froze, anger burning up my blood, then turned around. "Seriously?"

He blinked. "What?"

"What's wrong with you?" I put my hands on my hips. "We're at work. Remember the sexual harassment policy?"

"I…I didn't say anything." He frowned.

Oh, he was so good at the fake-innocent act. Too good.

"I heard you. Maybe *you* need to go back to the nineties and…and…" Damn it, I couldn't think of a single comeback. Why was I so bad at standing up for myself?

"And what?" His lips twitched.

"Never mind." I stalked away. I didn't need sex, and anyway, I owned a vibrator that did far more glorious things for me than Dave ever had. Maybe I should tell him *that* sometime.

Rounding the corner, I spotted Alex through the glass wall of his office. He stood at his standing desk, typing something on his computer.

He was an early arriver. Good. I rapped on the door, then shoved it open.

A cautious smile crossed his face. "Rowan. Good morning. What can I—"

I slammed the door. "Would you like to tell me how the hell you got hired here?" It all made sense now. His solicitous nature, the nice things he'd said to all of us, his supermodel cheekbones. It was all part of his magical power—charm. He oozed it.

His face fell. "I take it you saw the email. Listen, I don't know what you know about Stygians, but…"

"Oh, I'm intimately familiar with your kind." I crossed my arms. Beneath my blouse, the crystal was a warm slash against my skin. "My sister dated a Stygian. Two years ago, she disappeared, and a month later, council members found her body at the bottom of a ravine in Forest Park." The shock of that phone call ran through me anew.

I'm sorry, Rowan, but we think we've found Megan's body. There's a tattoo on the inside of the wrist that matches the photographs you sent us…

"I'm so, so sorry." He shook his head. "You have to understand—"

"I don't have to understand anything. Megan died because of a Stygian. She was my only family." Not technically true, but I hadn't spoken to our mom in years, and I didn't even remember my dad. According to my mom, he'd ditched us when I was a year old.

"Oh, Rowan," he whispered.

Were those tears in his eyes? No. He didn't get to cry over Megan. Someone just like him had been responsible for her death.

"So." My voice cracked. I clenched my hands into fists to stop them from shaking. "How many victims do you send Hades? One a month? One a week? How does it work?"

Stygians were demigods who used their magic to earn the trust of their victims. When the person had fallen completely under their spell, the Stygian opened a death portal to the Underworld and ordered the person to pass through. They obeyed without question, their souls traveling to the Underworld, their bodies left behind for their grieving families to find later.

He held up his hands. "I don't. Not anymore. And when I did, I…" He cleared his throat. "Listen, can we go get a cup of coffee somewhere? This isn't the best place to talk about this." He glanced past me, probably worried about someone overhearing.

The walls were thin here.

Alex would probably learn the hard way to use sound spells in his office for private conversations.

Good. I hoped someone overheard us. I hoped every last employee of the Firm freaked out about Alex and demanded his resignation. I hoped the partnership fired his ass and security escorted him out of the building.

"No, we can't get a cup of coffee. You didn't think about telling me this before?" I lowered my voice. "Before you kissed me?"

"I apologize. I got caught up in the moment."

Convenient. I glared.

He let out a heavy sigh. "HR wanted to send the email out on Friday, but I was hoping to meet everyone first. To get a chance to make a different impression."

"*Great* impression."

Alex glanced down. *"How can I make this right?"*

I started to tell him he couldn't, but then I realized his mouth was closed. Yet I'd heard his voice.

Had…had I just read his mind?

The crystal burned icy hot against my skin.

He shoved his hands in his pockets. "If you want to resign, I understand, of course."

I almost laughed at the idea. I had an apartment and bills and student loans. I couldn't just *not* earn a paycheck. "Not an option right now."

"All right. Then what can I do to make you comfortable?"

"There's one thing." I waited for him to look up and meet my gaze. "You can stay away from me."

The faint hope in his eyes crumbled and his shoulders slumped.

For half a second, I felt sorry for him. But no. That was just his charm, working its magic on me yet again. The whole thing—our connection, his kindness, our kiss—had been nothing but a magical side effect.

I lifted my chin and strode away.

****

Tabitha dipped a celery stick into a container of hummus. "Are you going to tell me what's wrong?"

I stared into the pool of pinot grigio in my glass. I'd only managed to avoid Tabitha until three p.m. today, when she'd cornered me in the break room to ask what the matter was. I'd spent the whole day researching my crystal instead of working, and I'd found nothing. It was time to get help.

The admission that I'd kissed Alex burned in the back of my throat, but I couldn't utter the words. I could already imagine the disappointment and shock in Tabitha's hazel eyes.

She sighed. "Ro." *"We've been friends for three years. Why won't she trust me?"*

My shoulders stiffened. There it was again. She'd only said my name, yet I'd heard two more sentences in her voice.

In my head. Or, in her head?

And what about earlier, when Dave said I needed to get laid?

Was I really hearing people's thoughts?

"Please talk to me," Tabitha said. Aloud, this time.

I set down the wine, flopped against the arm of the couch, and swung my legs across the back of it, draped like a sloth on a branch. Shutting my eyes, I tried to descend farther into the cushions, where I'd be safe from Tabitha's judgment. "Okay, I asked you over because…I can't tell you."

"You can tell me anything."

"I can't tell you this. You'll think I'm a terrible person." The kiss started replaying itself again. *His lips felt like velvet against mine. His hand caressed the small of my back.*

She patted my hand, ruining the fantasy.

No, never mind, I needed her to ruin the fantasy. I opened my eyes.

She touched my shoulder. "I'd never judge you. Even if you killed someone."

"How do you know I didn't?"

"Seriously. Talk to me."

"Okay." I took a deep breath, blew it out, took another one. "I, um…"

"Oh, for the goddess's sake." Tabitha snapped her fingers, and a tablet of hot-pink paper appeared and floated two feet above my face. "Just *think* it."

"What's that for?"

"It'll write your thoughts as you think them. I swear, no judgment here." She held up her hands.

The hot-pink notepad bobbed encouragingly.

I hesitated, but at least I wouldn't have to say it out loud. I clenched my jaw. *I kissed Alex.*

Tabitha shrieked and clutched the pink pad to her heart. "No wonder you wanted to leave so fast on Friday. Tell me everything."

I sat up and gave her the play-by-play, up through the moment we kissed.

To her credit, she didn't get screamy, but her face did turn a bit pink. She drummed her long nails against the notepad, then tossed it onto the coffee table. "You saw the email from HR this morning. Right?" Her tone was tentative, careful, like she thought the mention of the email might lead to a complete breakdown.

"Yeah, nice of him to tell me he's a Stygian before we kissed. Oh, wait, he didn't." His deception gave me an acid feeling in the back of my throat.

What helps anger heartburn? Snacks. I picked up a carrot and scooped out a blob of hummus.

"I'm sorry. It's not that I think he'd violate his non-reaping agreement. I just know what a sensitive topic this is for you." Worried lines appeared around her eyes.

"Yeah." I took a moment to mentally step back from memories of Megan. It required an extra sip of wine and a couple of deep breaths. "It gets weirder."

I told her about the aftermath of our kiss and showed her the crystal.

Her eyes were huge. "It's beautiful, Here, let me check it." She leaned toward me, held the crystal between two fingers and passed her other hand back and forth over it, the way Alex had done. "I think Alex was right. It *is* a magical object of some kind, and I don't sense a curse, either."

"Okay." I started to tuck the crystal back into my shirt, then realized I didn't have to hide it. I rolled it between my fingers, watching the light play off its depths.

Tabitha picked up her phone. "We need to do some research. Check all of the online grimoires. The

Association has forums we can post in, too."

I shook my head and let the crystal fall against my chest. "I've been doing research for three days. There's nothing out there. Big shock, no one else is hacking up objects after a make-out session."

She clutched my wrist so hard I winced. "You didn't say you made out! You said it was a kiss."

"A long kiss, a make-out session, what's the difference?" I drained half my wine. "Well. Tongue, I guess."

"Oh, my gods!" Tabitha's voice hit the approximate pitch of a dog whistle. "There was tongue?"

"Maybe."

She pursed her lips together, as if tamping down a squeal. "Okay. What about talking to my aunt Cora?"

Not this again. "Tabs, I don't want to see a healer."

She snapped her fingers, and her phone flipped to speaker and began dialing of its own accord. "We're just getting a little advice. She won't charge us."

"Tabs." I glared.

"Well, hello, my dear," said a voice almost identical to Tabitha's. "How are you?"

"Hi, Auntie. I have my friend Rowan with me here, and we have a weird situation to run past you." Tabitha nodded at me. "Go ahead, tell her what happened."

"Um, hi. So, I kind of kissed my boss." I recapped what had happened and explained my theory about my blocked powers causing bizarre and embarrassing side effects.

Cora asked for a description of the crystal, everything from the size and color to how many sides it had. "And have you noticed any other side effects since?"

I glanced at Tabitha. "I'm not sure, but…a couple of times I seemed to hear what people were thinking."

"What? You didn't tell me this." She gaped at me.

"It doesn't sound very believable." I shrugged.

"But that's huge! Auntie, what do you think?" said Tabitha.

"Hmm," said Cora. There was a long pause, then another, "Hmm." She cleared her throat. "It's against the Healer's Code of Ethics for me to diagnose someone without examining them in person, so this isn't a diagnosis. Just an opinion. What you're describing sounds like an unblocking. We have documented cases in medical literature of relationships between demigods and witches that resulted in the witch's power being amplified. The touch of a demigod can have some unusual side effects."

Oh, holy shit. I'd assumed the crystal was a side effect of my damaged magic. I'd only thought of demigods as soul-hunters. It had never occurred to me their powers could have any positive effects.

"Given your history, especially the exorcism that was performed on you as a teenager, and your difficulty in spell casting, it's entirely plausible that this kiss unblocked your power. The crystal sounds like a manifestation of power. I'd have to see it in person to know for sure, but I do agree it's unlikely to be symptomatic of a curse."

I glanced down at the crystal. It rested against my chest and once again pulsed with a tiny heartbeat. It did seem sort of friendly.

"That's great news." Tabitha squeezed my hand. "The Association doesn't seem to have any resources on this issue. Is there anything else we should do? Someone we should talk to?"

"Well, it wouldn't hurt to get a familiar," said Cora. "Air spirits are fairly knowledgeable about all kinds of magic. Plus, if my theory is correct and you're just coming into your power, a familiar would offer an extra level of protection. And if you do ever want to make an appointment with me, I'm happy to see you in person."

We both thanked her profusely.

After we hung up, Tabitha grinned at me, bouncing in her seat. "Ro, what if you're psychic? Do you know how rare and awesome that is? This is so amazing. We have to get you a familiar right away." Her eyes lit up.

Full of hope. She was always so hopeful about things. How did she do it? Probably, for starters, she hadn't been shipped off to boarding school by her mother at age thirteen. Parental rejection imbues a person with a certain cynicism.

"I don't know." I drained the last of my wine. "Aren't they risky? My college advisor's familiar stole her credit card and took himself on a Caribbean cruise."

"I'm sure that's highly unusual." Tabitha tapped her phone screen. "The agency that handles placements is open until eight. Do you want to call?"

I hesitated. The crystal pulsed against my chest. When I looked down at it, the blue surfaces glowed, lit from within by a filament of soft light, as if the crystal agreed with my friend's suggestion. "Let's call."

She flicked her fingers. Her cell phone floated into the air between us and switched to speaker.

"National Association of Witches, Familiar Placement Agency. This is Lee. How may I help you?"

Tabitha nodded at me.

"Hi, this is Rowan Baird." I leaned closer to the

phone. "I'm hoping to, uh, get a familiar?"

"The placement fee is $125, and it's non-refundable. Would you like to go ahead and start the application process now?" The alto voice paused.

There was an application process? What if I was rejected? I winced a little at the fee, but I guessed I could put one more thing on the ol' credit card. "Sure. How long does it take?"

"Once we complete the intake form, the process is almost instantaneous. We have a very extensive database of familiars."

Instantaneous? Was that good or bad? "Could I maybe see some pictures of them?"

Lee cleared her throat. "Now, this won't take long, I just need a little bit of information from you."

I braced myself for a slew of questions, but she only took down my Association registration number and asked what size my apartment was and whether I had a yard. I didn't. Then she asked about allergies to animal dander, and my preferences as far as species.

I gave Tabitha a helpless look. I didn't even know my options. Cats, obviously. My college advisor's vacation-minded familiar was a cat. What else could there be? Birds? Dogs? "I don't want one of those tiny, yappy dogs. You know, the rat-sized ones in sweaters?"

"Oh, we don't have any dogs," said Lee. "The air spirits don't like them."

Now that I thought about it, I'd never heard of a witch having a dog familiar. Well, at least I didn't have to worry about a dog peeing in my house.

"All right, just a few final questions so we can determine the best placement for you. Try not to analyze the questions too much. Just say the first thing that comes to mind, like a personality test, okay? First question. What would be your first choice for dinner—something homemade, a gourmet meal out, or takeout such as pizza?"

"You mean what would I feed the familiar?"

"No, what you yourself would prefer to eat."

"Pizza."

"Not a rabbit person, then," Lee declared. Before I could ask how she could tell from my choosing pizza, she launched into the next question. "Blue or red?"

"I like green better, but—"

"Blue, then. No rodents."

I shuddered at the thought of a small rodent running around my house and hiding in my cupboards.

"Utilitarianism or deontology?"

"Huh?"

She made a "tsk" noise. "No owls. And no elephants."

"Elephants?" Was that an option? Were there other large, untenable possibilities like rhinos and alligators? Oh, gods, what was I getting myself into?

She asked me three more equally random questions, and my answers eliminated, respectively, snakes, butterflies, and jaguars. I was a little disappointed about the jaguars.

"Last question. Would you rather befriend a cat, or a mighty beast with tiny knives in its feet?"

What the hell kind of animal had tiny knives in its feet? Was it a metaphor? I'd never been the biggest cat fan, so I shrugged. "Tiny knives, I guess."

"Okay, great. You're aligned to cats. Just a moment while I run this." Generic elevator music filled our ears.

"Wait, what? Those options were both cats?" I

rolled my eyes at Tabitha. "How are any of those questions supposed to indicate my preferences for a pet?"

She frowned. "A familiar's not a pet."

"You know what I mean."

Lee came back on the line. "All right, good news, you've been approved for a familiar. Her name is, um, I'm going to butcher this, Altocumulus Lenticularis? I think? And she appears as a black-and-white cat, weighing six pounds, eight ounces. I'm required to disclose that she sheds, and I quote, 'copiously.' There's a probationary period of thirty days, during which either you or the familiar can back out of the agreement. After that, the arrangement is permanent."

Permanent? I ran my hand over one of my hair-free throw pillows. I needed to hit up the nearest pet store, and I didn't even know where that was. Were you supposed to feed cats kibble or canned food or a mix of both? Where would I put the litter box?

"Just to clarify," Lee said, "once the arrangement is finalized, the familiar is bound to your life force as you are to hers. You live and die together."

"Wait, wait, wait. Don't cats only live to be about fifteen?" Gods, was I going to die an early death?

"Not familiars. They're air spirits, so their animal forms will last as long as your human body does."

"Oh," I whispered. This seemed like a bigger commitment than marriage. "Is there a handout you could send me, or something?"

Thunk. A two-inch-thick hardbound book dropped onto my coffee table out of thin air. *Getting Familiar, A Guide to Your New Soul Companion.*

"That's the manual," said Lee. "If you could please

sign the disclosure paperwork? Just trace your signature in the air."

Bemused, I did so.

A stack of paperwork dropped onto my coffee table on top of the manual. My signature marked the front page.

"So how do I get her, or pick her up?"

"No need, she should be arriving any minute," said Lee. "She'll supply her own food and bedding. Any questions?"

I eyed the contract and manual. "No, I guess not." Just like that, I had a lifelong companion.

"Thank you for using the Familiar Placement Agency, and remember, we're here seven days a week, eight a.m. to eight p.m., if you need anything."

Tabitha flicked her pinky finger, and the phone hung up and floated quietly to rest on the coffee table.

The doorbell rang.

Chapter Four

Tabitha and I glanced at each other.

"Should I…uh…" Obviously, I should answer the door, but what would I say? Should I try and straighten up first? Wait, no, this was a cat, not a British royal. I jumped up, my pulse pounding, and hurried across the room.

Tabitha followed, standing so close I could feel her breath on my left ear.

"Can you scoot back, like, a little bit?" The question emerged with more bite than I'd intended.

"Sheesh, okay." She stepped back an inch. "Are you nervous? Don't be."

"It helps my anxiety a lot, you know, when people tell me not to be anxious." I peered through the peephole. No one was there. Weird. Frowning, I opened the door.

"Greetings, witches," said a small, high-pitched voice.

A black-and-white cat sat on the doorstep, surrounded by cardboard boxes. Her brilliant green eyes stood out like jewels. "My name is Altocumulus Lenticularis. I am a lesser spirit of the air, of the seventh realm of the troposphere. I've been sent here for Rowan Baird to serve as her familiar on a trial basis."

The speech was preposterously formal for such a small, fluffy body. I pursed my lips, and Tabitha's fingers closed around my hand.

I cleared my throat and managed a response with only moderate lip-twitching. "I'm Rowan. This is my friend Tabitha. Uh, please come in."

The little cat leaped up and sauntered through the open door into my apartment. "I traveled a long way with no porter, so I'll need you to carry my belongings. My back is very tired."

Porter? What the hell? And how had she carried all of these boxes? I counted eight, and they must be twenty times heavier than she was. Then I remembered she was an air spirit and could probably do a spell to tote her stuff however far she had toted it. "All this is yours?"

The familiar didn't answer. She strolled over to the shoe rack in the entry way and touched her nose to my ankle boots. "Hmm. You don't own a canine, do you?"

"No, but there are lots of dogs around this complex." I picked up a box and struggled back inside. What was in this thing? Bricks?

"Dogs?" Alto-whatever-her-name-was bared her fangs, then closed her mouth and continued padding across the hardwood floor like nothing was wrong. She paused every few inches to sniff the air, whiskers quivering.

Tabitha set down a box next to the one I'd just brought in. Her eyes leaked tears of laughter. "Ro, I can't, her *voice*."

Snick, snick, snick. The familiar batted at my phone charger plugged into a power strip by the TV stand.

"Hey, now." I raced toward her. "That's not a toy." I bent to unplug it.

"Then why is it on the ground?" The cat pawed at the cord as I lifted it out of reach.

"It isn't now." I set it next to the TV. "Why don't

you keep, er, exploring while we bring the rest of your stuff in?"

"I suppose." She strolled across the room toward the couch.

I hurried back to the front door and grabbed another box.

"She's perfect," whispered Tabitha, as she stacked one box on top of another. "She couldn't be any cuter."

The cat reared up onto her hind legs and sharpened her claws on the couch.

Cute, but trouble. "Stop that!"

We carted the rest of the boxes inside. How many "supplies" did the familiar need, exactly? My apartment was less than 800 square feet. And what was I going to do to keep her from playing with cords and wires? Had she brought any actual cat toys, or would I have to buy those?

"Seriously, leave it alone," I snapped, as the familiar went for the couch again.

The cat stared at me, withdrew her claws, then strolled toward the bookshelf.

Tabitha and I set down the last two boxes, and I started for the kitchen to grab a pair of scissors to cut the tape.

A ripping sound stopped me in my tracks.

The tape peeled off all the boxes at once and the lids popped open. Supplies and objects levitated out of the boxes and zoomed around the apartment.

Within moments, my apartment contained one small cat couch; one cat tower in the living room and a second one in the bedroom; a bedazzled litter box in the bathroom along with a hefty supply of extra litter; what appeared to be a lifetime supply of canned cat food; bags of treats; a mountain of cat toys in a huge basket; and several fleece blankets, which arranged themselves over my couch, armchair, bed, and even on top of the washer.

A circulating water dish zipped past me and filled itself up at the kitchen sink.

I stared at the familiar, who was rubbing her head along the spine of a complete volume of Shakespeare. "Could these boxes have also moved themselves into the apartment?"

"Technically." She purred as she scratched her ear against the cloth binding,

I flopped onto the couch. What the hell was I supposed to do now that my entire apartment was a cat palace? Maybe this was a mistake.

Tabitha joined me on the couch just as the boxes disappeared into thin air.

The little cat trotted over to the couch and jumped up, landing on the middle cushion between Tabitha and me. She flopped onto her back. Her stomach fur splayed out in all directions, like a fluffy chocolate-and-vanilla cookie. "Pet me."

"So demanding." I petted her fuzzy belly.

"Careful," said Tabitha. "It might be a—"

The cat latched onto my hand, trapping it in a rigid four-pawed grasp. She kicked her back legs against my hand, her claws stabbing my arm.

"Ow, hey!" I yanked my hand away.

The cat rolled from side to side, delighted with herself.

"Trap," said Tabitha. "It was a trap."

"Clearly." I grimaced at the long scratches on my hand. I unfortunately now understood the question Lee had asked about tiny knives in feet. "Listen, Alto, um, familiar, if you're going to live here, you can't scratch me."

She rolled onto her haunches and tucked her head to her stomach, licking her fur. "There's nothing in the contract about scratching."

I wasn't sure about that, but I'd have to check later. "Are you hungry or anything?"

"Not now." She continued bathing. "I usually eat in the middle of the night."

I narrowed my eyes at her, but she steadfastly continued grooming her stomach. I suspected I was about to start down a path of severe sleep deprivation. "We can talk about bedtime later. Do you have a nickname?"

The cat lifted her head. "What's a nickname?" She licked her front left paw and swiped it over her ear.

"Something I can call you other than—how do you say your name again?"

"Altocumulus Lenticularis. Surely you don't dislike my name?" She flexed her paw. Needle-like claws jutted from the tiny pads.

"No, no, I love it." I held my breath until she went back to cleaning her face. "It's just really long. Maybe I could call you Alto, or…Lenti?"

The cat switched to cleaning her other ear. "Lenti is acceptable, if that's easier for your human tongue."

"Lenti. You're just the sweetest little thing, aren't you?" Tabitha stroked the cat's head.

Lenti purred. She flopped onto her side, the throaty rumbles getting louder.

I groaned. Of course my familiar instantly adored my best friend while treating me like a chew toy. *Well, she* is *an air spirit*. They were known to be unpredictable and liked messing with humans.

Tabitha buried her nose in Lenti's fur.

I cleared my throat. "Should I just leave you two alone?"

"Sorry." She sat up. "I miss having a cat. Paul's allergic. Can I come over and snuggle with you sometimes, Lenti?"

"Of course. I exist to be worshiped." Lenti stretched her front legs out and flicked her tail.

Tabitha raised her brows at me. "Aren't you going to ask her about the crystal?"

"What crystal?" The cat curled into a sitting position, ears alert.

I showed her my necklace and repeated the story, although it felt weird telling a cat that I'd made out with a demigod.

Lenti just blinked a few times, her gaze fixed on me. When I was done, she nosed the crystal, jiggling the chain.

"Careful." I shifted away from her, clamping my hand over the stone.

"I'm just going to examine it. Sit still, please," said Lenti.

I sat back and allowed her to sniff the crystal. Already it seemed normal to follow the orders of a six-pound cat.

After a few moments, Lenti sat back on her haunches. "It smells like you."

"Meaning?"

"All magic has a scent. This crystal smells exactly like you. I imagine it is the source of your power." She twisted her head at a sharp angle, licking her shoulder. "Power that manifests physically is usually a sign of eldritch magic."

My stomach clenched. Eldritch magic was the umbrella term for an array of mind-based and energy-based magical powers, most of which were poorly understood. Spirits, ghosts, and a number of gods and goddesses wielded eldritch magic, but the Association didn't strictly condone it or study it. As an eldritch witch, I wouldn't lose my license, but I also wouldn't find an Association mentor because, well, there were none.

"Eldritch magic is powerful." Tabitha shook her head. "But I can't help you with it, Ro. I don't know even know what kind you have."

I frowned at her and Lenti. "How could I even have eldritch magic? I've never studied it, and my sister was a regular witch."

Megan was eight years older than me, and already away at college by the time I figured out I could do magic. It was the first secret I ever kept from my sister. I was scared to tell her, afraid she would tell me I was sick or mentally ill and drag me to a doctor or a psychiatrist. Once I started attending boarding school, though, at holidays I stayed with Megan instead of going home.

My first Thanksgiving with my sister, I told her everything, and she admitted to her own powers. She'd never told me about them as a child because she didn't want to scare me, she said. Oh, and she wasn't attending a state college after all. She was enrolled at the Magical College of Oregon just outside of Corvallis.

It turned out she could do any spell involving fire. She could light candles with a glance, she could conjure a globe of flame the size of a tennis ball and bat it around her little apartment, and she could melt snow with a touch.

Megan had been a regular, albeit powerful, witch.

Or so I thought. Had she told me the whole truth?

"You must have an eldritch magician somewhere in your family line." Lenti yawned, revealing tiny fangs. "Such power can be inherited. We can test your magic later when I wake you for my breakfast. Right now, I must sleep."

One of the fleece blankets arranged itself on my lap in a neat square.

Lenti hopped onto it and circled a few times, like a dog, then settled down into a ball of fur, nose tucked against her paws. "Good night, witches." Her eyelids closed. A tiny snore escaped her lips.

I checked the time on my phone. It was seven p.m. I could have plucked Lenti off my lap, but I couldn't bear to move her content, sleeping form.

Tabitha and I turned on *Secrets of the Unseelie* with the volume on low, and we snickered as the Unseelie princesses' horseback-riding trip devolved into a series of screaming matches. There was something soothing about watching rich, spoiled faeries argue over who owned a bigger yacht.

The crystal around my neck no longer glowed, but it rested against my breastbone, warm to the touch, pulsing faintly in rhythm with Lenti's breathing.

****

Lenti flicked her tail, narrowly missing the base of my electric toothbrush. "Of course I'm coming with you."

"You're not." I leaned closer to the mirror as I applied mascara. "There are vampires and werewolves at my office. What if one of them tries to suck your blood?

Or eat you for lunch?"

"A vampire wouldn't touch me. My blood is poisonous to them. And I could outrun any werewolf."

I raised an eyebrow, then dabbed away a dot of mascara beneath my right eye. I'd started to read *Getting Familiar* last night, but between Lenti begging for food, head-butting me for pets, and trying to help me test my spell casting abilities at three in the morning, I hadn't had a lot of time. "I don't think we're allowed to take animals to work."

"So I'll hide." She batted at the mascara wand just as I was touching up my top right eyelashes.

I jerked away. "Watch it. That's my eyeball."

"But you're waving the stick thing and I want to catch it."

I set down the wand on the other side of the sink. "Are you sure you aren't just a talking cat?"

"Let me come with you. I'll be so bored here without youuuu." Her sentence ended on a sort of mournful yowl. "No one will even see me." There was a small pop, and she disappeared.

"You can go invisible?" Good to know. I leaned down to pet the space she'd just occupied but felt only the air. "Lenti?"

No answer.

My heart beat a bit faster. "Lenti?"

A set of claws swiped my bare forearm.

I yanked my arm back.

Lenti re-materialized. The trilling noise she made resembled a laugh. "See? No one will ever know I'm there."

"Damn it, cat." I examined the shallow scratches on my arm. I was going to complain to the Association, because they should give people time to read the manual before the familiars just showed up. If I'd had a week to prepare, I might have known important facts, like *Your familiar can disappear anytime she wants and will also claw your arm to shreds.*

She pawed my arm, this time without claws. "Please take me with you. A familiar can't be separated from her human for hours every day. It isn't natural."

I frowned and gently moved her paw off my arm. "What happens if we're separated too long?"

"I'll probably die." She leaped to the floor and rubbed against my ankles.

I eyed her skeptically. Grabbing my sweater, I yanked it on. I slipped the crystal necklace over my head and tucked it inside my sweater, then strode out of the bathroom.

Lenti followed, an inch from my heels.

"Fine, let's check." I picked up the manual from the coffee table and consulted the index.

Lenti leaped onto the table and nudged my arm, forcing me to pet her with one hand while I navigated the manual with the other.

After scanning a few pages, I glanced up. "There's nothing in here about physical separation."

"Maybe they forgot to write it down." She scratched the edge of the book. "Fine, I'll just amuse myself by exploring your cupboards. And what's the soft paper by the human litter box? The stuff on a roll?"

"Toilet paper." My stomach sank. Lenti had already batted at the toilet paper once last night, wasting about five feet of it before I caught her. She'd probably destroy the whole apartment before I was home from work. And what if she escaped and got hit by a car? Just because she was an air spirit, it didn't mean she understood traffic.

She tilted her head to the side and fixed her gaze on me.

The cuteness worked.

I sighed. "You can come with me, but at work, you have to do what I tell you."

"Excellent." She leaped from the coffee table to land lightly on the floor. Tail swishing, she sashayed toward the entry way.

Before I could figure out how to cart all of Lenti's necessities to work, one of my duffel bags flew into the room and unzipped itself. A small litter box, cat food, dishes, and a fleece blanket swirled into the bag in a brief tornado of activity. The fleece blanket folded itself in a neat square and the bag re-zipped itself with gusto.

Lenti nosed the front door. "Ready."

"Okay, then." The duffel bag was an unusual work accessory, but maybe everyone would just think I was going to the gym. That would be a first, since I loathed gyms. I was more a "stroll through the neighborhood to get a latte and a scone" type of person.

I gathered my own stuff. Sadly, my lunch didn't magically assemble or pack itself. In the entryway, I slipped into my shoes. "Don't go into the street, okay? Stay close to me."

Lenti wriggled her butt.

What was she doing?

She sprang up, landing on my shoulder.

I stumbled sideways. "Gah!"

"Let us go forth," said Lenti. "You shall bear me like the chariot of clouds I once rode in the sky. I am Altocumulus Lenticularis, spirit of the air, Fluffball of Doom."

I rolled my eyes. "Oh, for the goddess's sake," I muttered. Hefting Lenti's duffel bag, I stepped out into the hallway. The straps slipped through my grasp and the bag plunked to the floor. "Shit."

A popping noise told me she had gone invisible, but her weight settled onto my shoulder. "No cursing, Rowan. You have to be careful about language around me. I'm very impressionable. Haven't you read the manual yet?"

"No, I've been too busy attending to your every whim." I dug out my keys and locked the door, then grabbed the duffel bag and waddled down the hall.

****

I was waiting in the lobby for an elevator when Dave darted toward me. "Hey!" He chuckled and gestured to my duffel bag. "What's all this? You going camping after work or something?"

"Nope. Gym." I shifted my weight to the other foot, trying to counterbalance the bag against the invisible cat on my shoulder.

He snorted. "You belong to a gym?"

Thanks, asshole. "Just started."

"Which one?"

The elevator dinged and the doors slid open. Whew. As we stepped on, I searched for some topic to distract Dave from my supposed health kick. "So, how were the tunnels this morning?" Most vampires who worked on the eastside parked at one of two garages, then entered Portland's vampire-built tunnel system on foot. From there, they could navigate to most buildings from underground, avoiding the sun entirely.

A few of our newer associates simply got to work before the sun rose. One way to maximize your billable hours, I guess.

"Fine. They're not usually too busy this time of day." As the doors closed, he winked. "You remember."

"Do I?" I cleared my throat. Back when Dave and I were dating, he took me on a tour of the tunnels, explaining how in the nineteenth century, vampires had made quiet arrangements with the city of Portland to construct the tunnel system. They'd relied on the tunnels to allow them to move around the city with discretion. When the Firm moved to non-nocturnal hours fifty years ago, the tunnels became even more important. Admittedly, Dave's encyclopedic knowledge of the Firm's history was entertaining.

He'd told me about how the vampires used to store donated blood down there, then nudged me into an alcove, lifted me up, and we'd had sex there with my butt squashed against a dusty brick wall, the smell of mildew filling my nostrils as Dave grunted into my shoulder.

Charming, I know.

Dave smirked, but as the elevator shot up, his smirk depressed into a frown. "Do you smell that?"

"Smell what?"

"It smells sort of like a cat, but I can't quite place it."

I froze as Lenti's claws dug into my shoulder. I hadn't banked on the vampires being able to smell her. "Yeah, I don't know."

"Odd." He glanced around the elevator, as if a herd of cats was about to jump out of the walls.

I coughed and picked at a hangnail.

The elevator couldn't reach our floor quickly enough. I darted out and swerved the opposite direction of Dave, mumbling that I'd see him later.

In my office, the duffel bag unzipped, and Lenti's supplies unloaded themselves. Her fleece blanket tucked itself into a cozy square behind my filing cabinet, the perfect location where no one could see her from the hall.

She re-materialized, leaped off my shoulder, and plopped onto the blanket.

I logged into my computer, leaving her to conduct whatever grooming she deemed necessary.

"Good morning," said a female voice from my computer. "Alexander Kouris has sent you a chat message. Would you like to respond?"

Alex?

I opened Muse, our chat program, and clicked on the blinking window. A tiny version of Alex's headshot sat in the upper left corner, and was it ever a good picture of him. The sight of his full lips and bright smile gave me the physical sensation of his mouth on mine. My lips tingled.

Can you talk?

No. I couldn't talk to him. He'd lied to me about his identity and kissed me under false pretenses. If I knew who he really was, I'd never have made out with him.

Right?

An unpleasant hacking noise interrupted my thoughts.

I peered behind the file cabinet.

Lenti stared at a dark, wet mound on the carpet. "Enemy, I have defeated thee."

Ew. "Is that a hairball?"

"No." She swabbed her paw with her tongue. "It's an, uh, evil demon I exorcised from my body."

"Je…" I clamped my lips together, remembering her warning about cursing. "I mean, um, Juniper Christmas."

I grabbed a wad of tissues and mopped up the hairball, leaving a slight stain on the rug. Gross. No one told me having a familiar would be like having a toddler. Had to watch my language, had to clean up bodily fluids.

Lenti slinked back to her blanket and curled up into a little furball. She was soon snoring away, her lips twitching.

I minimized the chat window and checked my email.

Five minutes later, the Muse voice said again, "Alex's message is still waiting. It's rude not to respond. If you're busy, you can let him know. Would you like any assistance crafting a reply?"

"No." Rolling my eyes, I clicked on my long-standing Muse chat history with Tabitha and fired off a message. *You need to do something about Barbara. She's getting pushy.*

Barbara was the magical AI Tabitha had helped program into Muse. When we first rolled out the chat program two years ago, Barbara was intended to be a simple training tool to guide the attorneys and staff through basic functions in the program. In the ensuing months, though, as Tabitha added more tips and tricks to Barbara's knowledge, the AI took on a life of its own. Lately, she'd been awfully condescending.

I know. Tabitha wrote back instantly, her message accompanied by a sad-face emoji. *I'm redesigning some of her spells as fast as I can. Sorry!*

My mouth twitched. This was the only time I'd ever seen my best friend wrestle with magic.

"Here's a suggestion for a reply to Alex," Barbara said. "You could say something like, 'Hi, thanks for your message—' "

"I've got it." Clicking on Alex's message, I typed,

About what? I glared at my screen, daring Barbara to critique my wording.

She remained silent.

Three blinking dots appeared below my message. Alex was typing back.

Easier to explain on the phone.

I frowned. Part of me was still angry with him, but part of me wanted to hear what he had to say. I leaned back in my chair and glanced behind the filing cabinet.

Lenti was still napping away, her head tipped up in a peaceful expression.

"Would you like to respond?" said Barbara. "Here's a suggestion if you need help. You could say—"

I clicked into the chat window and sent Alex a thumbs-up emoji. That shut Barbara up.

The next second, my phone rang. The caller ID displayed Alex's name. What was he so anxious to discuss?

I tapped the button on my headset to answer. "Yeah?"

"Rowan, hi. Thanks for taking my call."

His voice brushed against my senses with a calming, cozy, safe feeling, the verbal equivalent of a sweatshirt. My shoulders relaxed.

I made myself tense them again. That was just his charm, and charm was how Stygians tricked people into trusting them. I wasn't falling for the nice-guy act. Swiping the cherry-red stress ball from my desk, I squeezed it as hard as I could.

"First, I wanted to see if you're doing okay. I know you were upset yesterday."

"Humiliated." I chucked the stress ball at the opposite wall. "You lied to me."

"I'm sorry. I understand how you feel."

His gentle, contrite tone almost made it worse. He didn't have the right to feel sad or upset, and how dare he be understanding?

"I don't think you get it." I lowered my voice, wishing I could do a decent sound spell on my office so I could be angry in a louder fashion. "Remember I told you what happened to my sister? After Council investigators found Megan, I had to go down to the morgue and identify her body. Do you know what it feels like to look at your sister's corpse?"

"No." His voice dropped to a husky whisper. "That must've been horrible."

"It was." Snagging a tissue, I blotted the tears that were trying to squeeze their way out. I wasn't going to lose it in front of my boss, not even over the phone.

"Did you know the Stygian who deceived her?"

I snorted. *Deceived* was just a neutral way of saying *manipulated, controlled, and kidnapped.* "Unfortunately, yes. He went by Angelo Pisani, but I'm sure that wasn't his real name. He posed as an investment banker. He and Megan dated for five months."

"Sadly, that's often how we—they—find victims. Through relationships."

"She was in love with him." I swallowed hard. "I thought there was something off about him at first, but I couldn't put my finger on it. And she just seemed so happy. If I'd listened to my gut—"

"You were up against a demigod whose entire job was to make everyone see what he wanted them to see. You can't possibly blame yourself for not knowing he was dangerous."

Logically Alex was right, but grief doesn't listen to

logic. "How do you do it? Lie to your victims every day, I mean? Does it just not bother you?" Questions I often wished I could have asked Angelo, who skipped town after Megan disappeared. *Do you have no soul? How do you live with yourself?*

He cleared his throat. "I don't do things that way."

I squeezed the tissue so hard my fingers ached. "What do you mean?"

"I don't trick people into giving up their souls. I make other arrangements."

"I'm not following you." I really hoped he wasn't about to tell me that he only preyed on serial killers who deserved to die anyway, like in several popular TV shows. I didn't buy the whole "criminal with a conscience" trope.

"Are you aware that all Stygians are contractually obligated to send souls to Hades?"

"No." I'd assumed it was just part of a Stygian's nature to hunt for victims, something like a vampire's need for blood.

"We sign a contract at age eighteen, agreeing to send Hades at least one soul a year. Of course, many Stygians enjoy the power they exert over others, and send many more than one soul per year. Hades even gives out an award for it. Reaper of the Year."

I grimaced. "That's disgusting."

"Agreed, which is why I don't work that way. I've always advertised openly on the Hades fan forums."

A laugh sputtered out of me. "I'm sorry, what? Hades has fans?"

"You'd be surprised. Faeries, especially, idolize him. There's a whole contingent that really got into his heavy-metal phase—"

"Back the train up. Hades had a heavy-metal phase?"

"Yeah, he signed with a supernatural-run record label, oh, thirty years ago. His first two albums did pretty well, and he was supposed to be working on a third, but no one's seen anything from him in a while."

I'd only ever seen Hades illustrated as a heavily bearded figure with a spear. I frowned at the image of the god of the Underworld rocking out on an electric guitar. "So, you find victims in the fan forums?"

"Not victims. I explain the terms ahead of time, and I only select someone who consents. A superfan gets to meet their idol, I fulfill the terms of the contract, and no one has to do any lying or manipulating."

I spun around in my chair, using my right foot to brake and then push off in the opposite direction. "If it's that easy, then why don't more Stygians do it that way?"

"Because soul-reaping is addictive. The power, the thrill of being in control of the fate of another. Many live for the hunt."

My skin prickled. Angelo must've been that way. He only dated my sister to gain access to her soul. The idea of him relishing Megan's death made my stomach heave. "And you don't live for it? Why?"

"Mostly because of my mother. I'll tell you about her sometime."

Huh. Well, I supposed even monsters had mothers.

Alex sighed. "The thing is, I haven't sent Hades any souls at all for the last five years. I've been trying to find a way to break my contract."

I stared at the phone console, watching the little counter on the screen that kept track of our call length. The numbers ticked up in the silence as I absorbed

Alex's words. A Stygian who wanted to escape the life? I'd never heard of such a thing. Could he be making this whole thing up just to earn my trust? "How does Hades feel about this?"

"He wasn't aware of it until recently. Someone on the inside helped me, altering records to make it seem like I was still reaping."

This was getting weirder by the minute. Next he was going to tell me he'd descended into a chamber attached to a wire and ducked around lasers in order to steal something. "What happened? Why isn't he helping you anymore?"

"She. And we broke up."

Oh. Of course Alex had dated someone else. What, had I thought he was just sitting around, waiting for me to kiss him? He was gorgeous. Women probably lined up around the block to go out with him. A slightly sick feeling washed over me, even though I didn't have a right to it.

"Rowan?"

I tipped my chair back and stuck my feet on the desk. "Send me a link to one of your ads on the fan forums."

"Why?"

"Because I don't have any reason to believe you or this ridiculous story."

His voice tightened. "Fair enough." After several moments of background clicks, he said, "There you go."

Our chat window blinked. I sat up straight and clicked the link he'd just sent me.

The link took me to an ad on a website called True Hades Fans.

Permanent Job in the Underworld, the post was titled. *Hey, Hades Fans, I'm back again! For those who are new, here's the situation.*

I checked the date stamp on the post. January second, six years ago. The username was *alexkouris1*, and the avatar was his photograph.

I didn't think even a demigod could spin up an entire website with a time-stamped chat history in thirty seconds. This looked legit.

"All right. I believe you about the fan forums." Taking my feet off the desk, I spun back and forth in my chair. "How are you supposed to break a contract with the god of the Underworld?"

"Good question. I'm hoping the Firm can help. You can't say anything to anyone about this. I'm not supposed to discuss it at all. But they've agreed to take my case. In fact, Noel is working on it."

The shell around my heart softened a tad. Noel Barfield, a founding partner of the Firm, was my favorite attorney. He was the only partner who ever complimented my user guides, and he always attended Tabitha's training classes, even though he struggled to understand spreadsheets. He treated everyone the same, from other partners to the receptionists. If he considered Alex a worthy client, then there must be some good in the man.

Heat bloomed against my sternum. I put my hand over my heart, feeling the hard edges of the crystal through my sweater. Was the crystal responding to Alex? Favorably? Ugh. "I should probably go. Good luck with everything."

Five seconds after we hung up, Muse blinked with another message from Alex. *Thanks for listening. And I hope we can be friends.*

I glared at the screen. It wasn't fair at all for Alex to

possess an earth-shattering degree of hotness *and* apparent moral fiber. How was I supposed to keep hating him when he was so likeable?

I typed into the chat window, my stomach churning with the sensation that I was doing something as dangerous as driving ninety miles an hour the wrong way without a seat belt. *Sure. We're friends.*

Chapter Five

An hour later, Lenti was snoring, and I'd completed a whole damn sentence in my revised OpenFang user guide. My conversation with Alex kept running through my head, along with more questions. I reread his ad on the Hades forum a dozen times. He was explicit about the permanence of sending someone through a death portal and gave numerous warnings that there were no guarantees once the person arrived. *Serving Hades could mean a glamorous job, like running one of his nightclubs, or it could mean cleaning the god's toenails with a toothbrush,* he'd written.

The Underworld had nightclubs?

I had to hand it to Alex. The guy didn't sugarcoat anything.

I was softening toward him, like a perfectly baked cookie. I couldn't afford to become a cookie. What if Alex was presenting this seemingly honest, kind side of himself specifically to woo me? What if he actually had me targeted as his next victim? He could be lying about wanting to escape his contract, or about the Firm taking his case. I could check the case files to verify his claim, of course, but if the Firm wanted to keep Alex's case a secret, they might be keeping the records on paper locked in the safe in Noel's office.

So, let's say Alex was telling the truth. How had he developed empathy when Stygian magic was built around manipulation?

He'd mentioned his mother. Stygians preyed on humans, so I supposed his mother could've been human. But how would that've been possible? Stygians were supposed to coerce the victim into passing through a death portal. Alex spoke of his mother in the present tense. How or why was she still alive?

My phone rang. I grunted and checked the caller ID. Reception. This usually meant an attorney emergency.

"Rowan, thank the gods," said Carina. "Do you know how to hook up the monitor in the Everett Room? Some of the partners are doing a presentation to a client, and I'm not allowed to leave the desk. I tried talking them through it on the phone, but they didn't get it, and no one's answering at tech support."

Probably because Dave was off flirting with his girlfriend and distracting her from work. Of course there were other support techs around, but I liked to blame things on Dave in general.

"I'll take care of it." Hanging up, I shoved my chair back from my desk.

Lenti popped up from her blanket. "Where are we going?"

"Upstairs, but you can't come with me. The vampires will smell you."

"No problem." She meowed a few times, then wriggled her butt and leaped onto my shoulder.

"What did you do?"

"Scent-masking spell. Should last all day." With the soft pop of a soap bubble, she disappeared.

Of course, a scent-masking spell. Now I could take my invisible cat literally everywhere at work. Would she insist on accompanying me to the bathroom?

We took the elevator to the thirteenth floor. I headed to the reception area, then toward the Everett Room.

Inside, several attorneys stood in a cluster, including Noel.

His assistant, Elizabeth, sat at the conference table with her notepad. As usual, she was scowling.

I slipped through the door, ignored Elizabeth's mutters, and approached Noel. "I heard you guys need some help."

"Ah, our savior is here." He took my hand and lightly kissed the back of it. He still acted like a genteel, late 1800s banker. I always wondered who turned him, but in the same way that you don't ask a human how they were conceived, you don't ask a vampire how they were made.

Letting go of my hand, Noel gestured at the presentation monitor. "None of us are sure how to connect this…contraption."

Every vampire in the room was at least a hundred years old. Modern technology tended to baffle them, and they could never remember what an HDMI cable was for.

I grabbed a cable out of the wall cabinet, plugged it into the monitor, and hooked it up to the laptop on the conference room table.

The screen filled with a presentation slide reading *Land Acquisition Project*.

"There you go."

"I'm eternally grateful to you." Noel gave me a fanged smile. He gestured to a statuesque redheaded woman who stood talking to Evelyn, another partner. "Melanie? I'd like to introduce you to Rowan, our technical writer. Melanie Harper is the CEO of The City

Elysium Group, Rowan."

The redheaded woman turned toward me and flashed the whitest smile I'd ever seen outside a mouthwash commercial. Her form-fitting tailored black suit jacket and pencil skirt with a pale green blouse were accessorized with black pumps with what looked like ice picks for heels. Seriously, how did she walk in those things?

I smiled back. Why had I picked today to wear faded flats?

With the grace of a ballerina, she extended a long-fingered hand toward me. "Nice to meet you, Rowan. Our company develops commercial real estate, and we're now extending into residential."

This explained Noel's presence in the room. He ran the Pan-Magical Regulatory group, which advised on any case where magic and the human world collided.

As I took Melanie's hand, my shoulders relaxed. She had a lovely smile, and emanated warmth and power. Too bad I couldn't sit in on this meeting. I'd love to hear more about her business, find out the secret of her success.

She smiled wider, her fingernails pressing into my palm.

Lenti pierced my sweater with her claws.

Several pinpricks of pain stung my skin. My eyes watered, and I dropped Melanie's hand. A shiver rolled down my spine. "I have to go, but it was nice to meet you."

Her smile faltered, then widened. "I'm sure we'll see each other again."

My stomach heaved. What the hell? I nodded, mumbled a, "See you later," to Noel, and rushed out of the room.

On the trip down in the elevator I sucked in deep, shaky breaths, trying to calm my sudden nausea. Where had this sudden sick feeling come from? I'd had my usual breakfast of oatmeal, which never upset my stomach. I didn't think last night's burrito had given me food poisoning. I *knew* I wasn't pregnant. Not having sex is a convenient way to scratch that worry off your list.

Back in my office, I sank into my chair, and Lenti's weight left my shoulder. A soft plop told me when she landed on my desk.

"Who was that creature?"

"What creature?" I logged back into my computer and stared at my user guide, not at all motivated to keep working on it.

"That woman who touched your hand. I disliked her greatly."

The keys on my keyboard clacked as an invisible Lenti strolled across my keyboard, inadvertently finishing a sentence in my document. *Click the Type drop-down to cdc5tjmo9l.*

"Can you move? Please?"

She hopped into my lap and rematerialized.

I erased Lenti's typo. "She's a client, and she's a powerful, successful woman." My fingers stilled on the keyboard. "Why did I just say that?"

"She reeked of magic." Lenti yawned. "Some type of influence." Pillowing her head on her front paws, she went to sleep.

My skin crawled. In retrospect, Melanie's magic was obvious. New clients didn't normally dazzle me, except last year when I met Samuel Ash, the famous warlock actor from a dozen superhero films.

He hired the Firm to manage his estate and did a meet-and-greet with the staff as a favor to his lawyers.

Tabitha and I both went a bit fangirl squealy.

I mentally ticked off a list of supernaturals who wielded influence. Vampires did it all the time. Werewolves? Occasionally. Could Melanie be fae? Maybe Seelie royalty? The Seelie court was more of a decorative formality these days than an actual power structure, and many of the younger fae had successful careers outside the realm. Or, hell. She could be an eldritch witch, like me.

None of those options were comforting.

Around eleven, my stomach grumbled.

I lifted Lenti off my lap, stood, and eased her curled form onto my chair.

She didn't open her eyes. No one would be able to see her from the hallway, so she was safe.

Maybe I could sneak off to the break room.

"Where are you going?"

I sighed and peeked over my shoulder. "The break room for lunch."

"Great."

Pop.

A moment later, her now-familiar weight settled onto my shoulder. If she was going to keep treating me like her personal pack animal, I might have to start wearing padded jackets or a back brace.

"Is there any cheese stuff for lunch?" she asked.

Letting Lenti lick my empty mac-and-cheese bowl last night was a big mistake. She'd already asked for more a few times. "No, and dairy's bad for you. The manual says so."

"It does not."

"You have your own food. You can't live on cheese. Cats are obligate carnivores, you know."

"I know. I'm the cat here."

I rolled my eyes, and we headed for the break room.

I opened the fridge and grabbed my lunch sack off the bottom shelf, flinching as Lenti's weight tipped forward and her claws sank into the back of my neck. When I straightened up, she re-draped her tiny form with her paws dangling dangerously near my collarbone.

"Die of separation, my ass," I muttered, as I began washing my apple at the sink. This was my life now. A six-pound cat was permanently attached to my shoulder and ordered me around, and my boss was a hot lowlife.

"What did that apple do to you?" said a deep, rich voice.

Speak of the Stygian.

I shut off the water and shook droplets off the fruit.

Alex stood at the other end of the break room, but he was close enough for me to drink in the sight of him. One of his tight black curls sat askew, and his deep-brown eyes sparkled to match the amused smile on his face. Ugh, that dimple again. It was too much.

"I'm not trying to interrupt your lunch." He put both hands up in a gesture of surrender. "I just have to, uh—the thing is, my food is in the fridge."

"I don't own the break room." I laughed. "I was just going back to my office, anyway."

"Oh, no. Of course."

He slipped past me, at a completely reasonable distance, but I still caught a whiff of the sea, wild and salt-laced. "Why do you smell like the ocean?" I blurted.

One corner of his mouth bunched up in a small smile as he opened the fridge. "Part of the magic, I'm afraid.

We smell like whatever your favorite scent is. So, different things for different people. I can't really turn it off."

"Huh." Megan used to say how incredible Angelo smelled, like cinnamon and Christmas trees.

"I hope it's not too distracting." He took a plastic container of chili out of the fridge and shut the door. "Do you need the microwave?"

"You go first." I set my apple on a small clean plate—the communal cutting board skeeved me out—and dug through a drawer for a knife. As I chopped, I snuck another glance at Alex.

He whistled to himself, watching his lunch rotate in the microwave.

His whistling was adorably off-key. The one thing about him that wasn't perfect, because everything else was, from his cut-glass jaw to the slope of his muscled shoulders. Shit, there I went again, thinking mushy thoughts about my boss the soul-reaping demigod.

What would Megan have said? The Megan before Angelo, the sister who had entertained me during Mass by drawing me funny cartoons on a church notepad. The sister who always cut to the heart of a problem. Who never judged me.

Would she have judged me for this?

Somehow, I didn't think so. I could almost picture her close-lipped smile, her eyes soft.

You're never alone, Ro, she told me during my first year of boarding school, when I was crying to her about not having any friends. *I believe your power will come back. And you'll always have me.*

I cleared my throat. The crystal pulsed against my chest as I tore a paper towel from a nearby roll. No crying today. If I'd learned anything from Megan's death, it was that the world kept moving around you whether you wanted it to or not. You had to try to keep moving with it.

Alex punched the microwave timer again. "Sorry. I'm almost done." He shoved his hands into his pockets and started whistling again.

As I watched him, the realization washed over me. I was looking at the one person who could do exactly what I'd wanted to for the last two years—get in touch with my sister.

I dropped the knife onto the counter with a clatter. "Hey. You can still get into the Underworld, right? You don't just send other people through?"

His eyes narrowed. "I told you, I don't *send* anyone. They go on their own."

"Yes, fine." I waved a hand. "Can you, yourself, still travel to the Underworld?" *Please say yes.*

"Why?"

I took a step toward him. "I'm not going to report you to the Firm. Can you or not?"

"I can." He glanced at the microwave. "Why?"

Oh, my gods. Why hadn't I already thought of this? "If I wanted to get a message to someone in the Underworld, you could deliver it, right?"

Confusion crossed his face, followed by recognition. He shook his head. "I'm sorry."

My heart fell. "It doesn't work like that?" I should've known. It would be too simple, too easy, too wonderful for me to finally have a conduit to Megan. There were probably rules and caveats, like everything in the supernatural world.

He gestured to the room in general. "Let's not

discuss this here. Come back to my office and we'll talk."

That wasn't an answer. My heart pounded as we finished heating up our lunches.

As I followed him into the hallway, Lenti smushed her tiny furry face next to mine, reminding me she was still there. As if I could forget I was carrying an invisible cat. I hoped her face wasn't making some kind of weird dent in my cheek.

Back in his office, Alex closed the door. "Do you want to sit?"

Nope. Couldn't get too comfortable. "I'm fine standing."

We stood on opposite sides of his desk, like it was a kitchen island. I waited, my heart thrumming, Lenti's warm breath on my cheek.

Alex stirred his chili absently and slid the bowl away. "I can pass into the Underworld through a portal, a different kind, not a death portal. I haven't been in years, though. Portals take at least a day to create. And you can only open them on the night of a full moon."

I inhaled sharply. "But you can still do it."

"I can get in. It doesn't mean I can find a specific person. There are millions of souls there, in multiple Underworld realms."

He could get in. To the Underworld. Megan's soul was there, and *he could get there*. "But it's not impossible?"

His eyes filled with a deep sadness. "You want me to contact your sister."

My throat hurt again, and I swallowed hard. "Yes."

"I'd like to help you, Rowan." He massaged his temples and blew out a breath. "The problem is, Hades is threatening to throw me in Tartarus for breach of contract. If I go back now, he'll have every demon in five realms after me. I wish I could help you. I really do."

I clenched my jaw at the unspoken "but" in his sentence. Boo-hoo, the demigod might get in trouble with Daddy.

I opened my mouth to shoot back a snarky reply, but the words died at the back of my throat. To be fair, Alex was my boss, not my friend. Why would he risk his personal safety for me? He didn't owe me anything.

Gods help me.

It was his voice, but his lips weren't moving. I was hearing his thoughts.

He sighed heavily. *I can't let this happen.*

Can't let what happen? I almost asked, but I didn't know how to admit I'd just read his mind. How had I done it, anyway? Was it the eye contact? Did that make it easier?

"I'm probably the last person you want advice from," he said aloud. "I can't imagine how hard it must have been to lose your sister. But the best thing you could possibly do would be to try and move on."

Heat flooded my body, and the crystal burned icy and fierce against my breastbone. Was he serious? "Move on? Now I know you have no soul."

I strode toward the door. Behind me, there was a crash.

Uh-oh.

I turned back around, jaw clenched.

Alex's bowl of chili spattered across the floor like the food version of a modern art painting, a mess of beef, beans, and shattered ceramic.

He looked from the chaos to me. "Did—did you do

that?"

"Not on purpose. Did I mention the crystal thing I hacked up might, um, be my power?"

"No, but that makes sense." He stared at the chili. "So, you're telekinetic then, yeah?"

"Guess so."

"Eldritch magic." He put his hands on his hips and contemplated the remains of his lunch. "Impressive."

"I have to go."

"Wait. Rowan." He moved toward me, then winced as his foot tracked through the chili. "I'm sorry for what I said just now."

I wasn't falling for his apology. "I don't want to talk to you about my sister."

I rushed out, my stomach churning with a nauseating combination of anger and humiliation. Back in my own office, I collapsed into my chair. Great, I'd left my lunch in Alex's office. Now I'd have to go out for food. I certainly wasn't going back there to retrieve it.

Lenti, reappearing with a pop, hopped onto the desk. "You have telekinesis."

"Lovely. I used to be able to levitate rodents, and now all I can do is break bowls of chili?"

"You just need to practice." She rolled back onto her haunches and stuck one hind leg straight out, leaning forward to clean her thigh. "Your boss smelled just like that lady. The one who gave us the ick?"

I froze. "Wait. You're saying Alex's magic smells the same as Melanie's? Are you sure?"

Her top lip lifted in a sneer. "You doubt my nose? I hail from the seventh realm—"

"Of the troposphere, I know. But are you sure it's the same? Not just similar? Maybe you made a mistake."

"I don't make mistakes." Lenti swiped her tongue over her leg. "They smelled exactly the same."

"But that would mean…" I leaned back in my chair, a cold weight dropping onto my shoulders.

That would mean the most obvious answer. The one I should have thought of already. Who else besides a vampire wielded influence?

Melanie was a Stygian, too.

****

Tabitha leaned in, pointing at a search result on my screen. "This one, maybe?"

"Elysian Fields Beauty Products. Probably a trademark application." I scanned through the list of twenty-five hits from our case database. Most of them had appeared only because they contained the word "group" or a few letters from the word Elysium. None of them were The City Elysium Group.

"Elizabeth must still be doing intake." Tabitha leaned against my desk, frowning.

I'd pulled her into my office half an hour ago and explained my theory about Melanie. Well, technically, Lenti's theory. Tabitha had suggested we search the City Elysium Group case file. Sadly, she was probably right about the intake.

Elizabeth kept a stack of files on her desk, and she frequently neglected to spell materials into the electronic case database.

Tabitha had been trying to train the assistants and paralegals on magical document management for three years, but Elizabeth was something of a losing battle.

Lenti, who'd taken up a post on my desk right next to all the excitement, head-butted Tabitha's arm.

My best friend smiled and scratched Lenti under her

chin, and the familiar responded by tilting her head to the side and purring.

I narrowed my eyes at Lenti, then checked the door. "Can you go back to being invisible now?"

"Fine." *Pop.*

The purring continued, and Tabitha's hand rested on the air.

I cleared my throat. "So do I need to ask Elizabeth for the file, or can you beam it down here?"

"Hmm. I have an idea." Tabitha glanced down at the space where Lenti was. "Do you know how to do a basic mirror spell?"

The little cat trilled. "Of course. Do you need one?"

I racked the cobwebby corners of my brain for remnants of Spell Casting 101. Came up empty. "What does a mirror spell do?"

Not seeming to hear me, Tabitha tilted her head to the side. She grinned. "Yeah. This'll work."

"You're going to use a perception spell?" Lenti said.

"Exactly. And then when I give you the signal—"

"I see."

"I don't." I looked at Tabitha, but she was already moving into spell casting position, feet shoulder-width apart.

Lenti popped into view again and stood on all fours, poised on the edge of the desk.

"I guess I'll block you from view." Getting up, I stood in front of Lenti so no one would notice her from the hall.

She stared at me, then head-butted Tabitha's arm. Total power move. Like she was taunting me with how much more she liked my best friend.

Tabitha lifted her hands, as if she were about to

conduct an orchestra. "Ro, what floor does Elizabeth sit on? Eight or nine?"

I didn't even have to check the directory. Elizabeth sat just outside Noel's office, and I'd been there dozens of times to help him with his computer. "Eight."

"Okay." She closed her eyes and lifted her hands palms-up toward the ceiling. She repeated a Latin phrase three times, each time lifting her hands a bit higher.

Something about seeing what was hidden, maybe? My Latin had never been the greatest.

The air around her rippled, as if she'd temporarily stepped into a heat wave. Eyes still closed, she kept one hand in the air and placed the other hand on Lenti's head.

"The thoughts of your mind become visible to your eyes." Lenti's voice dropped several notes lower than normal.

A bolt of purple electricity fizzed down Tabitha's arm and leaped to the top of Lenti's head.

With a crack, a violet flame appeared over each of Lenti's ears.

Tabitha and Lenti intoned together, "So it shall be."

The flames and electricity fizzed out with a zap, as if a dozen bugs had just hit a light. At the same time, my office printer whirred to life and began spitting out pages.

Well, holy shit.

Tabitha opened her eyes and grinned. "It worked! Good job, Lenti." She kissed the cat on the top of her head, and instead of swiping at her face, Lenti purred and licked Tabitha's chin.

What a little traitor.

I rushed over to the printer and grabbed the first several pages. Indeed, it appeared to be the City Elysium

Group case file. "How did you do this?"

"I used a perception spell to envision the file, and Lenti's mirror spell produced the copy. It wouldn't have worked without both of us."

"Nice job." I shoved back a pang of envy as I waited for the last pages to print. Tabitha was performing two-person spells with my familiar, while I was struggling to even understand my power.

I stapled the case file together and took a seat.

Lenti hopped into my lap and placed her front paws on the desk, her head close to the pages.

"You can read, Lenti?" said Tabitha.

What else was in that damn manual?

"Of course." Lenti tapped the page with her paw. "This says that horrible woman is...horrible, and a hundred cats should poop in her bed."

I traded glances with Tabitha. Both of us fought back smiles.

Lenti glanced up at me. "Right?"

"That's exactly what it says." Despite myself, I scratched her under the chin before continuing to scan the file.

The first page was just basic intake information—address of The City Elysium Group, phone number, business identification number. Melanie Harper was listed as the CEO, just like Noel had told me. Nothing in the first few pages screamed danger or made mention of Melanie's magical powers. "Wouldn't Noel have to know if she's a Stygian?"

"I guess. I mean, the Firm was aware of Alex." Tabitha shrugged. "Unless Melanie lied to him. But doesn't he scan prospective clients?"

Most attorneys used some variation of a magical

detection or scanning spell when meeting with potential clients for the first time. We'd all heard the horror story about the vampire at a firm up in Seattle. Six years ago, he'd gotten sloppy and failed to scan a client, only to have the client—a vampire hunter who hired him on false pretenses—stake him through the heart in the middle of a deposition.

"I'm sure he does." I flipped through the rest of the file, but Noel's elegantly scripted notes said nothing about Melanie's magic.

According to the notes, The City Elysium Group was brokering a deal to acquire a plot of land by the waterfront, which they wanted to convert into a high-rise condo building. It would be magically cloaked, appearing to the ordinary human world as a small park.

Not a bad idea. Vampires, werewolves, and witches could invest in real estate, and the building wouldn't block any ordinary human neighbors' views of the river.

It all seemed on the up-and-up. There was even a note about obtaining a sustainability certification for the building. Yet I couldn't forget the way Melanie stared me down, or her cold fingers gripping mine.

"Wait." I gasped and pointed at a note at the bottom of the last page. *Referred by Alex Kouris.* I looked down at Lenti, knowing she'd be curious what the document said. "Alex referred Melanie. He knows her."

The cat's tiny mouth curled up, and one of her fangs peeked out. "Why would he associate with such a dangerous individual?"

Good question. Why would Alex refer a fellow Stygian to the Firm? Come to think of it, why was a Stygian heading up a real estate group to begin with? A lot of people in the magical community distrusted them.

How was the group planning on marketing its real estate? What if they were trying to attract more Stygians to Portland, making our city a hub for soul-hunting? Alex might have a conscience, but other Stygians didn't.

I set the sheaf of pages down. There was something odd about this. Alex had just told me he wanted to end his contract with Hades, yet he was inviting another Stygian into our firm as a client. Shouldn't he be distancing himself from his fellow soul-reapers? Plus, he was the IT director, not a partner expected to build a client list. Why was he referring clients at all?

I gently scooped Lenti out of my lap and placed her on the desk, then stood. "I have to talk to him."

Tabitha nodded and scratched Lenti's tiny chin. "Do you want me to come with you?"

I chewed on my lower lip. Alex had mentioned in an all-IT email this morning that we were going to be starting a Firm-wide data security campaign. This might not be the best time to tell him two of his employees had stolen a case file. "I think I'd better go alone."

Lenti tilted her head up. "Excuse me?"

"Right." I sighed. "You'll die if we're separated, right?"

She began grooming her left ear. "Never said that."

"Are all familiars this obstinate?" I rolled my eyes at Tabitha.

"Haven't you read the manual yet?"

"No." I hefted the cat into my arms and let her climb onto my shoulder. "Let's go, gremlin."

She popped into invisibility.

Tabitha followed us into the hall. "Gods be with you. Text me when it's over."

I was going to need the gods, goddesses, and every

known deity to help me figure out what to say to Alex without getting in trouble. I ran through different scenarios as I trudged toward his office. Was there a way I could ask about Melanie without him realizing I'd nabbed a case file? Could anyone else reasonably have told me he referred Melanie? I could blame Noel, but he didn't normally introduce clients according to who had referred them. In fact, sometimes that detail was confidential.

As I passed the tech-support cubicles, Dave glanced up from his monitor. "I like your hair today."

I nodded to acknowledge I comprehended the words coming out of his mouth and kept moving. When we dated, I wore my hair short with blonde highlights, and Dave openly commented on his preference for long, dark hair. Rude. After we broke up, I let it grow out and dyed it back to its natural brunette, partly to spite him. He'd never commented on the color change before, though. He must be flirting or trying to get under my skin. Either way, *bye.*

Guess who else had long dark hair? Natasha, his girlfriend, the one he'd cheated on me with. A vampire frozen in time at twenty-five, made in the early 2000s. She was a runway model until a vampire photographer bit her after a late-night shoot.

The vampire thing alone wouldn't have halted her career, if she'd kept it under wraps and stayed out of the sun, but someone caught her sipping on a bag of blood backstage at a major New York fashion event, and her agency dropped her.

I'd heard some of the legal assistants gossiping about it one day in the reception area.

I guess if Dave was going to cheat on me with a

model, at least she was a model-turned-paralegal, which just didn't sound impressive.

I took the last few steps to Alex's door and peered into his office.

He stood at his desk, eyes on his leftmost monitor. His lips parted, and then he tapped a few keys on his keyboard and frowned. He closed his eyes for a moment, then did the whole routine again. Whatever he was reading was either pissing him off or he was thinking very hard about it.

It would've been cute if I wasn't still mad at him.

Through the half-open door, I checked the carpet. There was no sign of the deceased bowl of chili. He must've cleaned it up.

I rapped on the doorframe.

He flinched and glanced at me. "Oh. Hi. Are you here for your lunch? I put it back in the fridge for you."

Still thoughtful, even when we'd just argued. Why couldn't he have eaten my lunch or dumped my food in the garbage, like the asshole I needed him to be? I swallowed my anger. "Got a sec?"

"Sure."

I sidled into the office and shut the door as he stepped out from behind his desk.

His expression was guarded, but there was no anger there, even though I'd destroyed his lunch. He sighed, and regret flashed in his dark eyes. "I'm sorry for what I said earlier about you needing to move on from your sister's death. It was insensitive and ignorant. I've never lost a sibling, and I don't know what it's like. I'm truly sorry, Ro."

Most people called me Ro, but my nickname on his lips sounded like a caress, the brush of a hand over a cheek. His huge brown eyes drew me in. I felt safe and warm. I wanted to walk into his broad embrace and stay there, preferably for the next month.

On my shoulder, Lenti shifted invisibly. *Stop thinking about licking him.*

I almost shrieked. For a second, I thought she'd spoken aloud, but no, she was inside my head somehow. The crystal pulsed under my shirt. *How are you doing this?*

You're doing it. I can read your mind, but I wouldn't be able to communicate with you unless you were also a telepath. Like me. I can do everything, you know.

Yes, I know. Apparently. I really needed to read the manual.

Alex was looking at me strangely, and I realized I'd probably paused too long talking to Lenti in my head. "Uh, thanks. I appreciate it. That isn't why I need to talk to you, though."

"What's going on?" He leaned back against his desk and folded his arms, causing his forearm muscles to bulge slightly.

Damn it, he was making it hard to concentrate. I cleared my throat and took the conversational plunge. "Why did you refer Melanie Harper and The City Elysium Group to the Firm?"

He paused for what felt like an hour.

"Who told you?"

"I helped Noel set up for a conference with Melanie this morning, and Elizabeth told me." I held my breath as soon as the lie slipped out, waiting to see if it would stick. He didn't say anything and seemed to wait for me to continue. "Is Melanie a Stygian?"

His voice tightened like a tuned guitar string. "Yes."

Told you. Lenti head-butted my cheek.

I flinched and coughed, hoping to cover the slight twitch of my head. "I'm assuming she hasn't signed a non-reaping agreement, like you did. Or has she?"

"I can't talk about this right now." His voice dropped to a low volume. "Someone might hear us."

"That's what a sound spell is for. Everyone uses them." I lifted an eyebrow. "You know how to do one, right? Tabitha's really good at them if you need help."

"I know how to do one, but we still can't talk about this here."

Oh, no. He wasn't getting out of this so easily. "Then explain it to me somewhere else."

"It's complicated." He sighed and uncrossed his arms.

What was he thinking?

The crystal grew uncomfortably warm against my bare skin. A snippet of memory flashed across my mind, but it didn't belong to me—the image of Melanie's deep hazel eyes, and a feeling of fondness. It was as if, for a moment, I viewed her through an Alex-filter. There was a shared history there, a bond.

Oh, my gods.

Was *Melanie* his ex-girlfriend? The one who'd helped him cover up his lack of soul-reaping? *We broke up*, he'd said.

The crystal flared with heat, then cooled a bit. Could you get a burn from your own power?

My nose twitched, and I rubbed it with the back of my hand. I hoped I wasn't developing an allergy to cat hair, otherwise Lenti and I were in for a long sneezy ride. "Alex. Come on."

He heaved a sigh. "I'll talk to you, but not here. We

can do lunch. Or dinner."

Dinner?

I'd expected him to suggest we find a conference room. Or maybe take a stroll around the block. Dinner implied something else. Wasn't dinner a date? No, I couldn't date Alex. But could I go on *a* date with him? Just to window-shop? He'd be even hotter if he lost the suit and tie.

Hotter still if he lost them in my bedroom.

My cheeks flamed. "Dinner's fine. When?"

"Let me see." He stepped around to his computer, peeked at the screen, and frowned. "Saturday? I have Firm events and conference calls every night this week. It's gonna be hell."

I smirked. "Can a demigod of the Underworld say hell, or is that considered sacrilege?"

He rolled his eyes. "The Underworld isn't the same thing as Hell."

"I was joking." Sheesh, he was wound up tight. Wickedly, I fantasized about what I could do to help him relax, and then remembered Lenti could get into my head. I pictured a nice bowl of ice cream instead and cleared my throat. "Saturday is fine." My tone sounded casual, at least I thought so.

Inside, excitement clamored for an escape. Dinner with Alex. An actual date. Would he kiss me again? What if we went home together?

He nodded. "I'll text you details later, then. I have to get back to some things."

I started to ask how he had my number, but then I realized he could get it from the IT staff directory. "I'll see you Saturday."

I wandered back to my office, my mind racing.

Lenti? Can you still hear me?

Yes.

I grinned. The connection between our minds felt like a wire stretched taut between two hooks, an electric thing, alive and buzzing. *So, I wasn't imagining I could hear other people's thoughts?*

No. I told you. If we can communicate, then you're a telepath.

My hopes climbed. Telepathy would be awesome, maybe even more than telekinesis, if I could figure out how to control it. Right now the effects seemed totally random. I could tell the crystal was changing temperature when my magic flared up, but I couldn't seem to do anything on cue.

You'll learn.

Why haven't you mentioned you can read my mind?

It's in the manual, like everything else. Aren't you done reading it yet?

You know I'm not.

A faint trill, a cat-snicker, echoed in my mind. *Maybe you should've started with the table of contents.*

I sighed. *You're coming with me to dinner on Saturday, aren't you? I'm not going to be able to convince you to stay home?*

Nope.

The prospect of an intimate dinner with Alex fled. Ah yes, I could picture it now—a cozy meal, staring into Alex's eyes over a glass of wine, while my invisible cat made snarky commentary in my brain.

How romantic.

Chapter Six

I turned from side to side in front of the mirror, examining my half French braid. My dark-brown hair wound across the top of my head, like a crown. I tucked the end under the rest of my hair and twisted it into a side ponytail, tying it off with a clear elastic.

"Pretty." Tabitha stood in my bathroom doorway. With her flat tone of voice, she might as well have been describing broccoli or glue.

I plucked a beaded fringe earring off the counter and slipped it through the hole in my right earlobe.

Lenti, who sat on the counter, trilled and swiped the earring with her paw.

"Nope." I jerked my head away. "I got these at a craft fair, and you're not destroying them."

"What's that?"

"Never mind." Should've known this was going to happen. Gritting my teeth, I removed the earring and tucked it into a drawer. I tugged the neckline of my clingy black dress a little lower, then turned to Tabitha. "Is it too much? Should I wear my strappy sandals or my ankle boots?"

She crossed her arms. "Explain to me how this happened. You were supposed to talk to him, not go out with him."

Lenti paused in the middle of licking her chest fur. "Well, first he said—"

"It's not a big deal." I glared at the cat before continuing. "I asked him about Melanie, and he said he couldn't tell me at work."

"And what, he requires gourmet burgers and cocktails to tell you? He couldn't call you on the phone?"

"It's just easier this way. At least in person I can try reading his thoughts." I'd already told Tabitha I might be telepathic, and we'd tested my newfound powers a few times this week. I could read her thoughts, but not with any consistency or predictability. Lenti claimed I'd get better at control over time, but I wasn't sure. I might not be able to read Alex's mind at all tonight, in which case going to dinner with him was pointless.

I mean, other than the fact that I was going to dinner with a guy who made me drool, but whatever.

"What if he senses you invading his mind? He might be able to block you."

"I don't know. What if he doesn't sense me invading his mind, and I successfully read all his thoughts?" I leaned toward the mirror and wiped a small smudge of mascara from under my left eye. "Let's think positive here."

"You don't know anything about him other than what we've seen at work. He's already lied to you by omission. What if he's just charmed you into thinking he's a good person?"

I'd been thinking the same thing this entire week. I wasn't sure Alex was a *good* person, but I felt confident he wasn't *bad.* It made no sense, but I knew it was true.

I frowned at my reflection and picked cat hair off my boob. "But have you ever heard of a Stygian who wants to stop reaping souls? Anyway, I don't think he's going to open a death portal in the middle of the Pearl

District. It's not even a full moon."

She poked my arm a few times. "You *like* him!"

I slipped the crystal and chain over my neck. With the low neckline of my dress, the crystal pointed straight at my boobs. Should I wear a sweater?

Nah.

I slipped past Tabitha and headed for the living room. "Ankle boots, right?"

Lenti darted past me, racing toward the front door. "I've never been to a restaurant. I've heard about them. Do they really have giant pieces of fish?"

I followed her to the entryway and dug my vegan leather ankle boots out of the closet. "Yes, but this dinner isn't for you. You're going to be invisible the whole time. Remember? I can't order you an entrée."

She narrowed her eyes at me.

I slipped on the boots. Yeah, definitely a better choice. I wasn't the most coordinated person in high heels.

Tabitha rounded the corner. "You're treating this like a date."

"What if I am?" A date was just two people hanging out and getting to know each other. Was I not allowed to get to know Alex?

"I'm just pointing out facts, Ro." She reached past me for her jacket, which hung on the coat rack.

Lenti yawned, showing her little fangs. "Are you ready yet? I need to be home in time for my midnight snack. Also, I want to watch more of the show with the drunk faeries."

Tabitha cocked an eyebrow at me. "You're letting her watch *Secrets of the Unseelie*?"

"She's not a toddler." I shrugged. "We're in the

middle of Season One. The Summerlands cast trip." A few days ago while I was watching a cast reunion, Lenti popped awake. When she started asking questions, I decided to start her over at Season One. She blazed through the first several episodes and knew all the characters. Her interest seemed a bit unnatural, but who was I to stand in the way of a new fan?

I checked the time on my phone and gasped. "We should've left ten minutes ago." I shrugged into my jacket.

"Well, that's not my fault, is it?" said Lenti. "I was ready *hours* ago."

"You don't wear clothes." I grabbed my purse. "Okay, gremlin, hop on."

I braced, and Lenti leaped onto my shoulder. I was almost used to the landing by now.

With a *pop*, she disappeared.

I touched the crystal lightly, like a talisman. If this wasn't a date, I didn't need luck, but just in case.

Tabitha followed us out to my car. "Text me the second you get back." She squeezed my hand. "I'm just worried about you, that's all. No matter what happens, I want to know everything."

I smiled and hugged her. "You know I'll tell you."

"Farewell, sweet Tabitha," trilled the invisible Lenti. "YOLO."

I paused with my hand on the car door. The faeries in *Unseelie* said YOLO. Was that where Lenti picked up that phrase?

Tabitha's lips twitched. "Do you know what YOLO means, sweetie?"

"It's an exuberant goodbye."

"Right. Okay, love you guys, text me." She waved

and hurried to her car, which was parked on the street a block from mine.

"YOLO!" hollered Lenti.

Cringing, I ducked into the car before some passerby could hear the disembodied yell. Once again, I remembered Lenti's warning to be careful about how much TV she watched. Maybe I should show her a nature documentary or two.

I buckled up and started the car.

Lenti leaped from my shoulder. She re-materialized in the front passenger seat and stood with her front paws on the passenger-side door, her nose against the glass.

I ruffled her soft head, oddly glad to have her company tonight. I'd figure out later if I should impose TV limits for my cat.

Just as soon as I read my hot boss's mind over dinner.

****

Thirty minutes later, I sat across a table from Alex in one corner of Thirteenth Street Kitchen, an upscale but laid-back restaurant just north of downtown.

The place was one of those typically Portland industrial-chic designs—polished concrete floor, exposed ducting overhead, pendant lights in clear globes, and a brick wall running behind the long polished wooden bar.

The host seated us at a small table, close enough for me to notice that Alex smelled like the ocean. Beneath the light jazz and clatter of silverware and glasses, I swore I heard the surf.

Alex had smiled and greeted me when I arrived, but now he sat with his head bent over the menu, studying it like it was a Bible. Not talking.

95

This felt like the start of every awkward date I'd ever had. Great.

I already knew what I wanted. Tabitha and I loved this place, and the salmon mac-and-cheese dish was to die for. My general motto when ordering out was *eat all the carbs.* I played with my cloth napkin and hoped Alex wasn't ordering something virtuous, like a salad.

He finally set down the menu and graced me with a broad smile. "You look really...nice."

Nice? I was showing tons of cleavage. I'd put on actual makeup. I looked hot, and sue me, I wanted him to notice. I'd figure out the complicated reasons for that later. Then again, this wasn't supposed to be a date, and he probably wanted to avoid running afoul of the Firm's sexual-harassment policy. "Thanks. You do too."

He looked more than nice. His French-blue button-down set off his brown skin, and those black pants fit his lower body like a glove. What? I might've checked out his ass when he led the way to our table. His curly black hair was looser tonight, the curls a little wild, as if mussed by an ocean breeze.

Or like bed hair.

Sweating already, I gulped my ice water. I was going to need multiple glasses and a cold shower to stop lusting over Alex. Maybe this wasn't a good idea.

"Ah, at least you look nice."

Glancing up, I pinned the voice to a wiry server dressed in all black. He wore his hair in a tidy bun. I didn't usually hear servers express such relief when approaching me, but I imagined working with the public was exhausting. "Rough day?"

A hint of surprise crossed his face. "Yeah, the last table was one of those impossible-to-please groups.

There was too much pepper on the salad. The wine didn't taste right. You know the type." He laughed, although it seemed like the kind of forced laugh you used to combat the existential terror of your job. He clicked a pen three times and poised it over a small notepad like a brush over a canvas. "Anyway, my name's Damon and I'm here to make you folks comfortable. What can I get you to start? Maybe a cocktail? We have a fantastic cucumber martini right now."

Were we doing drinks? I glanced at Alex. That would definitely make this dinner a full-on date.

His gaze flickered toward me, and a tiny smile lifted one side of his mouth. "Yeah, I might do a glass of the, uh, the 2017 cab?"

"2017 cab, good choice." He pivoted to me. "And for you, Miss?"

Well, since Alex had ordered wine. "The house pinot. Um, a glass, obviously, not a bottle." I laughed and then wished I hadn't. It wasn't even a funny joke.

Fortunately, Damon joined in. "Ha, right? Are you sure? I'll get those drinks right up and you just let me know if you need anything, okay?" He stabbed the pen through his bun and walked away. "*At least you're chill.*"

"We'll try to be, anyway," I called after him, but he didn't seem to hear me.

Alex frowned. "Try to be what?"

"Chill. He said…" I stopped. The slight echo of Damon's words hadn't been restaurant acoustics, but his thoughts. The crystal warmed against my chest, seeming to confirm my suspicion that I'd activated my powers again. "Never mind. Sounds like he had kind of shitty customers before us."

Alex glanced toward Damon, who now stood at

another table. "I could never be a server. I don't know how humans do it."

The statement shot a cold jolt down my spine. For a second, we had been two normal people meeting for dinner, but of course we weren't. Alex was a demigod, and his power could kill me, if he ever used it on me.

"I like your necklace." He leaned toward me. "Is that *the* crystal?"

Right. He hadn't seen it since I hacked it up in his office. When I'd accidentally destroyed his lunch, I'd been wearing it under my shirt. "It is." I lifted the chain so the crystal caught the light. I might possibly also have leaned forward to boost my B-cups. "I didn't want to risk losing it."

"You're not going to break my wineglass tonight, are you?"

My face burned. "The chili was an accident."

"I know." He winked. "I deserved it."

I smiled and let the crystal fall against my skin.

"It must be strange discovering your power as an adult. How's that going?" He sipped his water.

"Up and down." I rolled my eyes. "The Association doesn't have any resources on eldritch magic. I'm just practicing when I can. Tabitha's helpful." A pinprick of pain in my shoulder. "And Lenti, of course. My familiar."

That's better.

"I didn't realize you had a familiar." He nodded. "Smart, especially in your situation. Eldritch magic is actually pretty unwieldy, and you weren't raised a witch, so be patient with yourself. You'll be smashing bowls left and right before you know it." His brown eyes sparkled with mirth.

"Well, thanks." I played with the edge of my cloth napkin. "How does eldritch magic interact with Stygian magic, anyway? Your magic is sort of a mental magic too, so can you cancel out mine?" What I really needed to know was whether he could sense me reading his mind.

"It's a good question, but no. Stygian magic gets its power source from the waters of the Styx. Your power source is your own consciousness, your own energy. To stop you from using your magic on me, I'd have to sense the attack coming. I wasn't expecting the chili, so…" He grinned.

"What about other kinds of eldritch magic?" I hoped I wasn't being too obvious in this line of questioning. "Like predicting the future or reading minds?"

He shrugged. "Again, I'd have to sense an attack coming to stop it. It's harder to sense someone invading your mind unless you're trained to recognize it. I've never spent much time on it, but Stygian magic is so powerful, it's kind of pointless to spend hours training to defend ourselves from rare magic. You know what I mean?" He grimaced. "Influence is arguably the most dangerous magic there is. Another reason to break my contract."

Guilt and relief flooded my chest. He likely wouldn't have any clue I was reading his mind. I could steer the conversation to Melanie and figure out his intentions. Yes, I should probably confess my psychic abilities right now, but I clung to the new-and-shocking notion that a Stygian couldn't fight my magic.

I thought I was defenseless around Alex. It turned out I wasn't.

And I needed to protect myself.

Our drinks arrived, and Damon took our dinner orders.

After he left, Alex held up his wineglass in a toast. "Cheers."

"Wait. What are we cheers-ing to?"

"Oh. Do we always need something specific for this ritual? I've never quite figured it out." He glanced up, lips pursed. "I suppose our friendship?" He smiled, meeting my gaze again.

His eyes varied between the grayer brown of smoky quartz, and the richer brown of coffee, depending on what he wore. Right now, they were deep brown. Inviting.

Bedroom eyes.

"To friendship." I lifted my glass.

We both drank.

"So when are you going to tell me about Melanie? You said it was complicated." I touched the crystal lightly as if I was just playing with the necklace, testing my theory that direct contact with the crystal made it easier to read minds. Beneath my fingers, its tiny heart—as I was coming to think of it—beat softly.

"Down to business, eh?" He cleared his throat. "You can't tell anyone what I'm about to tell you. Not a soul."

"Got it." I didn't feel connected to his mind, not yet.

Lenti shifted her weight on my shoulder and tucked her small head against the underside of my jaw. *Can we tell Tabitha?*

Yep.

Alex dropped his voice to a husky half-whisper. "I told you about the contract I signed with Hades. For years, I've been trying to find a way out of it. I discussed this openly with Noel and the other partners at my first interview. It's a condition of my continued employment with Ainsley Barfield that I get out of my contract. That's why Noel took the case. Long-term, I'm a liability to the Firm."

That made more sense than Noel deciding to take on a complicated *pro bono* case out of the goodness of his heart. Law firms usually wanted to minimize risk as much as possible, and a soul-reaping Stygian employee posed a significant risk. If nothing else, word might get around the supernatural community and clients could be reluctant to engage our services.

I took another sip of my wine, concentrating on sending my energy toward Alex and tuning in to his thoughts somehow. Nothing yet. Nothing so clear as a word or phrase, anyway. Just a general sense of anxiety. His or mine? It was hard to tell.

Alex stared into his glass. "The Firm is trying to set up an arbitration with Hades's lawyers. Unfortunately, there are some complications."

Hades had lawyers, too? I supposed that made sense.

When's dinner? Lenti's small and slightly hollow voice wandered into my brain again. *I'm hungry.*

You ate before we left.

But I'm hungry again. A purr vibrated against my cheek.

Stop being cute. I'll feed you when we're home. I promise.

"Ro?"

"I'm sorry. There's something in my eye." In a self-fulfilling prophecy, it started to itch. I rubbed it and reached for my water. "You were saying…complications?"

He nodded. "The Firm wants to negotiate a deal

where Hades lets me out of the contract, and I surrender my power. Unfortunately, Stygian magic can only be broken through bloodshed. Hades probably wouldn't kill me, but he'd take enough blood that he might be able to use it in some future ritual or spell. And we don't know what that would entail. It would work, maybe, but it's risky."

My stomach roiled. "If that's the only choice, though…"

"I'd lose all of my magic." He swept his hand through the air in a slashing motion. "Charisma is what allows me to spell cast. I'd be a demigod with no power. Zero."

"Oh." I, maybe more than anyone, knew what it was like to be powerless. I'd probably fight an emu to keep my own magic. Then again, his magic was deadly, and mine wasn't. If he really wanted out, shouldn't he take the only option he had? "There's no other way? There aren't any loopholes in the contract?"

He snorted. "There's one clause, sure. It states that the contract can be broken by the death of the one who truly loves me. That'll never happen, for two reasons. First, I charm people into liking me. It's impossible for someone to love me completely irrespective of and independent of my power."

Impossible? So the fondness I felt for him, the attraction—all fake? Manufactured, a result of his own magic? Gods, that was messy. "I thought you had a girlfriend."

"I did, but she was a Stygian too. It was enjoyable, and there were affectionate feelings, but love? No." Anger sparked, electric, in his gaze. "Second, even if falling in love was possible, even if I somehow met my soulmate, I wouldn't turn around and kill her. Hades is clever. And cruel. He made it impossible to escape the contract."

The sadness in his eyes made my chest ache. "So the Firm's idea is the only way out."

"If Hades will even agree to it, which remains to be seen."

"And Melanie?" I fixed my gaze on his face, channeling my energy toward him.

An image flashed through my mind. Long red hair, tanned bare shoulders, rumpled white sheets. It wasn't a fantasy, but a memory. Alex's memory.

Oh, gods, I was right, it was her. Melanie was his ex. No. Why did it have to be her? Literally anyone else would be better. A clone of Natasha would be better.

My nose itched and the image faded. I held my breath, waiting for a sneeze.

"She's an old friend." He swirled his glass, swishing around the last of the wine.

Liar. My chest stung with surprise and hurt. Why wouldn't he admit they dated? Did he not trust me?

I mean, yes, I was secretly reading his mind and he probably shouldn't trust me, but he didn't know that. So why wouldn't he confess?

He took a final drink and set down the glass. "She's been trying to break into residential real estate for years, so I referred her to the Firm. Ainsley Barfield's a logical choice. Our real estate group has won PMBA awards for the last eight years."

The North American Pan-Magical Bar Association, or PMBA, oversaw attorney licensing and best practices throughout the U.S. and Canada.

"And The City Elysium Group has been very

successful. Melanie built it from the ground up. She knows what she's doing."

The note of pride in his voice made me want to vomit. How long had they been together? Had they lived together? They'd probably had sex hundreds and hundreds of times. I almost wished I hadn't read his mind, because now the image of half-naked Melanie was burned into my brain. I was afraid to try again.

"I reached out to her a few days ago." He glanced over his shoulder, like he thought Noel might be spying on him. "I'm hoping she can help me find another way out of my contract, one that doesn't involve surrendering my power. She's very well-connected in the Underworld, and if anyone could do it, she could." Again that fond tone.

I needed to change the subject, stat. "The other day you said your mother is the reason you don't like reaping souls. What's she like?"

His eyes lit up. "Brilliant. Funny. And human. She was an art history professor before she retired. She fell for my dad when she was in grad school, when he was posing as a local gallery owner. She said he swept her off her feet."

I was right about his mom being human. "She's still alive? Like, on earth?"

"Yeah." He shrugged. "They dated for a few months, and then she got pregnant. That's somewhat rare, but it does happen. Usually, the baby is taken to the Underworld to be raised by other Stygians, but my father negotiated a deal. My mother could stay here on earth, and I could spend half of each year with her."

"Like Persephone."

"Yes. Persephone was actually the judge in my

mother's appeal. That's probably why the request was granted."

I tried to comprehend a Stygian advocating on behalf of his human lover. "He must've really cared for her, then."

"He had a soft spot for her, yes, though he also believed in mingling with human society more than some other Stygians. I believe he thought I'd be a better soul-hunter if I lived among humans." Alex frowned. "Anyway, I grew up in Seattle part-time, July through December of every year, and my mother made sure that during those six months my childhood was as normal and as human as possible. I went to school, we celebrated Christmas, we hiked." His mouth quirked up. "One year we rented a cabin on Shaw Island, in the San Juans, for two months. It was idyllic. I don't have a lot of respect for my father, but he did provide for my mother financially. It allowed us to live a semi-normal life."

The crystal thrummed against my skin, and I caught snippets of memory—a small child sitting behind a woman as she kayaked them across an expanse of deep-blue water. She twisted around to say something to him. Her large dark eyes and curly black hair looked just like his. In the distance, a seagull soared over a copse of evergreens.

The image faded again, but not the tender melancholy that accompanied it. "And when you were in the Underworld?"

"I was trained with the other Stygian children. We learned charisma, spell casting. It's like school. Really twisted school."

My nose tingled. I grabbed my linen napkin, barely clamping it over my face in time to contain a giant sneeze. "Ow."

"You okay there?"

"Um, yeah, allergies." I dabbed my nose with the napkin. Shit. This was happening directly after I wielded my power. Was I allergic to my own magic? "Where's your mom now?"

"She lives in Bremerton, outside Seattle, and she sells her paintings all over. I see her every other month or so."

A Stygian who loved his mother. Did he have an "I Heart Mom" tattoo on his arm, too? I sat back and dabbed my nose with my napkin, hoping I wasn't trailing any boogers. "You're full of surprises, Mr. Kouris."

"I hope that's a good thing." The warm light reflected in his eyes. "Ms. Baird."

"It is."

Another image solidified, one of clasped hands. Oh, my gods, did Alex want to hold my hand? I tested the theory, leaning forward slightly on the pretense of moving the salt and pepper shakers out of the way. I let my hand rest on the table next to Alex's.

The side of his hand touched mine.

I accidentally-but-on-purpose brushed his knuckles with one finger.

"Ro." He caught my hand in his, then slid his thumb over the inside of my wrist. "I think this dinner might've been a bad idea." His husky voice belied the words. In fact, he was gazing at me like he wanted to do very naughty things to me.

"Oh? Why's that?" I leaned closer.

The next second, cold panic washed over me. There was no six-pound cat on my right shoulder. No claws digging into my skin.

Lenti was gone.

I shot to my feet. "I have to hit the restroom."

"I'm sorry, I—"

"No, really, it's a bathroom emergency." I hurried toward the back of the restaurant, too distracted to be very worried by the fact that Alex now thought I was a person who experienced bathroom emergencies at restaurants.

I peeked under the tables and beneath the bar, scanning corners for a flash of black-and-white fur. Nothing.

"Lenti?" I shoved open the door to the women's restroom. My voice echoed off the tiled walls. "Lenti, where are you?"

Oh, gods. I'd lost my familiar. How did you lose your familiar unless you were completely incompetent?

The three stall doors were all unlocked. I checked behind each one, but Lenti wasn't there. I stood at the sink and took belly breaths to slow my heart rate. Where could she have disappeared to? The restaurant entrance, maybe? Had she gone outside for an evening stroll? She was an air spirit, after all. They followed their whims.

Closing my eyes, I placed my hand over the crystal. *Lenti, you better get your fluffy butt to the bathroom right now.*

I froze, alert for her reply.

Nothing. I was alone with my own thoughts.

A riptide of panic swept in. Lenti's bravery was oversized, but she inhabited a tiny physical body. Her claws couldn't protect her from a demon, a sorcerer, or—shit, what if she got outside and a hawk spotted her?

There was a telltale *pop*.

She appeared on the counter out of thin air. Her

small jaws worked the last of something pink and shiny.

"You little gremlin!" I scooped her into my arms. "I thought you ran off! What happened to you?"

"Jutht went to find food."

She struggled in my grasp, and I let her go.

As she plopped back onto the counter, I glared at her. "Food? Wait. You mean, in the restaurant kitchen?"

"That's where the food is." She licked her paw and swabbed her face. "Did you know they have raw salmon back there?"

I gritted my teeth. The damage was already done. It wouldn't help to run into the kitchen and apologize for my invisible cat stealing a hunk of sockeye. "You scared the shit out of me. Tell me next time you decide to randomly leave."

She swished her tail. "You seemed busy thinking about licking Alex. I didn't think you'd notice I was gone."

"Never mind. Let's get back to dinner." At least I now knew that my telepathy worked at some range. But if she ever did that to me again, I'd put her in a harness and make her walk on a leash.

"Cranky, cranky. You must be hungry." She did the butt-wriggle and leaped onto my shoulder. With a *pop*, she faded to invisibility.

The tightness in my chest eased at the now-familiar weight of her tiny body on my right shoulder.

I strolled back to the table, hoping my face wasn't flushed from my near heart-attack. I sat and tried to smile normally. "Sorry about that."

Concern washed over Alex's face. "Are you all right?"

"Oh, fine. Tiny bladder." Argh. No. Why had I just

said that? I did have a tiny bladder, but I didn't need to share that. It wasn't sexy to discuss your need to pee.

I guessed that meant I was trying to be sexy.

So much for this being a friendly dinner.

Damon served our meals, promised to check on us later, and bustled away.

We dug in.

I relished the salmon mac-and-cheese, but even more, I relished Alex's rapid-fire explanation of the sci-fi novel he was reading, the way he laughed at himself for dropping a piece of salad on the floor, the intimacy of his soft smile.

I sought his thoughts again, but all I sensed was contentment—a feeling that seemed connected to my presence. Alex felt comfortable around me. Relaxed? I touched the crystal, trying to interpret the emotion. Not safe, that wasn't quite the word.

Home.

The word sounded in Alex's voice, and my eyes widened.

"Something wrong? Or am I just boring you with a detailed explanation of the multiple-universes thing?"

"No! No, not at all." I smiled. "I was just thinking that I feel, well, comfortable around you. It surprised me, I guess." Okay, I hadn't exactly been thinking that myself, but I was thinking his thought, and that was almost the same thing. Anyway, it wasn't a lie. I did feel comfortable around him, and it did surprise me.

He grinned. "Same. You know the old cliché, 'I feel like I've known you my whole life'? It's true. There's something about you that just feels, well, like you said. Comfortable." He reached for my hand and traced a lazy path over my palm with his thumb.

The simple touch drew me into a warm haze, relaxed and slightly aroused. My mind jumped to fantasies of him sliding his hand up my arm, running his thumb across my collarbone and up the side of my neck, his hand wrapping around my ponytail.

How are you planning to get him alone? said Lenti. *I'll follow you everywhere.*

Get out of my brain. I squeezed Alex's hand, then picked up my fork.

He sighed. "Sorry. You're irresistible."

My insides did a kind of melting thing, and I almost grabbed his hand again. No. I didn't even know if I could trust him. And he was my boss. And a Stygian. Et cetera.

I knew the reasons.

I also didn't like them.

"You're the one who's irresistible." I shoved a forkful of mac and cheese into my mouth so I couldn't say more.

He laughed, then shifted back into telling me about the book.

Whew. Intimate moment averted.

The rest of dinner, our conversation stayed light. We didn't talk about contracts or ex-girlfriends.

Lenti behaved herself and remained quiet, although she kept her face smashed against mine. She only popped into my brain once to ask for *the stick things you're eating*.

I sighed and ordered her a box of truffle fries to go.

Finally, Alex paid the bill, and we gathered my container of fries and headed outside.

The temperature had dropped to sixty or so, and the crisp breeze hinted at fall.

We paused next to my car. I took a deep breath, but

underneath the clean mineral scent of the air, I smelled saltwater. The faint crash of powerful surf competed with the hum of cars zipping by. Damn. Alex's magic wasn't fair. I'd have lingered here for hours just to be near those sensations.

"Thanks for dinner." I smoothed back my braid, checking for flyaways.

"Of course." He smiled and started to lift his arms, then clamped them to his sides. Was he going to hug me?

Well, I was going to hug him.

Can you get off my shoulder? I asked Lenti. *Just for a second.*

What a rude request.

The weight dropped from my shoulder, and a soft padding noise tracked invisibly across the hood of my car.

You owe me.

I rolled my eyes and set the box of fries on the hood.

"Everything okay?" Alex ran a hand through his hair.

Oh, right. My strange pausing and eye-rolling probably made it seem like I was in a bad mood. I shot him a bright smile. "It's great. Here, um, let me at least give you a hug goodnight." Did I mention my middle name is "Smooth?"

I stood on my tiptoes and wrapped my arms around him. The competing smells of fresh shampoo and salty air overwhelmed my senses.

Alex drew me in tight and slid his arms down to my waist. He pressed his forehead to mine, his skin hot.

The crystal thrummed against my chest, or was that my own heartbeat? The air smelled of brine and sand and sea grass.

Alex lowered his mouth to mine…

Something crashed at close range.

I screamed and we jumped apart.

Lenti's claws jammed into my skin as she reattached herself to my shoulder, making my eyes water.

Alex glanced over his shoulder and clapped his hand over his mouth. "Uh…"

I followed his line of sight. My back passenger-side window had shattered, and the sidewalk was covered in green-edged shards of glass. "Motherf—ugh."

A faint cat cackle sounded in my head.

"You *are* telekinetic. First the chili, now this." He turned toward me and smirked. "Did you know that telekinesis is usually activated when you're emotional? Angry, for example. Or turned on."

"Stop." I tapped his chest. "I don't suppose you can fix this."

"Afraid alteration of matter isn't one of my talents." He ran a finger along my jaw and down my neck. "I'm better at other things."

I shivered.

It figured he couldn't fix the window, though. I'd have to call Tabitha over to repair it. Of course, that meant admitting the near kiss.

"It's probably a good thing." He stuck his hands in his pockets. "I think you're amazing, Ro, you know that, but this can't end well."

I braced against a sudden ache in my chest. "Can't it?"

He shook his head. "My charisma will always be an influence on how you feel about me. No matter how close we get or how much time we spend together, there's always going to be part of you that likes me because I willed it."

Well, that sucked. "Then stop. Turn it off. Unplug it."

"I can't. It's who I am." He glanced down. The streetlight overhead sharpened his profile, darkening the shadows under his eyes. "There's no way around it."

"You're telling me there are no spells anyone can do to counteract your magic? You're un-blockable?"

"Nothing that lasts very long. It'd take a strong psychic shield to withstand my influence for long periods of time. Almost no one has that kind of power."

A strong psychic shield?

My breath caught. *What about eldritch magic?* I almost asked him, but I didn't dare, in case it was nothing, in case I was incapable of forming whatever a psychic shield was.

His forehead crinkled. "Every moment we spend together will make this harder. You were very kind to have dinner with me, and I hope what I said about the contract sets your mind at ease about working for me. I promise to keep my distance after this." He dug his keys out of his pocket. "Thank you, Rowan, and again, I'm sorry. The last thing I want to do is hurt you. Whatever else you think of me, I hope you can believe that." His gaze held mine.

I tasted his regret, sharp and bitter, though I couldn't hear his thoughts. "Don't be sorry."

And then I sneezed. Loudly, without warning, and directly onto his shirt.

After I apologized for the three hundredth time, and Alex dabbed his shirt off with a paper towel that I hastily retrieved from the women's bathroom in the restaurant, we said our final goodnight.

I waited until he disappeared around the corner, then got into my car. Good thing this hadn't been a date, because breaking a window and sneezing on the other person didn't leave the best impression. Lasting, yes, but not exactly alluring.

Lenti re-materialized and perched on the front passenger seat, sitting back on her haunches in a vague imitation of a human. "I'll take those stick things now."

I put the container of fries in front of her and popped open the top. "Do you know anything about how to form a psychic shield?"

"Perhaps." She nosed into the box. "I have to think about it."

"What do you mean?" I buckled up and pressed the ignition button. "Do you or don't you?"

When she didn't answer right away, I glanced over.

Her face was buried in the container. In a garbled voice, she said, "It dependth on how many treath you'll buy me."

"What treats? You have a giant box of treats at home."

"Salmon. Cheese stuff. These stick things are good."

I glanced toward the ceiling. "Goddess, give me patience to bear the demands of my entitled familiar who wrongly believes she's a princess."

She hissed at me, but barely showed her fangs. It almost seemed like she was making a face at me.

I pulled away from the restaurant and cruised down the street. A cool wind blew through my now-decimated window.

"I can help you." Lenti surfaced from the box. Oil coated her nose. "It requires practice."

"I can practice." I pulled to a stop at a light and

flicked my turn signal.

This area was known as the Taphouse Blocks, and the sidewalks flowed with people streaming in and out of the various taphouses and restaurants that crowded this small section of the city.

I glanced at Lenti, who was once again snuffling into the fries. "How come you decided to be a familiar? This whole thing about being bound to me for life. Why would you do that?"

"I was bored."

Bullshit. She prepped for months to learn human culture. I searched out her mind, my curiosity piqued.

She remembered flying past dark clouds, her heart weighted by sadness.

"Don't do that." She hissed ferociously.

I flinched. "Sorry. I just wanted to know—"

"I don't want to talk about it. When we get home, we need to watch *Unseelie*. I want to know if Florinda and Emerald make up from their fight."

I frowned. This was an obvious ploy to distract me, but I couldn't resist a good *Unseelie* episode. "Sure. Are you okay?"

"Fine." She rolled over and started cleaning her face.

Behind us, a car honked, and the traffic signal glared green.

With an apologetic wave to the driver behind me, I stepped on the gas.

Chapter Seven

I told Tabitha everything the next day. I had to, because I needed her to fix my car window.

To my surprise, she didn't get either judgmental or squealy.

Instead, after repairing the window, she leaned against the car and frowned. "I don't like that he's involved with Melanie. Why not let the Firm do its job? And yeah, giving up his power would be a big deal, but how bad does he really want out? Shouldn't he be willing to do anything?"

"I guess it's not that simple." Wait, why was I making excuses for him? Tabitha was right.

"It does seem as if he's genuinely trying to protect you, though." She rubbed her eyes as if a headache was forming. "But do I think that because he's a good guy, or he's made me *think* he's a good guy?"

An invisible Lenti meowed from my shoulder. "Don't you want to know my opinion? He smells like catnip. You can't trust a supernatural being who smells like catnip. Too easy to let your guard down."

"Catnip?" I wrinkled my nose, but then remembered Alex saying Stygians smelled like an individual's favorite scent. "None of this matters anyway." I scuffed my right foot on the strip of grass next to the sidewalk, wiping away a clod of dirt stuck to my boot sole. "Alex and I aren't going out again."

Tabitha raised her brows and rapped on my newly minted window glass. "Never?"

I cleared my throat. "Well…probably never."

****

Lenti and I spent the rest of the weekend and all the next week alternating between practice sessions and episodes of *Unseelie.* Since I was starting from square one in my magical training, we focused solely on my mind-reading skills, though Lenti insisted I'd be able to control my telekinesis eventually.

By the following Sunday night, I could mostly control when I read her thoughts and when I didn't.

Psychic shielding proved much harder.

Lenti stared me down from her perch on the coffee table, communicating silently with me, reading my mind. *Buy me salmon. Make me mac and cheese. I know you like Alex.*

I could sense when she was intruding, but blocking her was almost impossible. She could come and go in my brain at will.

"Fight harder," she hissed. "Your shield feels like water."

"I am." The crystal pulsed and burned my skin, never leaving a mark. Once, when I managed to kick Lenti out of my brain for a full ten seconds, it glowed.

****

I stumbled to my desk, still half-asleep. A thick cottony feeling clogged my sinuses. While Lenti prowled over to her spot behind the filing cabinet, I popped an allergy pill and chased it with coffee. I probably should've called in sick.

Even as I thought it, I sneezed. I'd never had allergies this bad, and not in the fall.

My powers were making me sick.

I glanced behind the cabinet, where Lenti was already snoring. Maybe I should just shut off the lights, crawl under my desk, and do the same.

Five rapid knocks sounded on my door.

Tabitha stood outside, bouncing on her heels.

I waved her in.

She shut the door quietly and crept over to me, throwing glances over her shoulder as if she'd been followed. "Is Melanie six feet tall with red princess hair?"

"Yes." I sat up straight, my exhaustion dissipating. "Why?"

"She's in Alex's office. I knocked and he signaled me to come back later." She squinted at me. "What happened to your eyes? They're all red."

I sniffled. "I'm allergic to myself, I guess. Lenti helped me practice my magic all weekend, and this is what it does to me."

"Oh, sweetie." She aimed both palms at me and whispered an incantation, then snapped her fingers. "That should clear it up."

The back of my throat tickled, and I rubbed my eyes. "When?"

"Shoot." She leaned forward to examine my face. "That should have worked. Oh, gosh, maybe allergy spells don't work if the allergy is caused by magic. I'm sorry."

I shrugged. "Not your fault. I wonder what Melanie's doing here. Maybe she's here to talk to Alex about his contract." Or she was here to catch up with her old friend, and they were about to rekindle their romance.

Tapping the button on my headset, I dialed reception and asked Carina to check the calendar.

"The City Elysium Group has a meeting with Noel at eleven," I reported, hanging up. It was only nine. "She's here early, then."

Tabitha wandered behind the filing cabinet and bent to pet Lenti. "I know he said she's helping him, but so far she seems to be the only one benefitting from this arrangement. Did you know that land her company is eyeing for the condo isn't zoned for magical use? Elizabeth told me Noel is working overtime to get an exception with the Board of Supernatural Regulations. The board *he* sits on. That's a clear conflict of interest."

"Why would he do that, especially for a brand-new client?"

"I don't know."

My skin prickling, I stared at my computer screen. Just because Alex trusted Melanie didn't mean she was trustworthy. But I had power now, a way to suss out her true intentions. If only I could get closer to her. "Can you give Elizabeth some kind of magical emergency that keeps her from being in that meeting at eleven? Food poisoning, maybe? Getting stuck in an elevator?"

Tabitha's green eyes narrowed. "What are you thinking?"

"She always takes notes for Noel at those meetings. If I can sub for her at the last minute, I could try reading Melanie's mind."

Tabitha fiddled with the hem of her light-blue sweater. "This seems like a gray area. The Witches Code of Ethics says we can't do magic with malicious intent."

"It's not malicious intent. I'm not asking you to kill Elizabeth. I just want you to keep her from getting to that meeting. Food poisoning was just an example."

"I guess I could do a sleep spell on her." Her forehead wrinkled. "But how are you going to get Noel to let you into the meeting? Wouldn't he just ask another legal assistant to help?"

"Not if you wait until the last minute to take out Elizabeth, and I just happen to be passing by the conference room at the exact moment he needs me." I glanced at Lenti, who had lifted her head. "Do you want to come with me for some recon? Melanie's here."

"Ooh, the icky lady?" She sat up. "Can I scratch her? Bite her?"

"No." Tempting.

Tabitha scratched Lenti under the chin. "All right. I'll do it."

****

At ten forty-five, I took the elevator to the eighth floor. While Lenti invisibly staked out Noel's office, I hid in the small library, perusing the law reporters.

The leather-bound tomes extended all the way back to the 1800s and reported the decisions of magical courts on various cases.

I flipped through a volume from 1950 and amused myself reading the decision in *Smythe vs. Goodfellow*, in which an Oregon warlock turned his architecture-firm partner into a goat after the two had a fight. The goat proceeded to eat all the drawings for a new hotel in downtown Portland, causing the firm to lose the contract. Smythe took Goodfellow, still in goat form, to court. I snickered at the judge's analysis of the way Goodfellow had harmed his defense by eating a key document in the case.

Something familiar landed on my shoulder.

An invisible Lenti nudged my cheek with her small wet nose. "Noel's going up to the conference room now, and I just heard him ask some lady to send Elizabeth over when she's back."

"Perfect." I swiped a notepad and pen from the library's supply basket and headed for the thirteenth floor. On the way, I got a text from Tabitha, reporting that she was standing guard over Elizabeth, who was sleeping soundly in the back of the file room.

I found Noel in the Everett Room, sitting at one end of the conference table along with Peter, an associate, and Jessamyn, another partner.

Since the door was open, I strolled in. "Hi, Noel! You don't need any help hooking up a computer, do you?"

He glanced up. "Oh, Rowan. No, we don't have a presentation today, but I could use help tracking down Elizabeth. I asked Nora to send her up, but she isn't here. She's never late."

"Let me see what I can do." I smiled, wandered out, and took a lap around the floor to buy some time.

When I returned to the conference room, Noel snapped upright. His expression sank when I shook my head.

"No one's seen her in a while." I made a point of pretending to check the time on the grandfather clock. "You know, I have a break in my schedule. Do you want me to take notes, just until she gets here?"

He craned his neck toward the clock. "That might not be a bad idea. Only if you have the time, of course."

"Oh, absolutely." I settled into one of the brocade chairs at the opposite end of the conference table.

Lenti shifted her weight, her soft cheek snuggled

against mine.

A moment later, Melanie the Stygian sex goddess sauntered into the room.

Noel and the other three attorneys shot out of their seats to greet her.

I reluctantly stood as well. The sight of her made my stomach lurch.

She rocked couture in fitted black pants and a black suit jacket with a plunging neckline—and nothing beneath it, as far as I could tell. Her glossy red hair flowed down her back in waves.

Great. I sported a bulky sweater, collared shirt, and too-long pants with ragged hems. I always struggled to find pants that both fit my five-foot-three height and accommodated the fact that I had a butt, so I usually ended up with pants that dragged on the ground. Hence the hem issue.

Melanie was a person without hem issues. The kind of woman Alex dated. Another reason I couldn't be with him.

Noel gestured to me. "Melanie, you remember Rowan. She's very kindly filling in for my assistant, who got tied up in another meeting."

Of course, he wouldn't say Elizabeth was missing—he wouldn't want to lose an ounce of face in front of a client.

I smiled while focusing on Melanie's chin. Had to avoid eye contact this time. "Nice to see you again. You won't even know I'm here." This time I wasn't overwhelmed by inexplicable Melanie-worship, though her presence was like a magnet. I sat down and stared at the conference room table. *That's an interesting scratch. Look at that wood grain. Lenti, help me.*

She smells like a rotting mouse carcass.

I clamped my lips shut to keep a giggle from escaping. *I don't like her either.*

Oh, I don't like her, but that's a good smell.

Ew. Weirdo. I wrinkled my nose and pretended to take a note.

The group sat, and Noel asked one of the partners for an update on the Hades's certification process.

I scribbled a few more fake notes, then sneaked a glance at Melanie. After practicing with Lenti, I'd discovered reading minds was more art than science, a process of homing in on the person's energy, their essence. Like tuning into a radio station. It was still risky looking Melanie dead in the eyes, in case her influence overwhelmed me, so I focused on her left earlobe and tried to derive her essence from it. I mean, it was a nice earlobe. One of those small, attached ones.

I caught the fleeting sensation of Melanie's pride, then lost it. Frowning, I tried again, scanning the rest of her appearance. Since I didn't know much about her, I could only focus on outward things—her long shiny hair, her black suit.

Weeks…

One word. Better than nothing. I scrawled it down and tried again.

…not an option…

My nose tingled, but I didn't sneeze. Hopefully the allergy pill was kicking in.

I got nothing else. Five minutes ticked by on the grandfather clock.

I'd have to risk eye contact.

While Jessamyn kept talking, I scooted my chair back as quietly as possible and tiptoed alongside the table toward the small group. Noel sat at the head of the table, with Jessamyn on his left side, and Melanie and Peter on his right. I slid back the chair across from Melanie.

The conversation stilled.

"Did you need something, Rowan?" Noel pressed his thin lips together

"Oh, no, it's just hard to hear from that end." I dropped into the chair.

Jessamyn cleared her throat. "We'll want to use the sustainability scorecard throughout to make sure we're adhering to the standards."

I trained my gaze on Melanie. She adjusted her left sleeve, and a black wrist tattoo peeked out from the cuff. It was a tiny black bird, maybe a raven or a crow.

An alto voice drifted into focus.

...still have to find one...

Even as I wrote the words down, my nose started itching again. Oh no. I sniffed a few times, then held my breath and took the plunge.

I stared into her large hazel eyes.

...the alpha lyrae...

Not sure how to spell that one, I gave it my best guess.

The next second, I ran into a mental block, as if someone had slapped me across the face and slammed a door shut at the same time. My nose stung, and I tucked my face into my elbow an instant before letting loose a huge sneeze.

"Excuse me," I said.

"Bless you," said Noel.

Melanie glared, her gaze burning.

Invisible arms seemed to drag me from my seat.

Gritting my teeth, I clung to the sides of the chair. Sweat collected under my shaking arms. Slowly, my butt lifted off the cushion.

"Rowan." Melanie touched a hand to her mouth. "Are you feeling all right, honey?"

My stomach churned. *What a bitch.*

"I just need some water." I hated the way my hands trembled when I stood up. "I'll go see if Elizabeth is done with her meeting."

Melanie smiled at me, lips closed, her eyes predatory.

I hurried out of the room, swallowing back the nausea that threatened to eject my breakfast burrito all over the office floor.

When we finally got back to my office, Lenti hopped onto her blanket and I collapsed next to her, taking slow breaths. "She knew. She knew I was in her head." And she'd almost pulled me bodily from my seat. Why'd I think that practicing psychic shielding with a cat would protect me in the real world? Melanie's power almost flattened me.

I needed to dial up my training, but how?

Lenti burped. "She smells *so* strong. I don't feel so good." Her little body suddenly heaved, and with a few wet coughs, she hacked up a giant hairball.

Lovely.

I ripped off several paper towels from the roll I kept on my desk and blotted the carpet. "Any idea what an *alpha lyrae* is? I heard it in Melanie's thoughts."

Lenti flopped onto her side and licked her front right paw. "A musical instrument? A creature of the underworld?"

I sighed. I'd gotten one mysterious phrase out of my

recon mission, and a lesson in Stygian power. I could ask Alex what the phrase meant, but then I'd have to explain about my mind-reading powers.

Anyway, there was no point since we weren't seeing each other again.

I closed my eyes and thought back to our dinner, to the way his eyes had sparkled with kindness, the way he'd leaned forward listening to me as if I was someone important. Just for a few moments that night, I belonged with him.

I didn't, of course. How could I belong with a Stygian?

A girl can dream.

Chapter Eight

I flopped back against the couch cushions and picked the last bits of popcorn out of my bowl. I'd been researching *alpha lyrae* for three hours, with no luck. There were astronomy terms that came close, and a band called The Alphabet Lyricists, but no hits for *alpha lyrae.*

Tabitha had promised to do research too, but she was having a date night with Paul, so I doubted I'd hear from her this evening.

I grabbed a tissue from the rapidly depleting box on the coffee table. My sinus headache was slightly better, but now my nose was running again, and I'd already taken allergy medication today. Maybe I should try a nasal spray?

Whisk whisk whisk. Lenti sharpened her claws on the end of the couch.

"Seriously?" I tossed a balled-up tissue her way, expecting her to chase it.

She ignored it.

"You have multiple cat towers."

"I know." She eyed me, then resumed her vigorous scratching.

Maybe I should invest in some scratch-deterrent spray. Then again, it was futile to argue with an air spirit. I'd committed to decimated furniture the moment I matched with Lenti.

Gritting my teeth as I tried to ignore Lenti's attack on the couch, I opened an incognito browser window. If I couldn't find info on *alpha lyrae* on the regular internet, I was going to have to try something else.

I might be shit at an average spell and new to mind reading, but at least I kicked ass with technology. Last year I'd created a *Frequently Asked Questions* document for work on information security, and as part of the project, I'd learned more than I ever wanted to know about the supernatural dark web.

I installed a browser called Cloak and Dagger to keep anyone from tracing my IP address. When the browser opened, I hit up *The Beehive*, an online forum where some supernaturals went to trade all kinds of things their respective associations, guilds, and oversight committees wouldn't approve of—forbidden magical objects, blood-magic grimoires, information.

I wanted information.

The site resembled something out of the late nineties or early 2000s. Black background, neon title, blocky menu bar across the top. No one knew the identity of the person or people who ran the site. It sprang to life several years ago, out of nowhere.

I still had a free account with a throwaway email address, left over from last year's research. Not knowing quite where to start, I tried the *Resources* link, a collection of posts and articles about various topics. I searched for *alpha lyrae* in case it happened to be the name of a forbidden spell, but no results.

Well, that figured. I posted a message on the generic "looking for information" type board, explaining that I thought the term *alpha lyrae* had some connection to Underworld magic, and I was hitting a dead end in my research. I probably wouldn't even get a response but couldn't hurt to ask.

My phone chimed. I grabbed it off the table and checked for Tabitha's name.

—*Are you busy?*—

Alex.

I caught my breath, then glanced at Lenti, who was still occupied with chasing the pen around the living room. —*Do you need something for work?*— I typed back. Why else would he be pinging me at eight o'clock on a Wednesday night?

—*No. Are you free to talk on the phone?*—

I jumped up from the couch. "Hey, Lenti? I'm just going onto the balcony, okay? You'll be able to see me the whole time. I'm not leaving." Since last weekend, when I'd sensed sadness in her memory, I felt a bit more inclined to soothe her abandonment complex.

She glanced up from her battle with the couch.

Judging by the fraying threads, the couch was losing.

"Come back soon. I want to watch our show."

"You bet. I'll just be a few minutes." My stomach clenched, even though I wasn't lying to her. Or doing anything wrong. I had every right to speak to my own boss on the phone.

I texted Alex that I was free and scurried across the room and out onto the small balcony. I'd just closed the sliding glass door behind me when my phone lit up with an incoming call. I tapped the screen and answered. "Hi, it's Rowan." Wait, why did I say my name? He called *me.* Off to a great start.

"Thanks for taking my call." He cleared his throat. "I, uh, I know I said I'd stay away from you."

"Is something wrong?"

"No, not exactly." He half laughed. "Sorry. I'm at work right now, hiding out in my office. There was a partners' reception tonight, at seven. All the directors from the various departments were invited."

I vaguely remembered hearing about something, but honestly, it seemed like the vampires were always finding an excuse to break out bottles of vintage blood, so this could've been one of ten similar events in a month. "Did it go badly?"

"No, not at all. Everyone's very welcoming. No one's so much as mentioned—well, who I am. It's just that—" He sighed. "—law firms are very different from startups. I'm used to small offices. This is so hierarchical. All the partners, standing around in a stuffy conference room in suits, going on about how much they're billing and which clients they work with."

"Yeah, the shoptalk gets a little dry." I'd attended other Firm events, and unless you could catch someone like Noel in a mood to tell stories about history, they were pretty boring. Of course, I didn't like crowds to begin with. "How long do you have to stay?"

"I'm honestly not sure they'll even notice I've left. I just wanted to talk to someone normal."

I burst out laughing at the concept that I, a witch who until a couple weeks ago couldn't perform the most basic of spells, was normal. "I'm not sure you're talking to the right person."

"Oh, Ro."

His chuckle and the way he said my name made my skin tingle.

"I like that you don't take yourself too seriously."

I smiled. "It's a defense mechanism I've developed

after years of sucking at most things."

He laughed again. It rang like a bell, clear and crisp.

I'd have made a dozen more bad jokes just to hear that laugh again.

"I think you're underselling yourself. I seriously doubt you suck at most things. In fact, I have evidence that you excel at many things."

"Is it review time already?" I glanced over my shoulder to see if Lenti was okay.

She lounged on her side, lazily swatting a small stuffed mouse.

I waved, just in case she was watching me.

"You *are* very good at your job, from what I've seen so far, but that's not what I mean." He paused. "I shouldn't say this. In fact, I should probably warn you I've had a couple glasses of wine, so I'm being a little freer with my words than I ought to be."

My pulse jumped. Technically, he hadn't said anything yet, but I could feel something shifting, like a picture frame tilting sideways.

"You're quite good at being beautiful."

My whole body warmed, as if I were standing under a heat lamp. Alex had just complimented me. Alex had just called me beautiful. Alex thought I was attractive.

Oh, my gods, he was into me, and we were totally going to get married and have little demigod babies and—

"Ro?"

"Sorry." Now what? Did I tell him I thought he was hotter than lava? Proposition him? "Thank you." *Thank you?* I couldn't think of anything more coherent?

"You have no idea." His voice lowered, grew huskier. "Last week at dinner, I had to stop myself from complimenting you. Your dress. Your body in that dress…"

I silently congratulated myself for my $20.99 find at a local fast-fashion outlet. *Suck it, Melanie's designer wardrobe.*

I checked left and right, making sure my nearest neighbors weren't on their balconies. All clear. I leaned my elbows on the railing. "What about my body in the dress, exactly?"

"Your body is perfect. All tight little curves. I wanted to run out of the restaurant right then, take you back home, and tear the dress off you."

Well, okay then. My girl parts lit up like a Halloween light display. Open for business. "Then why don't you do that next time?" I whispered.

"You know there can't be a next time."

I felt bold. Was it the wine I drank while doing research? My magical powers imbuing me with confidence? Or just the sound of Alex's voice, breaking down my reserve? "Do I know that? It seems like you might want there to be a next time."

"Of course I *want* there to be one." He groaned. "I'm sorry, this is unfair of me. This is why I need to break my contract. I can't have a normal life as long as I owe my service to Hades."

Guess what? The mention of the god of the Underworld kills sexy vibes. Just when I was getting all tingly, too. I sighed. "Then I hope you can break it."

"Melanie's working on it. We talked today, and we're meeting again on Friday."

The jealousy flooded in. Would they meet at the office, or talk over dinner? It *better* be the office. Melanie seemed like the kind of person who would flirt with an ex just for funsies. I wanted to ask, but Alex didn't owe me anything. He could hang out with Melanie if he wanted to.

What if she tried to get in his pants, though? For old times' sake?

Something banged on the glass. Lenti stood on her hind legs, pounding at the door with her two front paws. Her little mouth opened in a silent yowl.

"I have to go. My cat is—I'm getting another call."

"Of course." He coughed. "What I said before was completely inappropriate. I'm so sorry."

"I'm not." Before he could respond—and before I could take it back—I hung up and stepped inside.

Lenti trotted toward the couch, her small fluffy tail alert. "You were outside forever. I thought you forgot about me."

"Gremlin, how could I forget about you?" I gestured in the general direction of the giant cat tower. "This whole place is a cat hotel."

"Well, you might." She leaped onto the couch but remained standing until I joined her.

By now I knew the routine. A fleece throw arranged itself over my lap and Lenti settled herself on top of it.

I flipped on the TV and navigated to where we'd left off in *Unseelie*, Season Two. The producer had stuck to the format of many human reality shows, and the opening credits consisted of cast members speaking taglines directly to the camera. Florinda, my least-favorite housewife, was first, clad in a shimmery gold ballgown that set off her iridescent wings. "Want magic? Look no further than *my lips*." She blew a kiss at the camera.

I snorted. Lenti head-butted my hand, and I

scratched her under the chin.

A purr rumbled in her throat.

My phone pinged again.

—*Okay. Then I'm not sorry either.*—

My belly zinged at Alex's text.

****

I gazed at Alex across the conference room, half-listening as he discussed the new email-retention policy he was implementing.

"All email will be magically moved to case files. We need to encourage everyone to follow good data-management practices and store email in the electronic files, not physical files."

Mm. His voice was so soothing. *I wanted to tear the dress off you,* I remembered him saying for the millionth time, and a little flower of desire bloomed inside me. If he could arouse me with mere words, imagine what he could do with his actual body.

Lenti shifted invisibly on my shoulder. *Is this meeting over soon? I'm hungry.*

It just started. You can go back to the office and eat, you know.

But I'm comfortable. She tucked her little head against my cheek.

Just in time, I stopped myself from petting her. I was getting way too used to carting an invisible cat around.

"Well, the assistants will love this," said Arjun, "and the vampires refuse to use email, so I don't imagine you'll get many complaints."

A few people chuckled.

A smile parted Alex's full lips, piercing my heart. He was so unbelievably gorgeous when he smiled and his eyes filled with that amused sparkle. Today, his light-gray shirt accented the grayer brown in his eyes.

He caught my eye for a second, and his smile stretched wider, or did I imagine it?

The next second he was all business again, talking about the data-management email campaign.

I let the general cadence of his voice wash over me. Lenti didn't seem to be actively traipsing into my brain, so I allowed my mind to wander, creating vague images of Alex and me in bed. Something that could never happen, unless…

Unless we didn't try dating. We could have sex if we agreed to a purely physical relationship.

Would that work?

Why not? Adults did that all the time. Hell, people took strangers home from bars and parties and had one-night stands. There wasn't anything wrong with two consenting adults agreeing to have sex.

To bang each other's brains out, more likely. Alex was a demigod. He probably had stamina to go with the skill.

A smoky tendril of anxiety curled in my stomach. I hadn't dated Dave for very long, and look how attached I'd gotten. How could I avoid getting attached to Alex? Then again, with Dave, I'd misread his charming exterior, allowing myself to see qualities that weren't there. If I truly accepted who and what Alex was and acknowledged the fact that he could never be a hundred percent emotionally open with me because of his power, then I could be satisfied with just sex.

I bet he knew his way around a woman's body.

My thoughts drifted to the fantasy of Alex and me in a huge bed. He probably owned silk sheets with a sky-high thread count. In a sexy color, like maroon or black.

I imagined the expanse of his muscular chest, his hands trailing down my sides.

I flinched, sensing Lenti nosing around my thoughts. Bracing, I took a deep breath and envisioned a massive steel wall, my psychic shield as a physical object. *Go back to your own brain, gremlin.*

Yours is more interesting.

I sighed and let the daydream go.

Alex was talking about data reimbursement plans for staff who had cell phones.

Nice perk, but not as exciting as imagining him naked.

After the meeting, Tabitha and I headed to the break room to hang out. She made us magical pumpkin-pie lattes, and we grabbed a table near one of the windows, overlooking the Larkspur Bridge.

Of all the bridges in Portland, I loved the Larkspur best, with its distinctive green trusses and the two towers that anchored a portion of the bridge, which could be raised and lowered to let boats pass underneath. I stared out at the cars and cyclists zipping over the bridge.

A man with curly black hair jogged past a cyclist. His hair looked sort of like Alex's.

Hmm. Alex…

"What's going on with you?"

I blinked and looked at Tabitha. "Sorry, what?"

"You seem really distracted."

Lenti let out a disembodied trill. "She's thinking about Alex."

"Thanks for that." I swirled my coffee in the cup and watched it slosh up the sides of the mug. "But, uh, yeah. I had an idea."

Tabitha's relaxed expression turned sharp and rigid.

"Oh?"

I dropped my voice. "Alex called me last night. He's as attracted to me as I am to him. He made that very clear. Had quite a few things to say about the dress I wore to dinner."

She looked like she didn't know whether to squeal or cry. "So…?"

"So…I think I might suggest that—"

She grabbed my wrist so hard that I flinched. "You cannot. Sleep. With him."

"Relax." I wriggled free of her grip. "I'm only going to suggest a friends-with-benefits thing. No strings attached."

She stared at me. "You're kidding, right?"

"No, why?"

"What's friends-with-benefits?" said Lenti.

Her consciousness nudged mine.

"Oh. Mating." She sounded bored.

"Ro." Tabitha waited for me to meet her gaze. "This is a bad idea. You understand why, don't you?"

"I don't see what you're worried about." I rolled my eyes.

"You. I'm worried about you. After Dave, you were a mess. I know you, and you're not going to be able to keep your feelings out of this. You'll get hurt."

"Not necessarily." *Totally likely*. "Not if we set boundaries from the beginning, like adults."

"It won't work. Plus, you have new power that you barely understand. The last thing you need is a distraction. You should be focused on training hard and learning to protect yourself. As long as your power is unfocused, you're vulnerable to attacks. I've been doing some research, and these kinds of powers can go wrong, especially if someone tries to attack you or, gods forbid, curses you. There are reports of telepaths losing their minds. Telekinetics who broke their own spines."

She doesn't know what she's dealing with. She's going to get herself killed. Fear filled her mind like a storm cloud.

So that's what my best friend thought of me. That I was weak. That I couldn't handle this. The pain of that knowledge burned deep in my gut.

Lenti nudged my cheek. "Tabitha's right. Eldritch magic is more unstable than other types. You probably couldn't handle a psychic attack right now."

"Thanks a lot." I stood, my face growing hot. "I *am* training hard. I've known about my powers for a couple weeks, not years. And in case you haven't noticed, the Association doesn't have a lot of *Eldritch Magic for Newbies* books. I'm doing the best I can." Swiping my mug, I whirled and headed for the door.

"Ro, wait."

"Let's talk later." I didn't want to be a complete bitch to my best friend, but sometimes she expected me to be Super-Witch. *She* should try being sexually frustrated by a demigod while grappling with unwieldy magical powers that gave her allergies.

Lenti's weight left my shoulder.

I glanced back. Tabitha leaned down, talking softly to what I presumed was an invisible Lenti.

Well, fine. If the two of them wanted to sit there and judge me, let them. At least I'd get some work done without a cat stepping on my keyboard.

I stalked out of the break room and back to my office. I slammed my office door and sat down, surprised at the tears that leaked out of my eyeballs. Lenti was a pain in the ass. I didn't care if she wanted to hang out with my best friend. Anyway, wearing a cat on my shoulder would probably give me carpal tunnel. At least it was quiet in my office.

Five minutes later, I was still staring at my email without seeing any of the words. Lenti would be back eventually, by the end of the day, at the latest. She did live with me.

The trademark soap-bubble *pop* sounded behind me.

It filled me with relief, more than I wanted to admit. I spun around in my chair. "What were you doing?"

Lenti strolled across the room, a large chunk of bagel and cream cheese dangling from her jaws. She dropped it into her dish. "Tabitha made me a snack."

"But dairy is bad for you."

"Only in large amounts." She crouched and began licking the cream cheese from the bagel. "Are you mad at me?"

"You're generally infuriating, but no."

She glanced up. A blob of cream cheese dotted her cheek. "Are you mad at Tabitha?"

"I don't know." I sighed. "Everything comes so easily to her. Magic. Relationships. Bonding with you. She's a great friend, but she has no idea what it's like to be a failure as a witch most of your adult life. And it's not my fault I like Alex. I'm trying to resist him, but I can't stop thinking about him."

"Do you think he'd take your soul?"

"No." The certainty in my own voice surprised me, but I knew, with the surety of steel, that he wouldn't. "I don't think he'd do anything to hurt me deliberately."

"That's good. I don't want to live in the Underworld. I hear it's cold there." She buried her face in her dish again.

I stared at her. "But if I died and was sent to the Underworld, wouldn't you go back to the seventh realm of the troposphere?" My death would release her from our contract, wouldn't it? Or I'd assumed so from the way the Familiar Placement Agency had explained things.

"Our souls are bound together. Where you go, I go." She tore off a small piece of the bagel.

"I didn't realize." Something in me broke at the sacrifice she was willing to make. To be bound to a person for eternity. It was a pretty big risk, pledging yourself to someone you'd never even met. I supposed that's why the thirty-day probation period was written into the contract. You'd have to be damn sure it was a good fit. *How many days left before it's permanent?*

Fifteen.

She'd slid into my mind without me realizing. My defenses were weaker when I was upset.

Okay, so Tabitha and Lenti had a point. I did need to practice harder if I wanted to control my power.

I caught a hint of sadness from Lenti. Huh. The crystal warmed against my chest as I reached for her mind.

She bared her fangs and let out a warning hiss. "I told you not to do that."

Mentally I backed off, but I got up and sat on the floor next to her. "Hey. What's wrong?"

"Don't want to talk about it." She ripped off another piece of bagel and chewed aggressively.

I gave her head a tentative pat. When she didn't scratch or hiss, I stroked her ears. "Come on. If we're really going to be companions forever, we have to be able to trust each other. What happened before we met?"

She finished her bite of bagel, then gazed up at the window. "I was placed with another witch, Lorna, five months ago. She lived in Florida. She didn't like me, so after a week, she sent me back."

My heart shattered. I scooped her off the floor and held her close to my chest. "I'm so sorry. I'm not going to send you back, I promise. You're a pain in my ass, but I actually like you a lot."

She rolled back in my arms and gazed up at me. "It's because I'm so small, isn't it? I was a bobcat before, and Lorna didn't ever let me on the furniture. All of the latest studies on familiars show that domestic cats have a higher placement success rate than wild cats, so I switched."

"You can change forms?" I pictured Lenti as a bobcat, all giant paws and fearsome fangs. It didn't stretch the imagination much. I could also easily picture her trying to sharpen her huge claws on someone's couch.

"Of course. You know I'm not actually a real cat." She wriggled out of my grasp and leaped to the floor.

"I know, but Lenti, I don't like you because you're small and adorable." I scratched under her chin. "I like you because you're…" Annoying, sassy, impossible, infuriating. "Yourself."

Curling onto her side, she stared at me with innocent peridot eyes. "I also ate one of Lorna's chickens."

"Lenti!"

"What? It's just what bobcats do. They hunt."

I petted her floofy belly. "And now you crave cheese for some reason. Which is not normal cat behavior, by the way. Hey!"

She latched onto my arm and sank her fangs into my hand.

I dragged my hand out of reach and glared at the puncture marks in my skin. "I thought we had a moment."

"I tricked you again." She cackled. "I'm so clever."

"Of course you ate a chicken," I muttered. "Take a nap, little gremlin. I need to get some work done."

Lenti finished her bagel, then curled up behind the file cabinet and went to sleep.

I didn't do so well holding up my end of the bargain. Alex's words from last night played through my mind like a never-ending chorus to a song. *I wanted to run out of the restaurant right then, take you back home and tear the dress off you.*

Gods, I wanted so badly for him to do that. I closed my eyes, allowing myself to wander into a scene where Alex backed me up against a wall and eased the black dress off my shoulders. He slid the dress down, tugged it over my hips, and allowed it to fall to the floor. I could almost feel his hands on my skin.

I sighed and opened my eyes. Maybe I shouldn't have sex with Alex, at least not yet. I should probably think through the ramifications before I offered the friends-with-benefits idea. Once I suggested it, I wouldn't be able to take it back without making things extremely awkward. You can't un-ring a sexy bell.

I glanced at the snoring furball behind my file cabinet. Lenti was a helpful practice buddy, but if I was going to learn how to put up a stronger psychic shield, I needed a teacher with influence. Charisma. Charm.

A teacher just like Alex.

I picked up my phone and texted him.
—*What are you doing tonight?*—

Chapter Nine

Alex opened the door halfway and gave me the same suspicious frown you give to a phone salesperson trying to convince you to upgrade your plan. "I'm still not sure about this idea."

"It's a perfect idea." I lifted my eyebrows at him.

After a moment, he opened the door all the way.

Alex owned an old house in southeast Portland, a boxy Craftsman with a large front porch and a gabled roof.

It was more traditional than I'd have expected—I'd pictured him in a sleek industrial loft—but as I stepped inside and looked around, it made sense. The sleek hardwood floors, elegant crown molding, and antique light fixtures were classic and polished. Just like Alex.

I hung my purse on a cast-iron wall hook and shrugged out of my jacket. The briny scent of the ocean flooded my senses, along with the sound of waves thundering across a distant shore. "Sound machine?"

He grinned. "Whatever you're hearing is just me, I'm afraid."

"Birds. I hear birds. Do you have birds?" Lenti strolled in behind me, nose sniffing, ears alert.

"Oh!" Alex jumped back. "I didn't realize you were bringing a cat."

"This is my familiar. Lenti, meet Alex."

She glanced up, eyes round and wide. "Pleased to

make your acquaintance. I am Altocumulus Lenticularis, and I hail from the seventh realm of the troposphere. You may call me Lenti, as Rowan does."

Alex's lips twitched, and he arranged his mouth into a flat line. Crouching, he held his hand out for Lenti to sniff. "It's nice to meet you."

Lenti sniffed his hand and dropped onto her back, rolling from side to side as she purred. It was like she'd suddenly landed in a field of catnip.

I opened my mouth to warn Alex not to fall for it.

"What a sweetie." Leaning over, he stroked her soft belly. Without incident. "Does she like to be held? Uh, do you like to be held?" he asked, redirecting his question at Lenti.

"Oh, yes, I adore being carried."

What the hell? "You do not. You barely let me—"

"Yes, please."

Alex scooped her up into his arms and held her like a baby.

She stared up at him with a contented gaze, her eyes half-closed.

"You're just a sweet little princess, aren't you?" he murmured to her, as he carried her into the living room.

Of course she was in love with him. Couldn't blame her, though. I kicked off my shoes, because he went barefoot, and followed him.

We sat on opposite ends of his large plush sectional couch.

With Lenti still cradled in his arms, he faced me. "So how do you want to do this?"

I'd told him I needed to practice resisting psychic influence. All eldritch magicians, including telekinetics, were vulnerable to psychic attack, so my request made sense. I didn't plan to tell him I was also telepathic.

I could almost hear Tabitha's voice in my head, encouraging me to tell Alex about the rest of my powers. If he knew everything, he could help me protect myself. But I hadn't suggested the friends-with-benefits idea yet, and it'd be nice to read his mind if I did broach the subject. Lying to him by omission gave me a weird feeling in my stomach, though.

I took a deep breath. "I think we can just start by talking, right? You turn on the charm, and I'll try to resist you. But not while you're holding her."

Lenti stared up at Alex with glazed eyes. "Why not? I'm very comfortable here. Anyway, he smells like catnip." She tipped her head back.

Alex obliged by scratching her chin.

I sighed. He'd charmed her. Now she'd never want to leave. Again, though, couldn't exactly blame her.

After a bit of finagling, we managed to settle Lenti onto a blanket next to Alex.

She curled up with her head nearly touching his leg and closed her little eyes. Within moments, she was snoring.

Alex eyed her warily, then scooted an inch toward me. "Maybe we should establish some ground rules first. I think we need to discuss boundaries. How far I'm allowed to push you."

I snorted. "What for?" The whole point of this was a fight, a battle. My nerves were on fire. I was ready.

"Think of my power as tectonic plates. On a normal day, the power stays under the surface. There might be some activity, but not enough for you to notice. Once I dial up the charisma, the way I would if I was trying to claim your soul, it's an earthquake. It's *going* to throw you off balance. You're going to fall."

"Unless I learn to resist it."

"Yes. But you're not a black belt yet, Ro, all right? Go slow. For my sake, at least."

"Fine. What are the boundaries, then?" I didn't want to spend hours discussing the rules. I wanted to work. Also, the sooner we got to practicing, the sooner I could distract myself from how good Alex looked. His T-shirt and jeans were the most casual clothes I'd seen him in, and I was there for it.

He ran a hand through his dark curls. "One way someone could try to break your defenses is by going for your emotional weak spots. They could force you to focus on something upsetting or sad. Your feelings about your sister, for example, should be off-limits, at least for tonight."

I sucked in a breath, riding out the ache. Megan's laughter rose in my mind and then faded, as if carried away by the wind. "Fair enough. What else?"

"I'm not going to influence you to touch me, and that's a standing rule. Nor will I make you embarrass yourself. Let's stick to mundane stuff, like getting you to pick a specific book off the shelf." He glanced at the built-ins on either side of the fireplace. The shelves were packed with books, some of the spines ragged and peeling.

"This sounds more like hypnosis." Uncertainty winged through me. I knew, in a distant, sort of academic fashion, that Stygians influenced their victims to trust them. I hadn't considered all the specific ways they might wield their power before stealing souls.

"It is, in a way." He stood and crossed his arms, broad shoulders and biceps outlined by his T-shirt.

"Anyway, let's get started. You're going to want to stand up for this."

I sprang to my feet.

He ran a hand over his chin. "Okay. Well, definitely starting at square one."

"What?"

"That was influence. You're already vulnerable."

I glared. "That isn't fair. You didn't tell me we were starting."

"And an attacker isn't going to tell you, either. They'll simply strike." His eyes flashed. "Sit down."

His words weighted me down, a physical force slamming me in my seat. I flexed my quads, but I couldn't break through the power gluing me to the chair.

Alex took a step back, relaxing his hands at his sides. His power dissipated like smoke. "Let's try it again. Stand up, Ro."

We repeated the exercise again and again. Sit, stand, sit, stand. I was starting to feel like I was doing squats. After the fiftieth round or so, I finally managed to block him, remaining standing when he'd told me to sit.

"Not bad." He rolled his shoulders, a slight frown on his flushed face. "Take a breather."

I flexed my legs, shifting from one foot to the other. Sweat beaded on my temples. "I feel like I'm at the gym."

"It's hard work, isn't it? Some people don't realize how physical magic can be."

Oh, gods, please don't talk about things being physical.

We stood there sweating and looking at each other until things felt awkward. I cleared my throat. "What else?"

"All right, let's try another tactic. Why don't you have a seat first, though? This could take a while to explain. Make yourself comfortable. Please." He smiled, his voice smooth as honey.

I plopped down, then realized what he was doing. "Hey. You tricked me."

"And your enemies are going to be perfectly honest with you at all times?"

"Asshole," I muttered. "Do it again."

We sparred for another hour. He ran through different methods of influence—begging and pleading, using a sultry voice, barking orders, even screaming, "Get away! There's a huge spider!" He influenced me to turn in a circle, touch my toes, and strike a downward dog pose.

By the end of our session, I was blocking Alex, but only thirty percent of the time.

He poured us glasses of ice water, and we sat on the couch. Alex clinked his glass against mine. "For your first try, that was good."

Lenti was still asleep; she hadn't woken once while we were practicing. Apparently being at Alex's house had put her into a semi-coma.

"Thanks." I took a long greedy drink of my ice water as sweat cooled on the back of my neck. "Maybe I need to do this more often. Might burn some calories." I brushed some damp strands of hair off my forehead. "How's your case going, by the way? Has Noel made any progress?"

"A little. They're trying to set up an arbitration." He shrugged. "We'll see."

"What about Melanie? Has she figured out a way to help you?" The mention of her name left a sour taste in my mouth, and I gulped more water.

"She's working on it. I'm hopeful." He smiled at me over the rim of his water glass. "Hey. I'm sorry I doubted your plan to practice together. This worked out pretty well."

I grinned. "So we can practice again?"

"I'd like that. Too much."

"What do you mean?"

"You probably won't believe me, because of what I am, but…" His dark eyes were soft. "I genuinely enjoy your company."

"I enjoy yours, too." My throat tightened. His gaze was melancholy and distant. I didn't know why he was sad, but I couldn't stand the hint of pain. Setting down my glass, I took his hand. "We're friends, whatever else happens."

He set his glass down, too, and took my other hand. "What if I don't want to just be your friend?"

My heart had stopped beating. I was sure it had. Time had frozen. "What do you want?"

"To be free," he whispered, "to do this."

He leaned close, but instead of kissing me, he trailed his lips close to my ear. His left hand let go of mine and traced a path up the inside of my arm. He teased along my collarbone as his breath grew uneven against my skin.

Holy shit. I didn't know it was possible to get this aroused when someone wasn't even kissing you.

He traced swirls down my chest and slipped his fingers beneath my bra.

Thank the goddess I'd worn black lace.

I bit back a gasp as he teased my breast and nipple with a light-but-sure touch. I could barely draw air; my body burned.

Sliding my hand beneath his T-shirt, I ran my fingers over his smooth, tightly muscled abs and soft skin.

He breathed harder and shorter, and on a groan, he whispered, "There's so much more I want to do to you, Ro."

"Avaunt!" cried a tiny but powerful voice.

The next second, Alex let out a yell and backed away from me. He batted at a ball of black-and-white fur on his head.

"Lenti!" I snatched her away, struggling with her snarling, hissing form.

She shot out of my arms and bounded toward Alex, then latched onto his ankle with her front paws and kicked.

Alex grimaced. "Please. Ow, by the Styx. Please stop. Please."

Lenti stilled and detached her claws from the leg of his jeans. "Oh. Hello." She purred and gazed up at him. He must have charmed her again. "Do you have any macaroni and cheese in this place, kind-and-lovely human person?"

So much for sexy moments. "We should go. Alex, I'm sorry for my familiar's violent behavior. It won't happen again, will it?" I gave her what I hoped was a look of death.

Lenti rolled onto her back, purring as loud as a fan.

"Impossible. I can't go anywhere with you."

Alex laughed so hard tears trickled down his cheeks.

****

Tabitha poured white cheddar popcorn into a small bowl. "So how are your sessions going with Alex?"

"Good." I'd had two more practice rounds with him this week—at *my* apartment to reduce the overwhelming smells of the ocean and catnip.

Lenti still acted enamored with Alex and spent our sessions perched on his shoulder.

There'd been no more hands-on-boobs situations.

I'd already decided not to tell Tabitha about our little slip-up the first time. I'd apologized for snapping at her the other day, and we were back to our normal Friday-night hangouts, but I felt cautious about telling her everything. She would just analyze the situation with Alex, wanting to know what my interactions with him *meant,* and I didn't even understand them.

I handed Lenti a piece of popcorn.

She batted it to the floor, then hopped down to chase it around. She didn't like the popcorn itself, but she enjoyed licking off the white cheddar coating.

"I'm getting better at shielding from his influence. Still breaking things at random, though." Last night I'd made a framed poster fall off my wall, and the glass had shattered. "And I'm still on a diet of allergy pills and eyedrops."

She nodded. "What about mind reading? Is that getting easier?"

"Um, yep." I stuffed a small handful of popcorn into my mouth.

She sat up, alert. "What? What are you thinking?"

"How do you always know when I'm thinking something?" If I didn't know her, I'd swear Tabitha could read minds, too. "The telepathy is getting easier. Alex doesn't know about it, though."

"What? Why not?"

"Well, we're already working on so many other

things. And mind reading is easier to practice on my own or with Lenti."

Liar, liar, hair on fire, crowed Lenti in my brain.

It's pants on fire.

She was right. The reasons I gave Tabitha were bullshit. I wasn't hanging onto my secret for any reason other than the control it gave me. If Alex and I kept hanging out, if we kissed again, or took things further, I wanted to know what it meant. What he felt. If I told him about my telepathy, he'd cut me off, I felt sure. Either psychically, by blocking my power, or physically, by never speaking to me again.

Keeping an ace up my sleeve was cheating, but I was willing to cheat if it meant I didn't get hurt again.

Tabitha opened her mouth as if gearing up for a lecture.

My phone saved me, chiming a new-email alert. I clicked through to the email, and my heart beat faster.

I'd finally gotten a response to my post on *The Beehive.*

"What's wrong?" said Tabitha.

"Nothing. Hang on." I clicked the email and read a reply from someone named Blaze352.

I don't have info per se, but I have something that'll get you access to do your own research. It costs $75, cash only. You can text me to set up a time to pick it up.

The message ended with a phone number.

The back of my neck prickled. This sounded like the start of a cheesy spy movie. What kind of "something" could this person have that would get me access? To what? Was there a Stygian Association website somewhere that I'd be able to break into? Plus, seventy-five bucks seemed steep. This person was probably scamming me.

But what if they weren't?

I showed Tabitha the email.

"Seventy-five bucks?" She snorted. "Not worth it. This person doesn't even say what they'll give you."

"But they're not asking for payment upfront, so maybe it's not a scam." I plugged Blaze352's number into my phone. "I don't have any other leads on the *alpha lyrae*. This is the first hit I've gotten."

"Still think it's sketchy."

"Oh, it is." I texted my possible benefactor. "But it's all I've got."

—UnseelieFan200 here. Setting up a time to pick up. Has to be in public.—

I certainly wasn't going to some stranger's house, or an empty parking lot, not even with Lenti and her claws to protect me.

Almost instantly, the three little dots appeared, signaling the person was writing back.

—Tomorrow night? I'll be at the Aspen Lounge for a show. You could go to the bar. Order a Waxing Crescent IPA so I can find you. Nine thirty?—

I let out the breath I'd been holding. The Aspen was a popular music venue in inner Southeast Portland. I'd be surrounded by people, many of them ordinary humans. Blaze352 probably wasn't trying to murder me, then.

—That works. How will I recognize you?—

—I'll wear a blue shirt.—

I wasn't sure that would help. Surely Blaze352 wouldn't be the only person wearing blue. But okay, if they thought a blue shirt sufficed for identification purposes, sure.

"Lenti?" I waited for her to look up from the popcorn. "We're going out tomorrow."

Chapter Ten

The next evening, with an invisible Lenti on my right shoulder, I showed my ID to the bouncer at The Aspen.

Admission to the bar was free; payment was needed to get into the concerts downstairs.

I sidled past the bouncer and peeked around.

About twenty people occupied the lounge, with warm, low lighting cast over their tables and chairs.

Just off the lounge, a young woman sat fidgeting behind a table, where a sign advertised the twenty-dollar admission to the show. Beyond her yawned the staircase that led downstairs to the music hall.

I'd been to a show here a couple times with Tabitha and Paul and remembered the venue as a cavernous basement with a huge stage and almost no place to sit down.

Only two people sat at the bar, so maybe it would be easier than I thought for Blaze352 to find me.

I took a seat at the end of the bar and ordered a Waxing Crescent IPA as instructed.

Nineties grunge played from a speaker overhead, clashing with the sounds of banjos and drums drifting up from the music hall.

I glanced at the brochure on the bar top that advertised October's shows. I hadn't heard of any of the bands. Either I was getting old or falling out of touch with modern-music culture.

While I waited for Blaze352, I spoke silently to Lenti. My ears itched a little, but allergy meds had tamed the worst of my sneezing. *What did you think of tonight's episode?*

We had just made it through Season Two, Episode Thirteen of *Unseelie*, in which the six main cast members rented a mansion in rural Ireland for three nights. Predictably, the first night's dinner had ended with Florinda throwing a drink in Daisy's face.

Lenti shifted on my shoulder, tucking herself in closer to my cheek. *I can't believe how selfish Emerald was being, kicking Daisy out of her room. And what did Florinda do to her face?*

I snickered remembering the scene. *That filler spell she did backfired, I think.*

"Rowan?" said a familiar voice.

I looked up.

Dave half-smiled, half-leered at me. Sweat flecked his pale forehead. He was pitting out, too, probably from all the body heat of the patrons downstairs.

Another reason I didn't love crowded venues. Lack of ventilation.

Then I realized he was wearing a blue shirt. Oh, gods. "Are you—?"

"Blaze352." He gave a small bow. "UnseelieFan. I should've known. You always loved that garbage."

Great start, insulting my taste in television. I ground my teeth and decided not to antagonize him, at least not until after I'd acquired whatever thing he was giving me. "How are you even here?" I glanced around, indicating the other patrons in general. "Doesn't this kind of setting…um, bother you?"

"You mean, why am I not drooling over all the pulsing jugular veins everywhere?" He grinned. At least he had the sense to keep his fangs retracted. "I take a little something to mute the bloodlust before I mix with humans. It wears off in a few hours, just enough time to take in a concert. Not that it's a problem if I'm out here longer than that. I can control myself. Most vampires can, at least the ones who manage their blood intake properly."

His condescending tone grated on me. *Yes, twenty-five-year-old child, please lecture me on the details of vampiric cravings, I so wanted to know.*

His voice hurts my ears, Lenti said.

I dated him. Trust me, I know. I took another sip of my beer, not for liquid courage, but for liquid politeness. I needed to be nice to Dave so he would sell me whatever this "resource" was.

"So." He tapped the black-and-red label plastered to my beer bottle. "I guess I know why you're here."

I set down my beer, the glass clanking against the polished wooden bar. "I guess so."

He waved down the bartender and ordered a stout. When the man turned toward the taps, Dave slipped something out of his pocket. He slid it into my hand and, with a clammy touch, curled my fingers over it.

Trying not to be too obvious, I tugged my hand away and peeked at the object.

A cat toy? said Lenti.

I frowned. "A flash drive?"

"That's a bootleg copy of a program called Wake. You wouldn't have heard of it before—it's not officially on the market." Dave paused to pay for his beer, then took a long gulp.

I dropped the flash drive into my purse and waited for him to explain.

Dave set down his beer, nodding in a satisfied way. "I don't know why anyone drinks anything other than dark beer, honestly. Before my rebirth, I was thinking of opening my own brewery." He put his nose to the bottle and his nostrils flared. "You can really smell the barley in this one."

I decided not to point out the foam on his upper lip. "So. The program?"

"Right." He leaned against the bar and unbuttoned the top of his shirt.

I wished he wouldn't. His close proximity was giving me a whiff of vampire BO. Trust me, it's not a smell you want to become acquainted with, unless you like the scent of rust and skunk.

Why does he smell so bad? Did you really used to mate with him?

Unfortunately.

Dave took another long draw of his drink.

"Careful, turbo. Shouldn't you be pacing yourself?" Vampires were more sensitive to alcohol than humans. Something about the altered chemical makeup of their blood, though I couldn't remember the details. Supernatural Biology 101 had been a long time ago.

"Oh, I don't think I have a problem with my timing." Dave lifted an eyebrow.

I rolled my eyes. Why did he have to turn everything into an innuendo?

"No? Nothing? I thought that was a good one."

I slipped off the barstool. "Okay, we're done here."

"Wait, wait. Here's the deal."

I leaned against the bar and made a show of

dropping a ten-dollar bill where the bartender could see it. I wasn't sticking around to finish a beer with Dave. He was wasting my precious time.

He leaned in, giving off another whiff of rusty skunk. "Wake is a software program that gives you access to other dimensions. You need a dimension key to use it, so I put that on the flash drive in a text file. Once you're in, you've got access to the prophetess of the Underworld. You're on your own after that. No guarantee you'll get answers."

I perked up. Maybe this was worth seventy-five bucks after all. The prophetess of the Underworld? I wasn't sure what prophetess he meant—the only one I remembered from Greek mythology was cursed Cassandra—but a prophetess would have access to divine wisdom. They could surely explain the meaning of *alpha lyrae.*

And a prophetess would know how I could get a message to Megan.

I dug out seventy-five dollars in cash and passed over the bills. "Here you go."

"Sweet. You just paid for all my drinks this evening." He laughed. "You want to stick around? The band's really good."

"Natasha's not meeting up with you?" In other words, *where's your girlfriend, buddy*?

"Not really her scene." His eyes flashed. "You and I always had fun at these types of things, though."

Wow. He truly had no shame. "Oh, I really can't. I have to get up so early tomorrow." I groaned. "Thanks, though. Have fun."

Time to get out of here. I adjusted my cross-body purse and zipped it tight. Lenti's weight on my right shoulder was reassuringly familiar.

"Hey, one sec." Dave touched my arm with damp fingers. "I'd appreciate if you could keep this between us. The code of conduct at work doesn't officially prohibit me selling software on the side, but I have a feeling HR wouldn't like it. Wake isn't exactly a sanctioned form of magic."

"Trust me. This is off the record. And I assume you won't tell anyone I bought it, right?"

He put a hand up in a gesture of surrender. "I don't ask questions about this stuff. As far as I'm concerned, we ran into each other at the bar and had a drink. Just two co-workers catching up."

"Good."

"Can I have the rest of your beer, if you're not going to drink it?"

"Knock yourself out."

I hurried out of the bar. Sometimes I wished he would actually, literally, knock himself out, but right now I was grateful. He might've just given me the key to figuring out this whole situation.

Fricking Dave. Who'd have thought?

Back home, I fed Lenti, changed into my pajamas, and settled down at my laptop at the dining room table. It was already past ten, but I couldn't wait until tomorrow to see how Wake worked. Or if it worked.

As promised, Dave had included a text file with a twenty-character code.

I copied it, then ran the installer for Wake.

By the time it finished, Lenti had scarfed her snack and hopped into my lap.

The start screen popped up, with a prompt to enter a dimension code.

I pasted in the code and idly scratched Lenti's head.

A new window popped up and filled my screen. A kaleidoscope of deep blue shapes spun and twisted on the screen, slowly resolving into…

Lenti stood up on her hind legs, her front paws on the table. "What is it?"

I frowned, studying the image. "I'm not exactly sure."

It appeared to be a video shot underwater, maybe in a tropical setting. The water progressed from a deep dark blue at the bottom of the screen, up toward a light brilliant blue toward the top. A few rays of light shone down into the water, and the surface undulated gently.

"Is this it?" I tapped a few keys. Nothing happened. I tried pointing my mouse at different regions of the screen, thinking maybe the program used hotspots. Nothing. "Um, hello?" I sighed. "If Dave sold me a seventy-five-dollar screensaver, I swear—"

"Oh!" squealed a high-pitched female voice. "Who's there?"

I gasped and shoved my chair back.

Lenti leaped onto the table, all the fur on her back standing up. She hissed at the laptop.

"Dear, I can't actually see you," said the voice in a posh British accent, "so you're going to have to introduce yourself. Have you just arrived? Oh, here, let's go to the top."

The image on the screen changed, and the camera rose through the water, breaking through the surface into a huge cave. It wasn't sunlight that had been shining on the water, but an otherworldly light emanating from huge white stalactites that dripped from the ceiling.

And what I'd mistaken for an ocean was a wide,

calm river. What was this place? "What the hell?"

"The Underworld, actually, not Hell. I hope that's not a surprise. Some people aren't expecting it."

I clapped my hands over my mouth to keep from screaming. Bloody Dave. His software had actually worked. Which meant I was speaking to the prophetess of the Underworld. "No, that's what I was hoping for. Um, I have some questions."

"Oh, most people do. Now, let's start with introductions. I'm Susan, and you are?"

A prophetess named Susan? Well, okay. "I'm Rowan, and this is my familiar."

Lenti pawed at the corner of the laptop. "Altocumulus Lenticularis, of the seventh realm of the troposphere. If you hurt Rowan, I'll claw your eyes out."

I placed a warning hand on her head.

Susan laughed. "A feline, how delightful. I thought I sensed two of you here. Now, I know this may be quite unexpected, but I can assure you there's nothing to be afraid of. Your forms will become more corporeal as you get used to things. This, as you can see, is the River Styx. It's a lovely place for a swim. And there are no restrictions or anything like that, so you can have a dip whenever you'd like."

Understanding dawned. Susan thought Lenti and I were *in* the Underworld. Did she not know about Wake? "We're not dead. We're still on earth, in my apartment."

"You mean you're still on the mortal plane? But how…Can you see me?" An arm appeared in the camera and a hand waved.

Oh, shit. But that meant… "We can see your point of view. I think, uh, I think we're inside your head."

"*Really.*" She drew the word into several syllables.

"How did you accomplish that?"

"A spell." I wasn't sure if I should explain about Wake; I wasn't even sure I could explain it. What mattered was that it had worked.

"You must be quite a powerful witch. Well, this is unexpected. You see, usually I connect with new arrivals and give them a tour. But you won't be staying with us, so, can I help you with anything?"

A tour? The prophetess gave tours?

"Oh, I want the tour." Lenti nosed the screen. "I've never seen the Underworld before. It's forbidden to air spirits."

I scooted the laptop away from her. "We don't have time."

"The full tour does take an hour, but I can at least show you around this area."

The point of view shifted as Susan slogged onto the riverbank. An arm and hand veered into view again as she pointed at the ceiling, her skin and pale-gold sleeve mysteriously dry. "Now, this is called the Cathedral of the Styx, and it's one of my favorite places in the realm. The Styx is at its widest here, about 150 meters. Do you know how many rivers we have here? I'll give you a hint, it's more than one." She laughed, a tinkling sound like a sleigh bell.

"It's five. The others are the Archeron, the Lethe, the Phlegethon, and the Cocytus." Lenti sneered at me.

I ruffled her back fur. "Show-off."

"That's right, very good," said Susan. "The rivers of remembrance, forgetfulness, fire, and wailing. Some people think the Archeron is the river of pain, but that's a misconception. Swimming in its waters actually keeps memories of loved ones alive. And the fire isn't fire so much as a hot spring. I'm afraid the wailing is accurate. The waters of the Cocytus induce grief, though it is incredibly good for your skin. All the sulfur."

A series of yappy barks blasted out of the speakers.

Lenti arched her back, and my eyes widened.

Susan crouched just as a fluffy three-headed Pomeranian bounded toward her. "Oh, hello, sweet poochie." She reached out to rub each of its heads.

"A demon!" Lenti sprang off the desk and shot across the room.

Why was she so scared of a weird-looking dog? "Gremlin?"

The only answer was her tail disappearing into the hidey-hole in her tower.

"This is Cerberella," said Susan.

The dog sat back on her haunches, her three fluffy heads panting happily.

I burst into giggles. "Like Cerberus?"

"Yes. She's the great-great-some-indeterminate-number-of-greats-granddaughter of the original Cerberus. He's retired now, you see. Oh, who's a good girl?" Susan scratched Cerberella under her middle chin.

"Okay, she's adorable in a creepy way, but how does she keep the dead from leaving the Underworld? Isn't that what she's for?"

"No, it's more of an honorary position these days. Hades has really changed his approach, and almost none of the dead even want to leave. I mean, why would you go anywhere when we have our own restaurants and resorts? It's really more like a vacation."

Restaurants and resorts? And Alex's long-ago post on the Hades forum had mentioned nightclubs. The Underworld sounded more like Vegas by the minute.

That didn't mean it was a playground, though. "But what about everyone who's forced into servitude by Stygians?"

"I assure you, everyone here is perfectly happy."

I doubted that, but I didn't have time to argue with her. "So, how does this work? Do I get a set number of questions?"

"I'm not sure what you mean. Questions for what?"

The bottom of my stomach dropped out. "Aren't you a prophetess?"

She laughed. "I'm sorry, no. We have several prophetesses, but most are on vacation right now, and the remaining two are booked for months. And only one does mortal plane appointments. I'm afraid it may be spring before you can get in to see her."

I clenched my jaw. Not only had Dave wasted my money, he'd lied to me. What an ass.

"I'm sorry, I'm being paged." Susan stood. "There's a new arrival, and I need to greet them."

"Wait, wait, wait. Do you know someone named Megan Baird? Could you get a message to her for me?"

"Megan Baird," she drawled.

My hopes rose.

"No, I'm sorry, dear, but I don't keep the rosters, I only give the tours. I really do have to go. It was lovely chatting, though. Feel free to come back anytime."

And with that, the screen darkened.

Chapter Eleven

I marched down the hall, Lenti's whiskers brushing my face every few steps. By now I was used to her riding my shoulder like a parrot in a pirate movie.

You're really mad. Her voice in my head sounded gleeful.

Because Dave knew this program was worthless when he sold it to me. I bet he wrote it himself.

Can I bite him?

No.

A scratch?

Maybe.

I stopped in front of the block of cubicles where our tech-support specialists sat.

Dave was the only one there right then, and he stared at his computer screen, his eyes shadowed.

This section of the floor had no windows, and instead of overhead lights, the cubes were lit by bankers' lamps. The yellowish light cast a waxy pallor over his face.

I glared until he noticed me.

He removed his headphones. "Hey." His voice was scratchy. "You should've stuck around last night. You missed an amazing show. Two encores. And then this other band, kind of a nineties alt-rock type sound, did an after-show."

I leaned over the top of his cubicle and dropped my

voice to a furious whisper. "Did you think it would be funny to scam me? Did you think I wouldn't find out that Wake is worthless?"

His brows wrinkled. He craned his neck, checking behind me. "Remember the whole 'nothing happened, we met for a drink'? What're you talking about? The code didn't work?"

"No, it worked fine." I came around the cubicle and pulled up a chair. "You told me I could talk to the prophetess of the Underworld. I ended up in the head of someone called Susan who's a tour guide for the newly dead. What's the deal?"

Dave leaned his forehead against one palm. "You thought Wake would get you to a prophetess, like a Greek mythology type prophetess? That's not what I meant. I said it connected you to the Prophetess of the Underworld. As in, Prophetess, the software company? The cloud service that hosts all of our apps?"

I stared at him. "Are you telling me Wake is just a supernatural connector?"

"Right. It hooks you up to the magical infrastructure of whatever dimension you're accessing. The cloud-hosting service of the dimension, if you will. The Prophetess of the Underworld or the Eighth Realm or wherever you're going. You see what I mean?"

Embarrassment heated my face, but I also wanted to punch him. Why would he use a convoluted metaphor like that and expect me to get it? "So just to clarify." My voice cracked. "Wake is like a VPN, and it gets me onto the Underworld wi-fi, but after that, who I talk to is just, what? Pure chance?"

"Pretty much." He shrugged. "I'm a little surprised you didn't know what I meant, since you're the technical writer."

I fought the urge to yell at him for the next five days solid. Instead, I sought his mind, which opened like a sliding glass door.

I'm gonna puke. Please leave before I puke.

I smirked. He'd clearly enjoyed one too many beers last night. I hopped up and walked away.

"Rowan, wait."

I glanced over my shoulder.

"Hey, I'm sorry. Are we good? Is this still between us?"

"Yeah, we're good, I'm not gonna throw you under the bus to HR. Relax." I strode down the hall. *Sanctimonious ass.*

I was rewarded by the sound of Dave retching into the nearest garbage can.

I spent the rest of the morning revising a quick reference guide on word processing that Tabitha needed for a class she was teaching next week.

Around eleven, my stomach growled, reminding me I'd only had coffee for breakfast. The sandwich and apple I'd brought sounded sad and unappealing right now. Could I get by with buying a food-cart burrito for the sixth work lunch in a row? Checking my bank app, I frowned. My account balance suggested it wouldn't be in my best interests to drop another nine dollars on lunch.

Sad and unappealing, then.

I tapped Lenti lightly on the head.

She was sitting on my lap, eyes closed, folded into a duck pose—belly to the ground, all four paws tucked under her body so she appeared to have no legs.

"I need to grab my lunch from the break room. Are you coming?"

She hopped onto my shoulder and dematerialized.

The break room was on the opposite end of the floor, and the quickest route went straight past Alex's office. Was he there? *I'm not going to check.* He was probably in a meeting. Or talking to an attorney. Or doing other more important things than hanging out in his office waiting to run into me.

As I strode past his office, I peeked in anyway. Damn all these glass walls.

He stood inside, profile to me, talking to a tall redhead in a tight black dress.

My heart lurched as Melanie leaned forward, her fingers on his forearm as she said something. She brushed her hair back from her ear with two delicate fingers and then shook her long, thick, cinnamon locks.

Alex's laugh rumbled through the glass.

Oh, hell no.

I yanked open the door and plastered on a broad smile. "Oh, hi, Melanie. I didn't know you were coming by. Do you have another meeting with Noel today?"

Her smile locked into place, and she blinked. "Alex and I are going to lunch."

Of course they were. I pictured them sitting in a cozy corner, sipping iced teas while Melanie tossed her hair around like a shampoo commercial. "Sounds fun."

"You're welcome to join us, if you'd like."

Huh? The last time I saw her, Melanie made it clear she didn't like me. What kind of power play was this, inviting me to lunch?

"Oh, I'm sure Rowan has her own lunch plans." Alex smiled casually at me, but his eyes screamed panic.

Okay, what was going on? Alex didn't want me there? I mean, yes, eating lunch with the two of them sounded like Dante's second circle of hell. But I already knew Melanie was helping him, so presuming she was there to talk about his contract, it wouldn't matter if I heard the conversation.

Of course, maybe he hadn't told her I knew about the contract. *Stop panicking.* Alex was probably trying to keep the situation low-key, especially since the Firm most likely wouldn't approve of a fellow Stygian helping him with his case. Still, the idea of them sitting together at lunch made me feel like I had norovirus.

I looked from Alex to Melanie, careful to focus just below her eyeballs so I wouldn't get zapped with another of her influence spells. "I'd love to, actually."

"Well, we actually have some business to discuss." Alex grabbed his jacket off the back of his chair.

"We can talk later."

Melanie patted his arm in a way that made my blood boil.

"Of course she can come."

"Of-of course." Alex shot me a *what are you doing?* look.

I gave him a breezy smile and a little wave. "See you downstairs."

In my office, as I slung my purse over my shoulder, Lenti said aloud, "You really think Ick Lady is trying to mate with Alex again?"

I giggled at the nickname. "Probably. For all I know, she's done it already. Why does he trust her at all? She's clearly the worst."

"I don't know if I can be around her. She smells delicious, but she makes me want to throw up hairballs."

I paused with my hand on the door. "You could always stay here, take a nap."

"No." Her grip on my shoulder tightened. "I shall suffer the presence of your greatest enemy."

I smirked and we headed for the elevators.

Five minutes later, I was following Alex and Melanie down the sidewalk toward Campground, which despite the name was actually an upscale bistro.

Lenti rode on my shoulder, her whiskers tickling my face. *Why are there so many pigeons here? Can I chase them? Why don't we have pigeons at home?*

The restaurant was just opening for lunch when we arrived. The hostess seated us at a square wooden table by the window, and Alex and Melanie studied the menus. I never got anything here besides the grilled cheese, so I didn't bother.

Oh, I should probably order a snack for Lenti, otherwise my feline boss would guilt-trip me for not sharing all the delicious food. *What do you want? I'll order it to go.*

Do they have salmon?

They did, but it was twenty-seven bucks, so I told her no and to pick grilled cheese or fries. She insisted on both. In a sign of my complete and total servitude to a six-pound cat, I agreed.

We made small talk until our server took our order. When I asked for a second grilled cheese and fries to go, Alex chuckled. "Dinner for later?"

"What can I say? I'm a hungry girl."

"So, Rowan." Melanie folded her hands and tapped her long nails together.

The clacking sound gave me goose bumps.

"Noel speaks very highly of you. I'd love to know more about your background. Have you always lived in Portland?"

I stalled with a long drink of water, suspicion churning in my stomach. Melanie didn't care about getting to know me. What was she doing? "For the most part, but I'm not that interesting. I'd actually love to hear about your business. I understand you focus on commercial real estate. What got you interested in residential?"

She dragged a manicured, polished nail across her paper napkin, leaving a gouge. "I think it's important to diversify. Our building will have magical amenities that residents can't get in human-run buildings, like warded doors and an energy-replenishment bar. We'll even stock donated blood for the vampires."

"You didn't tell me about the replenishment bar. How did you arrange that?"

Alex looked impressed, which illogically pissed me off.

"I called in a few favors." She shrugged. "A warlock in Seattle, one of my clients. He owed me."

As she discussed the design of the bar, I sought her mind. If she was talking about the condo, she might be distracted. Which meant I might be able to sneak in her mind to search for information about the mysterious *alpha lyrae.*

My left temple suddenly throbbed, and I clamped my napkin to my nose just in time to contain a sneeze.

"Are you all right?" Melanie frowned, her voice all light and sympathetic.

Too sympathetic. Had she just kicked me out of her brain? Again? I sniffled and gulped some water. "It's just allergies. Probably ragweed."

"How unfortunate."

"I have allergy meds back in the office. No big

173

deal." I smiled.

"So, you're allergic to ragweed." Melanie folded her hands together and raised her brows, as if this was the most interesting thing she'd ever heard. "What else? Do you have any pets? Are you married?"

"Nope. Single as a dollar bill. What about you?" I narrowed my eyes at her.

Why did you deny my existence? Lenti dug her claws into my shoulder.

I winced. *You're not a pet, and I don't trust her.*

"Oh, I'm much too busy for a relationship. I'm completely married to my company. Alex knows that."

Melanie shot him an intimate smile that made my stomach turn.

Alex coughed and changed the subject.

We managed neutral conversation until our food arrived.

As I bit off a chunk of gooey grilled cheese, I tried again to read Melanie's mind. It was like trying to pry open an iron door with a toothpick.

She flicked an eyebrow at me as she sipped her lemon water.

When Alex excused himself to the restroom, I leaned toward her. "What do you want? Why did you invite me to lunch?"

One corner of her mouth tilted up in a wry half-smile. "Not very subtle, are you? I can feel you trying to penetrate my mind. Not going to work, pumpkin."

"I want to know what you're doing with Alex." I narrowed my eyes. "Are you actually trying to help him break his contract?"

"I'm not at liberty to discuss Alex's situation," she purred. "He's asked me not to. I can tell you, though, that

I do have his best interests at heart. Why are you so concerned?" She tilted her head, and the concern on her face screamed insincerity. "You have feelings for him. Oh, sweetie. It'll never work with him."

Oh, wouldn't it? I smiled tightly. "I usually don't take life advice from a murderous demigoddess."

"Sassy." She dabbed her mouth with her cloth napkin, leaving traces of red lipstick on the paper. "You're cute enough to be Alex's plaything, but let's be realistic. You aren't someone who could ever give him what he really needs."

My nose stung with the effort of holding back sudden tears.

Lenti let out a disembodied hiss.

"Christ, was that a cat?" Melanie glanced behind me.

Lenti's weight shifted. *I'm going to chew off all her hair, and then claw her purse.*

Do you want your fries and grilled cheese? Then stand down. As satisfying as it was to imagine Melanie with ragged hair and a decimated designer purse, it might cause a slight scene in the middle of the restaurant. Plus, Melanie would probably sue the Firm if Lenti attacked her. I didn't need both of us getting in trouble at work.

Lenti grumbled a series of curse words in my brain, and I sat dabbing my eyes and scarfing the last of my grilled cheese until Alex returned.

He frowned. "You okay? Your eyes are a little red."

I dabbed my nose with my napkin. "My allergies are still really bad."

"That's too bad. Have you tried a healer? They have anti-sneeze potions."

"What are you allergic to?" Melanie raised her

175

brows as she speared a cherry tomato with her fork.

"I'm allergic to this lunch, actually." I threw my napkin down. "Sorry, Alex, I need to get back to the office." I didn't have cash, and I didn't feel like waiting awkwardly at the table while I settled my bill. Alex could figure it out. I'd pay him back later.

Or maybe I wouldn't.

"Are you sure?" He stood at the same time I did. "Do you want to go outside and talk for a moment?"

"Nope. See you at the office." I locked gazes with Melanie, then stalked out of the restaurant.

To her credit, Lenti remained silent until we reached my office. Then she hopped behind the filing cabinet and reappeared. "Why wouldn't you let me attack her? She insulted us. Also, I'd like my lunch now."

I set the to-go box in front of her and opened the flaps. Sitting next to her, I slumped against the wall. "Because Alex is my boss, and if you attacked Melanie in public, I could lose my job. She's a client."

"But she's so awful." Lenti stuck her nose into the box and tore off a chunk of grilled cheese. "Thith tathty. Can you make thith at home?"

"No, I've tried. Their grilled cheese is literally the best." I sighed. "Alex probably thinks I'm a huge bitch because I left."

"Tho what?" She licked her chops.

I shrugged and picked at a hangnail while Lenti snuffled her way through the food. I shouldn't care what Alex thought of me, but that would require me to have no feelings for him. The fact was, I did have feelings, or at least, a feeling. Comfort. Warmth. The feeling that for the first time, a guy recognized me for my authentic self, and didn't want to change me.

If I really cared about him, I should go talk to him. Like an adult.

I logged in to my computer and flipped between reading my email and checking Alex's status in Muse every several seconds. When the little light next to his name flipped from yellow to green, I stood and glanced at Lenti. "I need to talk to Alex. Could you just stay—"

Wriggle. Spring. Land. "What are we talking about?"

"—put." I sighed. "Don't know why I even asked."

Lenti dematerialized, and with her safely tucked on my shoulder, I strolled down the hall toward Alex's office. My mind raced, sorting through different options of what to say. Should I explain why I'd left? Apologize?

Alex was frowning at his computer, but when I knocked, his mouth and eyes softened at the corners. He motioned me in.

Before I could say anything, he hurried out from behind his desk. "Are you okay? I'm sorry if you felt trapped into going to lunch with us. She was here to talk about my case, but she doesn't know you're in the loop, so I couldn't mention it."

My anxiety about his earlier caginess fled. *See?* He was just trying to keep things quiet. "I didn't feel trapped. What do I owe you for lunch?"

"Please." He waved a hand. "Lunch is on Ainsley Barfield. Are you okay? You seemed upset when you left."

"Sorry." I shrugged, wondering how much to tell him. "Uh, Melanie sort of reminded me that I'm not a demigoddess and it probably wouldn't work between you and me."

"That's what she said to you?" His eyes narrowed.

177

"Gods. I'm sorry, Ro. It's not like I've discussed you with her. We go way back, and she's protective."

A cold tendril wound its way around my heart. Why wouldn't Alex tell me they had dated? Melanie wasn't protective, she was manipulative. But he seemed protective of her.

Why?

I placed a hand on my chest, over the crystal tucked into my shirt, and sought Alex's mind. It was open, but like trying to watch a movie in fast-forward. Conflicting thoughts and emotions clashed and fled. I backed away.

"She's not wrong." I hated agreeing with anything Melanie said, but a mortal and a demigod wasn't a match made in heaven. "I mean, we've already agreed that you and I aren't a good idea."

He clasped my hand, his skin rough and warm. "That doesn't mean I don't want you."

I took a step closer to him and gazed up into those huge brown eyes.

His long black lashes lowered slightly.

I waited, barely breathing.

He seemed frozen, too. We were close enough to touch, if I dared. I brushed one finger down the side of his jaw.

My mind filled with the image of dove-gray walls, an antique nightstand, a warm yellow lamp, and a king-sized bed. Alex leaned over me, silken sheets rumpled around our naked bodies. The vantage point was through Alex's eyes, staring down at…me.

This wasn't my fantasy. This was his.

I supposed that should have been obvious, because he'd made my boobs a full cup size larger than they were in real life. Apparently he wasn't very good at recognizing padded bras.

With his free hand, Alex cupped the side of my face in his hand. He leaned down.

Lenti let out a warning hiss at close range.

Wincing, I stepped back.

Pop. She rematerialized on my shoulder. "Hello again."

"Oh, Lenti." He blinked. "Uh, how long have you been here?"

"All day. I'm invisible most of the time." She slipped out of view again. A moment later, she popped up on the top of his bookshelf. "It's me again. I can teleport, too."

Alex stared at me. "She comes to work with you every day?"

My heart sank. "Please don't tell anyone. I can't leave her at home."

"Rowan is very attached to me." Lenti licked her shoulder in a disinterested fashion. "I've tried staying home, but she feels more secure when I'm around."

I rolled my eyes at Alex. "Trust me, it's better if we're not separated."

"I suppose she isn't hurting anything. Was she at lunch, too?"

"Yep."

"I see." He rubbed his chin. "If we were to go to dinner again, she would come, too."

"I thought we weren't doing this again."

He held my gaze, his eyes deep and inviting. "I did too, but I can't resist you."

"Ooh, dinner?" Lenti paused, her tongue half-sticking out. "Will there be salmon?"

His lips twitched. "There certainly could be."

"You may have noticed we're a package deal." I shrugged.

"Then the invitation is to both of you." He gave Lenti a nervous glance before turning to me, his smile widening. "What about Wednesday?"

Chapter Twelve

I hugged Tabitha. "Thanks for doing this. I owe you a hundred favors."

"Now hold on," piped up Lenti from her spot cradled in Tabitha's arms. "Let's review the rules one more time, shall we?"

I sighed and checked my phone. "I'm going to be late." I stuck my phone into my purse, crossed my arms, and waited for my cat-boss to do her thing.

Lenti, curled up in the crook of Tabitha's left arm like a baby, gave me her lime-green stare. "You'll return at what time?"

"Eleven p.m."

"How many times will you text Tabitha to check in?"

"Five." I'd talked Lenti down from her original demand of seven. "Once when I arrive, once every hour, and one when I'm heading home." I bent to kiss her on the forehead.

"You forgot the most important one." She batted at the crystal around my neck. "You won't change your mind and stay the night with Alex."

I yanked the chain away and tucked it inside my coat. "Yes, I swear, I won't stay the night. I'm coming home. I *promise.*"

"And if you break any of the rules, what will happen?"

"You'll throw up hairballs in the shower and poop on my pillow. I've got it." I ruffled her tummy fur, narrowly escaping the wrath of her claws. I was getting faster at snatching my hand away. I reached past her to hug Tabitha. "Are you sure you're okay babysitting?"

"Of course." She smiled down at Lenti. "We're going to start *Unseelie* Season Three. You won't believe the first episode."

The little cat trilled. "Hurray! Drunk faeries."

"Okay, you two, have fun." I hugged Tabitha again and hurried out the door.

I had to give Tabitha credit. She didn't entirely approve of me going on a date with Alex, but when I'd explained my dilemma, she'd immediately offered to babysit Lenti. And I was shocked Lenti had actually agreed to the plan, though it probably helped that I'd promised her a wedge of cheddar cheese.

As I drove into the city across the Welter Bridge, I smiled at the last of the sunset glinting off the towers of Portland.

A few clouds in the sky shimmered pink and gold, and the Willamette River sparkled in the late evening light. A speedboat churned past, leaving a foaming track in the water. In the distance, the forested West Hills stood watch over the city. Portland was damp and rainy much of the year, but there was nothing like the city on a clear early October night.

Alex had made reservations at Chrysalis, a restaurant and lounge on the top floor of the Broadway Pearl, a ritzy hotel.

I'd technically stayed there once last year, by which I mean Dave rented a room for a friend's wedding, and I met up with him late at night after he drunkenly called me from the reception.

That's right, we were dating at the time, and he didn't even invite me to the wedding, even though he had a plus-one available. Fricking Dave. The room had been gorgeous, though—gold brocade wallpaper, a huge bed with a soft down comforter and plush pillows, and a giant shower.

Dave passed out two minutes after I arrived, so I ordered room service and ate a burger in bed while watching late-night talk shows. Minus the Dave situation, it was kind of fun.

In the middle of the night, though, I found a pair of someone else's high heels under the bed. In retrospect, they were probably Natasha's. I left before Dave woke up. The beginning of the end.

My jaw muscles ached, and I unclenched my teeth. I didn't need to wander down memory lane. Dave was a shitty boyfriend, but I'd survived just fine, and now I was going to dinner with a kind, handsome, demigod of the Underworld.

Whose powers were so dangerous he'd had to sign a contract that he wouldn't murder his employees.

Why didn't I just stay away from him? I should be asking Tabitha if Paul had any ordinary friends he could introduce me to, or at least I should get on a dating app and swipe whatever direction you were supposed to swipe.

Instead, I couldn't get Alex out of my head. His sensitivity, the way he knew how to challenge me during our practice sessions, his self-deprecating sense of humor.

Oh, also his six-pack abs, and the way he kissed.

I flipped my turn signal and switched lanes as soon

as I exited the bridge. As I traced the tidy grid of Portland's streets toward the hotel, I wondered what Alex was wearing tonight. Whatever he chose, it would show off his sculpted shoulders and chest. I lingered on the image. Sexy thoughts were safe thoughts. *Remember, girl, you're here to get laid, not get feelings.*

I found parking at a garage a few blocks from Broadway Pearl. Since I was fifteen minutes early and didn't want to stand around waiting for Alex, I stopped at Miles Away, the farm-to-table restaurant on the fourth floor of the hotel. The building had originally housed a boarding school, and you could still see it in the restaurant layout—the open space, and the atrium rising past curtained hotel windows. Blocky booths surrounded by plants gave the place a sort of greenhouse-cafeteria feel.

The long waiting benches were unoccupied, so I sat on one and scrolled through my phone for ten minutes. Then I found a bathroom and spent another six rearranging my hair.

At one minute after seven, I decided I was good. I texted Tabitha and took the elevator up to the fourteenth floor.

I entered a narrow hallway with a high ceiling.

One of the walls formed a sharp angle down to vertical panels covered in tropical wallpaper. At the end of the hall, a white pedestal served as the hosting station.

I gave Alex's name to the hostess, and she led me through the entrance into the restaurant.

It was brightly lit and done in shades of cream and green, with green floor tiles, bright wood paneled pillars, and cream walls with angled accent beams.

It made me think of a mid-century modern Palm

Springs house. Long windows everywhere provided a view of the blue twilight settling over the city.

The hostess led me to a table tucked into the corner next to a tall window.

Alex, who was already seated, sprang up to greet me. "Hi. You look amazing." He leaned down to kiss me on the cheek.

The smell of saltwater filled my senses as he slid back my chair for me. "You look pretty great yourself." As Alex sat down, I took in his freshly-shaven face—ah, he was self-conscious about the tiny cut on one side of his jaw—and his collared dark-green shirt that hugged his chest and shoulders.

He grinned, his left cheek dimpling.

The dimple just killed me. Uh-oh, caught staring. I picked up the menu.

"Is Lenti with you?" he asked softly.

"No, Tabitha's babysitting her, but I'm required to report back every hour. Let's see." I checked my phone and laughed. Tabitha had already responded to my text with a selfie of her and Lenti curled up together on my couch. I showed Alex.

"Cute. Tabitha seems like a good friend. How long have you known her?"

"Three years, but it seems like longer. We basically became friends my first day at the Firm." I told him how our offices had been next to each other, and how we'd ended up chatting on Muse all day. "She knew I was crap at spells, so she offered to help teach me. It evolved into a regular Friday night thing, except now it's not spell casting. Mostly wine-drinking and watching bad reality TV." I shrugged and sipped my water. Predictably, I was already sweating. Why did I always overheat when I was anxious?

"Oh? Like one of those dating shows?"

"No." I set down my glass and wiped some of the condensation off with my napkin. "Um, *Secrets of the Unseelie.*"

"I have a confession." He drew it out, taking a long swig of his water and dramatically leaning toward me. In a stage whisper, he said, "I love that show."

I stared at him. "Are you actively trying to be perfect or is this just your natural state?"

"I didn't know I was perfect." His dark eyes sparkled with amusement. "What else do you like about me, Ro?" He traced one finger down the side of my hand.

I shivered. "You-you…" I sputtered.

"You're a little flushed."

I shook my head, trying not to laugh. "You're terrible." I slid my hand into his.

He squeezed my fingers and kept hold of my hand while he examined the menu.

I extended my consciousness toward his again. I sensed a few nerves, which shocked me. Alex, the demigod, got nervous? My heart melted. My nose twitched, but I'd popped some extra-strength allergy meds before leaving the house, and they kept me from sneezing all over him.

Already did that once. Didn't want to do it again when I was actively going to try and seduce him.

Our server sauntered over to take our drink orders. She was tall and curvy, with thick dark-brown hair and full lips. "What can I get you folks?" She was only looking at Alex.

"How about a bottle of the 2012 merlot?" He glanced at me. "Are you a red-wine person?"

"I'm an *any* wine person, but I did drive here."

"I'll make sure you get home safely." He waited for my nod before he confirmed our order with the server.

His charm worked wonders. Our server returned less than a minute later with our wine and a plate of coconut shrimp on the house, which we hadn't ordered.

"You get a lot of free meals, don't you?" I picked up a shrimp.

He pursed his lips. "I do. One of the perks, I guess."

"What are some of the others?"

"I don't know, Ro, I'd rather talk about you." He caught my hand again. "And how incredible you look. Did you wear that dress to drive me out of my mind?"

"You remembered." I grinned and smoothed down the skirt. Perhaps I also leaned forward a little so my cleavage looked fuller.

"That dress has been in my thoughts far more often than I should admit to you."

"Just the dress, huh?" I made a face at him.

"Well, yes." He leaned across the table and whispered in my ear. "When I think about it, it's usually on the floor of my room." He dropped a kiss on the side of my jaw before sitting back in his chair.

Oh, hi. All of my nerves were alive and tingling. I blew out a breath and took another long gulp of my water. "We're going to hell, aren't we?"

"Probably." He grimaced. "This is strictly against Firm policy. Superiors and employees dating, I mean."

I'd suspected as much, but I'd never checked. It sounded as if Alex had researched the policy, though. Which meant—what?

No. I wasn't going to ask, or even think about it. I took a few deep breaths in and out, which I'd discovered helped a bit with casting a psychic shield. If I could block Alex during practice, surely I could block my own anxiety now. I imagined the doubts and insecurities being trapped behind a steel wall, one with no door or lock. This situation didn't have to be anything more than two consenting adults, who were attracted to each other, enjoying each other's company.

And having sex.

The crystal's warmth spread across my chest and through my core, filling me with peace. I could handle this. There was freedom in not caring too much. Freedom in remaining in the moment.

I ran my fingers along the inside of his wrist. "If we're going to hell, then let's enjoy the ride."

He coughed and made an exaggerated show of tugging at his collar. "Wow, Ro."

I laughed and dropped his hand. The next hour flew as we ate and drank. We talked about Firm gossip, about how Elizabeth had gotten spoken to for being rude to the other legal assistants on her floor, about the new wave of winter associates the Firm was expecting in January.

I told Alex how Lenti stole the salmon during our first dinner at Thirteenth Street Kitchen.

He snorted with laughter.

We lingered over our final glasses of wine long after the server had cleared our dinner dishes.

Alex finished his first and interlaced his fingers with mine. "So. When you're not risking eternal damnation by going on a date with me, what else occupies your social life? I know you and Tabitha hang out quite a lot, right?"

"We do." Where was this going?

"What about any other, you know." He cleared his

throat. "Romantic interests?"

Oh, gods, were we going to spoil this dinner by talking about my sad dating life? *Keep it light, Ro, keep it light.* "Worried about the competition?"

He held my gaze. "What if I am?"

I swallowed hard, my throat dry. "There's no competition. Trust me. My last relationship was several months ago."

"Nothing wrong with that." He tipped his head to the side, studying me. "What's the matter?"

Damn it, maybe he was psychic. I didn't want to rehash my past, but it felt weird tiptoeing around the issue of who, precisely, I'd dated. "The last person I dated was, uh, someone at work."

"Oh?" He flicked one eyebrow up. "Someone I know?"

"Unfortunately, yes." I pulled my hand free from his and reached for my glass. "I shouldn't have mentioned this. It's too weird."

His gaze grew wickedly amused, and he leaned toward me, hands folded, the picture of active listening. "Well, now you *have* to tell me." He dropped the pose and his brow crinkled. "You don't actually. Not if you don't want to. But I'm wildly curious now."

"Oh, gods," I muttered. "It's Dave."

"Ah." He leaned back, his expression suddenly flat. "*That's* why he gives you such a bad time about your magic."

I snorted. "No, he teased me before and after we dated. It's a department-wide hobby." I forced a smile. I was out of wine now, so I guzzled water. Why did I have to mention such an awkward topic? "Anyway, it's way over now. I don't even know why I went out with him."

Desperation, loneliness, low self-esteem. But Alex didn't need to know the reasons right now. Let's at least go on a few more dates before he uncovered my massive insecurities.

He put up a hand. "Hey, I can respect it. Dave's…a smart guy."

My lips twitched. "He's a bombastic ass. He and Natasha deserve each other."

"Who's Natasha?"

"The paralegal he cheated on me with. They're still together, so maybe it's true love." I shrugged.

"Oh, Ro." He squeezed my shoulder. "I'm so sorry."

"It's not a big deal now." I rubbed my temples, trying to ward off the start of a headache. "So, now that I've ruined this date talking about my ex, can we talk about something else?"

"Hey. You didn't ruin anything. I asked." His dark eyes were full of nothing but kindness. "Humans seem to have some concept that being vulnerable in the early stages of a relationship will ruin the whole thing. Maybe it does for some, but not for me."

"You're not human." I tried to ignore his reference to the early stages of a relationship. He meant our fling, or whatever this was. Not a real relationship. Not long-term.

"True." He grinned. "But I want to get to know you, Ro. Your experiences, good and bad, are part of you."

I stared at him for a moment, then shook my head. He was too perfect, too good to be true.

Wait. Wasn't this just his Stygian charm working its magic on my brain? Making me think he was the most-understanding person ever?

Which didn't matter because we weren't going to be

in a relationship. We were going to have fun. No strings attached.

"What are you thinking?"

I smiled. "Let's go outside."

He settled our bill, and we meandered onto the patio.

Bordered by glass walls, the patio provided a spectacular vista of eastside Portland.

We wandered near the edge and gazed out over the city—the stately gray stone of the distant courthouse, spires of steel and glass, the blocks of trees and grass stretching along the sidewalks.

Lights winked in various windows and in the distance, blue lights cast a cool glow over the Salmon Crossing Bridge.

I slipped my phone from my purse to see if Tabitha had responded to my second check-in.

She'd sent a picture of Lenti curled up on her lap, eyes closed, and it was captioned, *Sleeping like a baby*.

I tipped the phone toward Alex and snickered.

"I'm glad to see Lenti is surviving your absence." He sidled behind me and slid his arms around my waist. "It means I get you to myself for a little bit longer." Dropping his head, he kissed the side of my neck.

"Alex." I sighed, not caring if anyone saw us. I leaned against his chest, and he pillowed his chin on the top of my head.

We stood there, buffeted by the breeze, as lights winked on like fireflies across the buildings, and the city awoke to the night. The wine we'd shared at dinner buzzed in my blood and lingered on my tongue.

He sighed heavily and slid one hand along my stomach, his fingers playing with the fabric of my dress. "How much time do you have?"

I shivered, my brain going hazy with his touch. With some difficulty I extracted my phone again and checked the time. "Two hours."

"I have a suggestion." He kissed my temple, then trailed his lips down to my earlobe. Another kiss. "If you wanted to go somewhere a little more private, they have rooms here."

My heart raced. I twisted around in his arms so I could see him. "Those rooms are expensive, especially if you aren't staying the night." I remembered Dave complaining about the cost last year.

He lowered his head, barely brushing his lips against mine, teasing me. "Worth it."

"You can't."

"What? Let this be my treat, Ro." He trailed his lips down the side of my neck and murmured against my collarbone, "Let me make you feel good."

I sighed softly. My brain started to go slightly mushy.

Out of the corner of my eye, I glimpsed a woman with short gray hair frowning at us. I pulled back and patted Alex's shoulder. "We're being judged."

"Oh?" Keeping one arm around my waist, he glanced over his shoulder and directed a smile and nod at the woman.

I expected her to roll her eyes, but instead she smiled and waved.

Actually waved, like she'd spotted a celebrity. She leaned toward her friend and whispered something. Both stared at Alex, eyes wide.

I lightly batted his arm. "You charmed her."

He shrugged, his dark eyes glinting. "It won't last. I only smiled at her. But I bought us enough time to get out of here without her staring."

"Your power comes in handy." I looped my arm through his. I was the one who'd said if we were going to hell, we should enjoy the ride. And let's be honest, I wore the dress hoping something would happen. Not that I'd expected him to book us a room at Broadway Pearl, but hadn't I wanted him to want me?

I wasn't going to hold back any longer or worry. Tonight I'd live in the moment.

Chapter Thirteen

We crossed through the restaurant toward the hallway. On the way, I texted Tabitha for my nine p.m. check-in. *Going well. Getting drinks on the patio.* I didn't even feel guilty about lying. It was my business what I did with Alex, and if it was against Firm rules, then it was better she didn't know about this anyway.

Of course, Lenti would figure it out right away, because she could read my mind. But I'd deal with my cat later.

We stepped into an empty elevator. As soon as the doors closed, it was like a firecracker exploding. Alex and I dove at each other, making out and feeling each other up like horny college kids. I was as thirsty as a vampire, and I couldn't get enough of his mouth.

The elevator dinged to announce its arrival on the first floor, and we jumped back. Giggling, we hurried to the front desk, where a young man stood behind a computer.

I brushed back my hair, trying to tame the frizz.

Alex's top button was undone, and his face was flushed. Subtle.

"Hi, how's your night going?" He smiled as he slid a credit card out of his wallet. "I'd like to book a room, please."

"Certainly." The young man took Alex's name and his credit card, then keyed something into the computer.

His face lit up. "Great news, Mr. Kouris. You're eligible for a free upgrade to our Luxury Pearl Suite. Would you be interested?"

"That would be great." Alex glanced at me. "Do you happen to have a champagne package of some sort?"

"I could have room service send up a bottle."

"Thank you so much." Alex chatted with the man while he booked the room.

I maintained a blank expression when he told Alex the final price, but secretly I was wondering what the room would have cost *without* the free upgrade. Sheesh.

We took our keys and headed for the elevator again. On the way up, I nudged Alex's side. "Does this place normally include bottles of champagne?"

"I don't know. I've never stayed here before."

"But you got a free upgrade."

He smiled. "Charm has its perks."

We kissed again until the elevator let us off on the eleventh floor. Our room was just a couple of doors down.

Alex swiped the keycard across the door and pushed it open, gesturing for me to go ahead.

I felt a bit guilty that he'd conned the hotel into the free upgrade, but the second I stepped inside, I forgot the guilt.

The Luxury Pearl Suite was nicer than my apartment.

The door opened into an entryway leading into a kitchenette with stainless steel appliances and a small dining area.

We kicked off our shoes and entered a living room with a gas fireplace and floor-to-ceiling windows opening onto the city below. Leather chairs and a soft beige love seat invited us to curl up and enjoy the view.

The bedroom featured a king-sized bed with a tufted headboard and clouds of pillows. And the bathroom…was the pinnacle of luxury. It accommodated a marble-topped counter with his-and-hers sinks, a huge jacuzzi tub, and a large shower with glass doors and multiple showerheads, everything tiled in white.

Alex chuckled. "It's pretty nice."

"Pretty nice? It's a palace."

There was a knock at the door, which proved to be room service with our bottle of champagne and two glasses.

As soon as he'd set the champagne on the kitchenette counter, Alex looked up at me with a wicked hunger in his eyes. "Do you mind if we come back to our nightcap in a bit? You're distracting me."

"Oh, am I?" I eased down my left shoulder strap and slipped my arm free. "What are you going to do about it?"

He strolled toward me and caught me in his arms. "You'll see." He slid his mouth down to my right shoulder and grabbed the other strap in his teeth, then slid it down my arm as I eased out of the strap. He straightened up, kissing along my shoulder and across my collarbones, then up the side of my neck.

I wasn't wearing a bra under the dress. What? I'd planned ahead.

The fabric slipped lower over my breasts.

Alex drew his hands up my waist and sides and tugged the dress down until it slipped over my hips and to the ground, leaving me standing in only my black-lace underwear.

He took my hands, stepped back, and gazed at me

from head to toe. "I was right. This dress does look spectacular on the floor. Damn."

I laughed and dove for his belt buckle, but he laced his fingers through mine and draped my arms around his shoulders. "Not yet. I have plans for you, Miss Rowan." He eased me backward into the bathroom, pausing to kiss me every few moments. At the tub, he coaxed me into a sitting position on the edge, then leaned past me, deliberately rubbing his chest across my breasts before turning on the tap.

I let out a soft moan. "I like your plans so far."

Alex smiled wickedly. "It's going to take a minute for the tub to fill. I wonder what I can do in the meantime. Hmm…".

He unbuttoned his shirt, and I caught a flash of his thoughts, and I knew exactly what he planned to do next. In response, my center tingled and hummed, already going wet for him.

He peeled off his shirt and tossed it on the floor, then knelt in front of me.

I vaguely registered that he had a lot more tattoos than I'd expected, but then he spread my legs apart and I lost the brain power to study his ink. Hazy and tingling, I held tight to the edge of the tub.

He slid his hands up the insides of my bare legs as he kissed my calves, my knees, and my thighs. Then he hooked one finger around the thin fabric of my underwear and yanked it aside. His head dropped between my legs, and his tongue slid inside me.

I gasped and gripped the tub as the water thundered behind us, or was I hearing the ocean? Saltwater filled my senses. I couldn't tell where I was anymore. I only knew Alex's mouth was on me, sucking, licking, teasing, and spirals of pleasure were already building. I groaned and opened wider for him.

A minute later, he lifted his head.

"What…no," I moaned, "don't stop now."

"Tub's ready." He winked and shut off the tap, then switched on the jets.

"Are you trying to torture me?" I stumbled to my feet. Between my legs I was swollen and aching with incompleteness.

"I'm trying to pleasure you, my darling." He kissed the top of my head. "Climb in."

The endearment did something strange to my heart. I told myself it had just slipped out, probably something he always said to women when he was driving them out of their minds in the sack. It belonged in a mental safe, along with dangerous items like feelings. I shoved it away and sought his mind again. Why was it easier to sense images and emotions rather than words with Alex? Just the way his magic worked in combination with mine?

All I got from him now was raw lust.

He slid his pants and boxers to the floor.

My jaw came unhinged.

So this was the body he'd been hiding under those fitted work clothes. He was all lean lines and taut curves, from his rounded calves and the bunched muscles in his thighs to broad shoulders. The tattoos I'd not had time to admire while he was going down on me, covered most of his left arm, curled across his chest, and spread down his left side. They were all black linework—a flock of ravens, vines, skulls. He had an actual eight-pack, and the V of muscles on either side of his stomach drew my gaze down to his erection.

Alex chuckled and stepped into the tub. He slid down into a sitting position and made a patting motion on top of the water, inviting me to sit.

I kicked off my underwear and got in, settling between his legs with my back against his chest. Jets bubbled around the tub, and I stuck my aching left foot against one. Damn high heels. I was going to start wearing sneakers on my dates.

He wrapped one arm around my waist and kissed my jaw.

I half-turned my head. "Weren't you in the middle of something?"

He laughed. "I was indeed." He kept one arm around my waist, holding me close. His other hand slid down to cup my left breast, his fingers teasing my nipple.

I sighed and closed my eyes.

He slid his hand down my side and in between my legs, his fingers teasing my soft outer folds as he kissed my neck.

I squirmed, ready for him to do more. The crystal throbbed against my chest. I didn't even have to try to reach his mind now. His lust was as palpable as a fire, inflaming my own. It made my body even more sensitive to his touch, and when he just barely slid a finger inside me, a new wave of tingles washed over my body.

When he withdrew his finger, I groaned. "You're such…a tease."

"Not a tease." His lips pleasantly tickled my shoulder. "Just taking my time. It's rude to rush your partner."

"It's rude to make a girl wait so long."

"All right, then." He chuckled and slid two fingers inside me.

I strained to take him in deeper, rocking with him as he slid his fingers back and forth, his breath heavy against my neck.

"Yes," he whispered, in rhythm with his hand. "Let go, Rowan…let go."

Hot pleasure built in my core, radiating outward. I gasped as sensation spiraled through me, propelling me to a shuddering climax. I grabbed his hand and rode out the aftershocks as he covered my back with kisses.

Blowing out a slow breath, I settled back against his chest, and he eased his fingers out of me. As he rubbed my shoulders, I shivered. "That…was…"

"It was."

I leaned against him, feeling his erection against my back. "Anything else you want to do?"

He leaned down and kissed my neck. "I want to take you to bed."

"Then take me."

We climbed out of the tub, and he shut off the jets. We didn't towel off so much as barely patted ourselves dry.

Alex wrapped me in one of the soft white towels and lifted me into his arms.

He carried me out of the bathroom and into the bedroom and, instead of tossing me on the bed the way I'd expected, set me down gently, like I was breakable. We rolled under the covers and into each other's arms.

For several moments, we just kissed. I sought his mind, my insides tingling again as I searched for images. The possibilities suddenly hit me. I could figure out exactly what he wanted, touch him the way he liked it most, help him carry out his fantasies without him having to say a word. He would think I was some kind of sex goddess.

I drew back, studying his kind, warm gaze. A line I didn't even know existed rose up in front of me. If I used my power to mine Alex's brain for his sexual fantasies, what would that make me? A manipulator. A liar. No better than the Stygians who used their charm to make their victims trust them.

He touched my cheek. "Are you okay? Where did you go?"

I smiled and sat up. Lifting the chain over my head, I dropped the crystal onto the nightstand. "Nowhere. I'm right here." I cupped his face in both hands and kissed him, slipping my tongue into his mouth.

He flipped me over so he was on top of me. Sliding a hand between my legs, he gave me a satisfied smile. "You're already wet."

I dragged his hand away and stared into his eyes. "I want you inside me."

He groaned and kissed me again while he stroked my breasts, his fingers playing with my nipples.

I ran my hands up and down his body. I couldn't get enough of his hard muscles or smooth skin, of hearing his breath come in short bursts when I kissed his chest and down the flock of ravens tattooed into his side.

He paused to grab a condom from his wallet and rolled it on.

I nestled back against the pillows and opened my legs.

He slid between them, pausing to kiss me, tracing a line with his mouth diagonally down my stomach and then sliding his tongue across my center.

Pleasure began building again, and I was going to come without him if he didn't get busy. "Alex." I grabbed his shoulders and dug my fingers into the firm landscape of his muscles. "I need you. Please."

A guttural noise sprang from his throat, almost a growl of pleasure, as he repositioned. His tip nudged my folds apart, and then he slid into me, strong and hard and thick.

My pussy tightened around him, shuddering with nerves as he thrust against me. Wrapping my legs around him, I drew him deeper, wanting to feel every movement to the fullest. The ocean crashed in the distance, and I could smell the salt air, sharp and wild, as we writhed together, our bodies shivering and vibrating as one. I moaned as I climaxed, and a second later, he gave one final thrust and cried out.

He slumped against me, holding me close. When we'd caught our breaths, he pulled away and kissed me. "Damn." Shaking his head, he got up to dispose of things.

I snuggled under the blanket and sank into the mountain of pillows while my heart rate dropped back to normal. My whole body was flushed and damp.

When he returned, Alex slid in behind me and wrapped me in his arms.

Somehow I wasn't surprised he was a cuddler.

He kissed the back of my neck, then nestled his face against me. "So is this how you thought our date was going to go?"

"I didn't know. I might've been hoping."

He chuckled. "Me, too."

We snuggled quietly for a minute.

Suddenly my heart seized. "What time is it? I'm supposed to check in with Lenti."

He shifted against me. "It's not even ten."

I relaxed and texted Tabitha. *Still hanging out!*

He tucked his chin into my shoulder. "Does something bad happen if you don't check in with Lenti every hour? Will she destroy your apartment?"

"Probably." I set the phone on the nightstand. "But no, she has an abandonment complex. The last witch who adopted her only kept her for a week. Poor thing."

"But she's so cute."

"Well, she was a bobcat before, and apparently she ate a chicken." I shrugged against him. "Anyway, the last I heard from Tabitha, Lenti was asleep. I swear, I feel like I have a small child."

He laughed. "But so much fluffier and she doesn't have to be toilet-trained."

"True."

I snuggled back against him and closed my eyes. This was comfortable, dangerously comfortable. If I wasn't careful, I'd fall asleep and miss curfew.

Alex sighed against me. "Sure you can't stay the night?"

"I wish." I rolled over in his arms. "Maybe we'll have to plan ahead next time."

Shit. Should I have said that? I started to check his thoughts to see if I'd scared him off, and then remembered the crystal was on the nightstand.

He just smiled, though. "Sounds like a good idea."

I cradled his left cheek, tracing my thumb over the dimple there. "You know, my sister would've really liked you."

He brushed my hair back from my forehead. "I'm sorry I couldn't have met her. If she was anything like you, I'm sure we would have gotten along."

"She was and she wasn't. She was more serious than

I am, I think. Definitely smarter. A math whiz. Her day job was in finance. And she was one hell of a witch." I took a breath, let the ache settle. "I've wished every day for the last two years I could talk to her again."

Alex kissed my forehead and held his mouth there, like a blessing. "When I'm out of my contract, I promise to help you try and find her."

"Really?"

"Really. I can't promise I'll succeed, but I'll do everything I can."

"Thank you." I clung to him, fighting back tears. The first month after Megan disappeared, I'd mentally send messages to her, almost like prayers, willing her to be safe, to come back. Once I learned she was gone for good, though, I stopped. I thought about her all the time, but I didn't try and send mental messages into the ether. No amount of will or energy could pierce the veil to the afterlife.

But Alex could.

I searched for something, anything to take my mind off Megan. I didn't want to burst into tears right now. "So, how's your case going?"

He shifted to lie on his back, and I snuggled into the crook of his arm.

"It's about the same. Noel's still negotiating with Hades's lawyers to set up the arbitration. They have all kinds of weird conditions about times and dates and lunar cycles. But Melanie's still trying to find another way. She thinks she might have something, but she said it'll take a few more weeks to put together. Some kind of spell, I think?"

I lifted my head. Could the spell be the *alpha lyrae*? "Did she say what it was called?"

"No, but she said it requires a lot of preparation. If it doesn't work, though, I'm going to have to go the arbitration route. The Firm isn't going to keep me on if I can't break my contract."

I gently rubbed his chest. "It'll work out. It has to."

"Hope so."

We cuddled a while longer, and finally at ten-thirty, I dragged myself out of bed to get dressed.

Alex stretched back against the pillows, arms up like a cat. "Don't hate me, but I think I might sleep here. I'm not sure I should drive home right now, and this bed is pretty amazing."

"I don't blame you. Wish I could stay."

As I slipped on my shoes, he rolled over and picked up his phone. "Let me call you a cab, Ro. Unless you've sobered up?"

"Not entirely. I can, uh, bring you cash tomorrow…"

He waved his hand. "Please. This is on me. Do you want me to move your car for you tomorrow morning? I could drop it at our parking garage."

"That would actually be amazing." I could take public transit from my apartment into the city. I wrote down my license plate and gave Alex my garage ticket and car key, explaining which section of the garage I'd left my car in.

"I'll take care of it." He kissed me on the forehead. "You just get home safely. Text me when you're back."

He insisted on getting dressed and taking me downstairs, then waiting with me until the cab arrived. As the driver got out to open the door, Alex wrapped me in his arms one last time. "Sleep well, darling. See you tomorrow."

"Good night." I leaned my head on his chest, inhaling the scent of the ocean one more time. Then I got into the cab.

Alex handed a bill to the driver.

I didn't see the denomination, but the man grinned and nodded. I told the driver where to go, then slumped against the window.

As we pulled away, Alex waved.

There it was again. *Darling.* He'd shelled out a few hundred bucks to spend a few extra hours with me, snuggled me close, paid for the cab, and offered to get my car to the office.

Not fling behavior.

The feelings I'd kept at bay during our roll in the hay flooded back now. The way Alex had set me down on the bed so carefully, like I was something precious. How giving he'd been physically. The tender kisses, the way he'd brushed my hair out of my eyes and stroked my face. All of it made me like him. Far too much. It made me want to see him again, and do this again, and spend lazy Saturday mornings together sitting in cafes and eating scones.

Shit.

These fantasies led nowhere good. I'd had them with Dave. Yes, Alex didn't appear to be a cheating man-whore, but there were still reasons we couldn't be together. As the cab rumbled over the Larkspur Bridge, I recited the reasons to myself.

One, Alex was my boss. Two, we could get in trouble at work. Three, if he couldn't break his contract, he'd have to go back to reaping souls to avoid a pissed-off Hades chucking him into Tartarus. Four, even if he could break his contract, he'd still be a demigod and would live for hundreds of years. I'd die at ninety if I was lucky. Five…I wasn't sure what five was.

You're cute enough to be Alex's plaything, but let's be realistic. Melanie's words drifted back to me. *You aren't someone who could ever give him what he really needs.*

Was I Alex's plaything? He didn't act like it. But maybe that was his Stygian charm, influencing me even if he didn't intend it to. He'd said he couldn't turn it off, that it was like the shifting of the earth. Which meant he was never, ever, one hundred percent just being himself—because he was built to make people like him.

Which meant I could never fully know or trust him.

There was the fifth reason. I knew it was there somewhere.

Chapter Fourteen

Tabitha didn't even knock the next morning. She barged into my office, closed the door, and murmured a spell, frosting the glass wall as well as the windows. "There." She folded her arms. "No one can see or hear us. What happened last night?"

Lenti hopped up and emerged from behind the filing cabinet. "I know! I know! I know!"

I heaved a sigh. Last night, I'd arrived home at eleven sharp, just as promised. Tabitha had begged me for the details, but I said I was too tired, and I'd tell her at work.

Lenti was already asleep when I arrived, but this morning when she woke up it didn't take her long to read my mind and learn exactly how well my date with Alex had gone. She kept staring at me, then chortling to herself.

"Well…" I began.

"They mated," said Lenti.

"I'm going to stop letting you read my mind," I snapped.

Tabitha clapped her hands to her mouth and let out a strangled squeal.

I couldn't tell if it was a scandalized or happy noise; it could've been either.

"Oh. My. Gods." She perched on the edge of my desk, and Lenti leaped up to sit beside her. "I knew it. I

I Dream of Demigods

knew you were acting weird last night! What happened? Tell me everything."

"You can't tell anyone else." Even though she'd sound-spelled my office, I lowered my voice. "Alex says there's a policy against supervisors dating employees. We could get fired."

"Wait, you're dating?" She grabbed my hand.

"No, but same thing as far as the Firm is concerned." I leaned my head into my hands. "I don't know what I'm doing. This was a huge mistake. I shouldn't even have gone to dinner with him, but he was so sweet, and he paid for everything and even rented a hotel room…"

Tabitha squealed again.

"Please stop making that noise. It's too early." My head ached from the wine we'd drunk last night, and I felt like a vampire had drained all of my life's energy. Worse, I'd been binge-watching the mental movie of last night's date all morning. I kept shoving Lenti out of my head so she wouldn't witness the most intimate portions. She might've studied human culture, but I didn't want to explain the finer points of oral sex to a cat.

"Sorry." She pursed her lips. "Please talk. I'll be quiet."

I told her and Lenti the whole thing, although Lenti kept interrupting to tell the parts she knew. "And then they licked each other in the elevator…"

When I'd finished the story, Tabitha said, "So just to clarify—you didn't pay for anything? Not dinner, not the hotel room, not the cab ride home?"

"No. Nothing."

"And he kissed you goodbye and called you 'darling' and offered to move your car."

"Pretty much." I slumped back in my chair and

closed my eyes.

"It sounds like a date. An elaborate one. Sweetie, it doesn't sound as if he just wants a fling. I think he really likes you."

I shrugged. "It doesn't matter even if he does. I can't date a Stygian."

"Can't you?"

My eyes flew open. "You're actually advocating for this?"

"I mean, it's not ideal, but…he sounds so sweet."

"He is. Too sweet." I petted the top of Lenti's head. "Can you make it so I don't have feelings for Alex?"

"Nope." She lifted her chin so I could scratch underneath it. "My magic doesn't cover human emotions. I could give you a new hair color, though."

That did sound useful, and my roots were coming in. "Good to know."

"What're you going to do?" said Tabitha.

I touched the crystal on its chain, as if it could somehow give me the answer.

It pulsed faintly, steadily, but offered no enlightenment.

"I'm going to focus on me. I still don't know much about my magic, and I need to keep practicing. It would help if I knew more about my family history. Megan and I grew up thinking our dad was a regular human, but I've never even met him, so I have no idea where to start."

I'd long ago searched the Association's genealogical databases, as had Megan when she was still alive, in case we'd inherited our magic from a grandparent. We found nothing. As far as the Association's records were concerned, Megan and I had sprung forth from the ether.

Tabitha drummed her fingers on her thighs, then hopped down from my desk. "I know you're not the biggest fan of healers, but a healer is probably your best bet. My aunt isn't a specialist, but she'll know someone who can help. I can ask her for a referral if you want."

I hesitated. I was hitting dead-ends everywhere else, and healers could perform advanced scanning spells to identify my magical DNA. "Can I think about it?"

"Of course." She leaned over to kiss Lenti's head, then headed for the door. "Do you want me to leave the privacy spell? It'll last for several hours."

"Please."

She paused with her hand on the doorknob. "It'll be okay, Ro. Just don't run away from something because you're scared."

"But that's my special talent." I tried to smile, but my face felt a little stiff.

She smiled back, but her eyes were melancholy. Or maybe it was pity. "I have to set up for a class. Just think about it."

Lenti lifted her head. "YOLO, Tabitha."

"YOLO, sweetie."

She left, and the door clicked shut.

Hey, with the glass of my office frosted, no one could see me from the hallway. I could definitely take a nap under my desk.

I bundled my coat into a semblance of a pillow and stretched out on the floor. Closing my eyes, I mumbled, "Night, Lenti."

Four paws padded onto my chest.

I squinted at the cat. "Yes?"

"Why aren't you working?"

"Because I'm tired."

"How long are you going to sleep?"

"I don't know, gremlin. As long as my body wants to sleep." I closed my eyes again, hoping she'd get the hint.

After a moment, she settled down onto my chest, and let out a quiet purr.

I stroked the top of her head.

Don't be sad, Ro.

I smiled and scratched her ear.

The floor wasn't especially cushy, but Lenti kept my core warm. I drifted into unconsciousness, lulled by the hum of the HVAC, slipping in and out of images from last night. Alex sliding my legs apart. Alex curled up against me. *Darling.*

"Rowan?"

My eyes flew open, and Lenti leaped off me as I scrambled to my feet.

Alex stood there with the door half-open, a confused look on his face. His black polo and khakis were casual attire for him. In one hand he held a reusable cloth grocery bag. "Should I come back?"

"No, you're fine." I motioned for him to step inside, then shut the door. I didn't want anyone to see him going into my office, even though he was my boss and could have a dozen legitimate reasons for doing so.

He ran his fingers across the frosted glass wall and door. "What happened here?"

"Tabitha spelled it for me. It's soundproofed, too. Temporary, sadly."

"Huh. Cool." He motioned to the ground. "So were you meditating?"

"I was napping." I smiled sheepishly. "I'm wiped out."

He chuckled. "Me, too. The bed was comfortable, but I couldn't fall asleep after you left."

He did look tired. I'd never seen shadows under his eyes before, nor stubble on his jaw. On instinct, I started to hug him, and then remembered I was supposed to be cool and casual about this whole thing. Stepping back, I scurried around to my desk. "I don't normally sleep on the job." My voice sounded too loud to my own ears. I logged into my laptop. "I'm usually productive. I just…last night was…"

"Rowan." He set the bag on the desk and placed his hands over mine, stilling them. "I'm not worried about it. You always get your work done."

"Excuse me." Lenti pawed at his leg. "You haven't greeted me yet."

"Oh, I'm sorry." Alex crouched down and picked her up.

She snuggled against him, purring.

Alex rubbed her ears. "I hear you and Tabitha had a fun hangout last night."

"Yes. We watched faeries throw martinis in each other's faces. It was delightful." She gazed up at him, adoring.

"Season Three? Good one." He winked at me. Still petting the cat, he nodded at the bag on my desk. "We forgot the champagne last night." A wicked smile flashed across his face.

My chest and neck sizzled with heat as I peered into the bag. He'd wrapped the bottle in several layers of tissue paper, and two gourmet chocolate bars leaned against it. My car keys sat at the bottom. "Thanks for moving my car. You don't want the champagne?"

"No problem. I left your car in level 3C. And the

champagne is a gift." He cleared his throat. "I thought you might want some good chocolate to go with it. Something for your next girls' night, maybe."

My stomach twisted. Why did he have to be so fricking caring? And adorable, too, cuddling Lenti to his broad chest.

She closed her eyes, her head lolling back.

Okay, well, he was being super-nice, which meant we could remain friends, instead of dealing with post-fling awkwardness. I smiled at him and tucked my keys into my purse. "That's very sweet."

"Are you, um…" He glanced down at Lenti. "Could we talk somewhere private, maybe?"

I waved a hand. "Oh, she knows everything already."

His eyes widened. "Everything?"

"Most of it. The gist, anyway."

"Rowan and I are one," pronounced Lenti from her prone position, her eyes still closed. "You may speak freely in front of me." She yawned.

Alex raised his brows. "All right. I just wondered if you're okay. If we're okay. After…" He stroked Lenti's head. "I can't do this while I'm holding a cat. Does she have a bed somewhere?"

I pointed to the spot behind the filing cabinet.

Lenti hissed when he set her in her cat bed, but he bent and whispered something into her ear. She curled into a tight little ball and squeezed her eyes shut.

"Charm comes in handy again." He leaned against my desk, facing me. "Funny story, by the way. When I went into the hotel-room kitchen to get the champagne, one of the glasses was in pieces on the floor." He raised his brows suggestively.

I sucked in a breath. "Crap. You think I…? But I didn't hear anything break."

"I didn't either, but we were a little preoccupied."

My whole body flamed hot as a sunburn. I nodded and glanced down, rearranging the handles on the bag. "We were."

"Ro, I know our situation is complicated, to say the least, but I want you to know I had an amazing time last night. I don't regret any of it. In fact, I'd do it all again."

For the first time since I left the hotel last night, the tightness in my ribs eased up. Since no one else could see us, I laced my fingers through his. "I feel the same."

He sighed. "We technically shouldn't see each other again, since it's against policy."

"Totally." But he wasn't letting go of my hand.

"If we did…" He captured my other hand and massaged my palm. "We'd have to keep it quiet. No one could know."

My heart jumped. He wanted to see me again?

"Except Lenti, I suppose." He glanced toward the snoozing cat. "But I wouldn't want to jeopardize our positions here, or the Firm's involvement in my case. We'd have to be extremely discreet. Not even Tabitha could know."

I cleared my throat. "Right. Ah. Yeah, see…"

"She already knows." His eyes closed for a moment, and he exhaled sharply. "Okay, but no one else. Seriously, no one."

"I get it." I stepped closer to him, daring to slide one hand up his chest. "Believe me. I understand. This can just be a low-key, no-strings-attached situation. All under the radar." I slid my fingers farther up, trailing them just under his collarbone, a touch he'd responded to last night.

His eyes glazed over, and then he grabbed my hand and held it still. "Is that what you want? No strings attached?"

Of course it's not what I want, I wanted to yell. *You've made me like you and now I can't get you out of my head!* But regardless of what either of us felt, it was safer this way. His situation was way too complicated, and I couldn't afford to let him hurt me. If we could both keep it chill, we could just have fun for as long as it lasted. "I think it's for the best." I traced one finger around the edge of his mouth.

He gently caught my finger between his teeth and sucked on the tip, making eye contact with me the entire time.

Damn. I was tingling already. "You're making it hard for me to think." I pressed my body against his. With the privacy spell in place, I was ready to rip off his clothes here in my office.

"You're making it impossible to think about anything besides you." He slid an arm around my waist and drew me in tight. "When can I see you again?" He kissed down one side of my neck, across my chest, then up the other side of my neck.

"As…As soon as possible."

He pecked me on the cheek and stepped back. "I'll text you to arrange something, Miss Baird."

"You don't have to go." My body tingling with anticipation, I followed him to the door. "Did I mention there's a sound spell on my office?"

He laughed. "Let's not risk it. We'll talk soon." He dropped a kiss on the end of my nose and left.

Great, now I was too sexually frustrated to go back

to my nap. And Lenti was snoring, lulled into a deep sleep by Alex's charm, so I couldn't even talk to her about it.

I was contemplating discussing my relationship woes with a six-pound cat. This was what my life had come to.

I dropped into my chair, leaned back, and put my feet on the desk.

Through the frosted windows, the light was gray and drab. Clouds had rolled in overnight, and the weather app on my phone warned of a ninety percent chance of rain by noon.

It was a day to curl up on the couch with a book and mope about my feelings for a soul-stealing demigod, not write instructions for submitting a client intake form.

I groaned. This was exactly what I didn't want to have happen—for Alex to dominate my thoughts, for a hollow space to open up in me when he wasn't physically in the same room. I didn't want to miss him.

What would Megan tell me to do? I could almost picture my older sister sliding her large round glasses into place, her heart-shaped face serious and contemplative. *You need to stay in the moment,* I imagined her telling me. *You can't let one man dictate your whole life. You're stronger than this.*

At least, that's what she would have said before she met Angelo, before she burned for him and then flamed out like a dying star. I remembered how she used to check her phone every few minutes for messages from him. When they weren't together, she'd seemed restless and incomplete. I'd never seen my sister so obsessed, and naively, I'd chalked it up to her being in love.

It wasn't love, of course. It was addiction.

If I started pining for Alex, was I really any different?

I sat up straight and squared my shoulders. I wasn't going to fall under anyone's spell. I had work to do and magic to learn.

I opened Muse and sent Tabitha a message. *Please ask your aunt for a referral.*

Chapter Fifteen

I stopped in front of the drab building and eyed the paint flaking off the siding, the color neither brown nor gray. The blocky two-story might've been a small apartment building before it became a commercial space. A window on the second floor held a *For Lease* sign.

When Tabitha's aunt Cora referred us to Dr. Freya Marks, supposedly the best healer in Portland, I expected a sleek glass-fronted office in downtown. This reminded me of my college apartment. "This is her office?"

Tabitha glanced at her phone. "Yep. Let's see, number two twelve…"

We strolled past the entrance to a nail salon, its open door giving me a whiff of the sickly-sweet smell of polish—like sugar and metal.

The next door advertised an acupuncture clinic, with a *Closed* sign across the front.

We stopped in front of the final door, which was made of solid wood, unlike the other businesses' glass doors. It sported a hand-lettered sign for Crescent Moon Alternative Healing.

Tabitha opened the door. "You first."

I stepped inside and glanced around. We were in a small cozy waiting area, with a couple of chairs and a love seat tucked near a window. A distressed wooden vanity held an assortment of tea bags, mugs, and a carafe. A few magazines and books fanned across a small side table. The front counter held a set of business cards, a terrarium, and a bell with a sign reading *Please Ring When You Arrive.* A musky, spicy aroma filled the room.

Lenti popped into visibility, her claws burrowing into my shoulder. "What's that smell?"

"Incense, I think." I tapped the bell twice.

"Something else." Her nose wriggled.

"Just a moment!" called a woman's voice from somewhere in the back.

Tabitha made herself a cup of tea, while I picked up one of the books and studied the back. *Finding Your Moon Phase, What Lunar Cycles Say About Your Personality.* It seemed a bit...*squishy* for a healer. I hoped this Dr. Marks lady was legit.

"Hello. Sorry to keep you waiting." A werewolf with black-and-rust-colored fur lumbered toward us. "I'm Dr. Marks. You must be Rowan and Tabitha."

Lenti burrowed her claws into my shoulder. "A DOG, A DOG, A DOG." She scrabbled across my collarbones and dove inside my sweater, where she clung to my torso like a spider.

For a second, I thought she was reacting to Dr. Marks's appearance, which was strange considering how many staff meetings she'd attended with me. Half the IT staff were werewolves. But then I spotted it—a tiny chihuahua in a blue sweater, trotting next to Dr. Marks.

The werewolf stopped cold. "I'm sorry to have frightened your familiar. Has she not seen a werewolf before?"

"She's not scared of you. It's the dog. She hates them." I patted Lenti through the cable knit, cupping my hand around her rear so she would ease up with the claws. "Gremlin, the dog is a pet. She isn't going to hurt you."

Inside my sweater, Lenti shivered.

"He, actually, and he's very friendly. His name is Ferdinand." Dr. Marks looked down at the tiny creature. She must've communicated something to his teeny little dog-brain, because he barked and raced over to Tabitha.

"You can hold him," prompted Dr. Marks.

Tabitha emitted a series of gurgling, cooing noises as she picked up Ferdinand. He nestled in her arms and licked her shoulder. The thing probably weighed no more than four pounds.

She stared at the dog with the level of wonder I'd imagine her giving to her firstborn child. "Should I stay with him while you go back and talk?"

"Do you mind?" I hated to leave Tabitha behind since she was the one who'd arranged all this, but she looked pretty happy. When she shook her head, I turned to Dr. Marks. "Is that a problem?"

"Of course not. Please come into my office." She turned and strode back the other direction, her form dominating the hall. She was the size of a small horse. I wondered if she was also tall in human form.

As I followed her, I glanced down at my sweater and sent a silent message to Lenti. *You can come out now. The dog isn't going to hurt you.*

It's a demon.

Why are you not scared of vampires or werewolves, but you're terrified of an animal the size of a rat?

Because dogs can steal your soul.

I frowned, wondering where she'd gotten this idea. Some air-spirit myth? No wonder the placement agent had said familiars didn't choose dog forms.

We entered through the first door on the right, into

a cozy office cluttered with plants.

I sank down onto a suede love seat and leaned back against the plush cushions.

Dr. Marks nosed a small rectangular object on her desk. "I hope you don't mind if I record our session? I don't like to take notes the first time I see a patient. It's easier if we can talk freely."

"Of course." I patted Lenti again. "Gremlin, the dog is in the other room. It's perfectly safe to come out now."

Lenti poked her head out of the top of my sweater. "I think I'll stay in here for a while."

"Whatever you'd like," said Dr. Marks. "Lenti, is it? You're absolutely beautiful." She extended her paw.

"I do have exceptional fur." Lenti nosed the woman's paw a few times. A small purr rumbled through her throat, and she settled back against me, her head peeking out of my sweater. "Why do you insist on keeping a harpy as a pet? Aren't you worried about your soul being ripped from your body in the middle of the night?"

"Not in particular, no." With Dr. Marks's elongated wolf's face it was difficult to tell if she was trying to hold back a laugh. "I've had Ferdinand since he was a puppy. But since he makes you uncomfortable, we'll leave him in the waiting room." She turned on the recorder with a short spell, then settled into an enormous chair and trained her large pale-blue eyes on me. "You said on the phone you're trying to find the origins of your power. Tell me more."

I gave her the whole story, starting with the exorcism when I was thirteen and the way my mom had shipped me off to boarding school. I talked about how college had made me feel like a failure, how top grades in communications and writing hadn't mattered when I was failing basic spell casting. My history usually filled me with residual shame, but Dr. Marks's attentive, ice-blue eyes set me at ease. I even told her about my conflicting feelings about spending time with Alex. The only story I glossed over was Megan's disappearance. We didn't need to dive into all of my trauma in one session.

"You said you haven't told Alex you can read his mind." Dr. Marks tilted her head to one side. "Why do you think that is?"

I shrugged. "I just…I've been burned in the past. I want to be sure how he feels about me, I guess, and…If I tell him, then he'll shut me out." I could already imagine him cutting me off, becoming cold and distant.

"Perhaps you don't want to lose your power." Her voice was soft and calming. "Your personal power, I mean. It sounds as if much of your childhood was beyond your control. Your magic was blocked for years. You also mentioned being hurt in a previous relationship. Now, for the first time, you have real control."

"Are you a healer or a therapist?" I cleared my throat.

She opened her mouth in what might have been a smile or a pant. "A little of both. All right, I think we can do a few scanning spells now. Would you mind scooting forward a bit?"

I shifted to the edge of the couch and sat up straight.

With a quick spell, Dr. Marks produced a slender pine branch which she held in her mouth. She waved it in front of my body in various configurations as she recited spells in a throaty language I'd never heard before.

Lenti, still tucked into my sweater, tracked the branch, her head snapping back and forth.

I willed her not to attack it, and thankfully she stayed still.

When she'd finished, Dr. Marks studied the pine branch thoughtfully, as if she were reading a medical chart. "I can suggest a couple of things. First, I'm going to mix you a potion that should stop your allergic reactions to your power. Second, a close friend of mine is a private investigator. His name is Tomás González. I'll contact him on your behalf, but I think he'll be able to help you."

"How so? Do you not know what kind of magic I have?" If the best healer in town couldn't figure out my power's origins, how would a PI have any luck? I was a mystery to everyone, it seemed.

"I know what you *don't* have. Your power isn't rooted in nature, so you aren't related to a wood nymph, a tree spirit, or anything of the like. I can tell your magic is based in the spirit world somehow, but—"

"Hold on. What do you mean in the spirit world?"

"Any realm but this one. Any of the atmospheric dimensions—"

Lenti eased a little farther out of my sweater. "Like the troposphere. There are over a hundred realms. Rowan's too klutzy to be from one of the Ten, but maybe the lower fifty…"

"Klutzy?" I sputtered.

Dr. Marks nodded. "Yes, any of the lower fifty. Or the Underworld."

Chills rushed down my back. "I'm sorry?" I couldn't be associated with the Underworld. Not when it had taken Megan.

"It's simply one possibility. There are also other realms, twilight realms, any of which could be the source of your power. The trouble is, without knowing more about your family, it's hard to pin down. The magical signatures, at least the ones I can detect, are very similar to any of a dozen. Since your mother was an ordinary, I'd guess your power is inherited on your father's side, but sometimes it skips a generation, so I can't be sure. I don't have the resources to dig into genealogic records, but Tomás does. And he'll take you on my recommendation, so I don't want you to worry about the cost."

"Oh, thanks." I was still dazed by the idea that my magic could possibly come from the Underworld somehow. Did Megan and I have a demigod or demigoddess in our family line? A Stygian, even?

Dr. Marks hopped down from her chair and went over to her desk. Murmuring a series of spells, in short order she mixed a potion called Sneeze Away, printed out an instruction sheet, and emailed me the private investigator's contact information.

I left with a sheaf of paper, a bottle filled with murky-green liquid, and a million more questions.

Tabitha and I had driven together, so Lenti and I told her everything on the way back to my apartment. My best friend was ready for me to email the private investigator right then, but I convinced her to come watch *Unseelie* with Lenti and me instead. Paul was working on his dissertation, so Tabitha didn't have anywhere to be.

Back at my apartment, we binged a few episodes, but I struggled to concentrate on the antics of the cast. I was no closer to understanding my magic than before. My dad, or possibly a grandparent, had left me eldritch powers and no answers. What if I was the child of someone or something evil? What if Megan and I didn't even have the same dad? Our mom said he left when I was young, but she could've been lying.

By four p.m., my head ached from entertaining conspiracy theories about my family origins, and we were all starving. I gave Lenti a can of cat food and ordered a pizza.

We paused the latest episode to eat, and I fed Lenti tiny bits of gooey cheese from the top of my slice.

Lenti sat back, a string of cheese dangling from her chin, "We should talk to Susan again. I liked her. I didn't like the demon, though."

Gremlin, that's a secret.

Tabitha looked from Lenti to me. "Who's Susan?"

"Oops." Lenti swiped the cheese off her chin and licked her paw in an unconcerned manner.

I sighed. Lenti had heard Dave's warning that Wake wasn't on the market, but she probably didn't understand the concept of sanctioned versus unsanctioned magic— or the risk of using it. Air spirits did whatever they pleased, no consequences.

"She's talking about Wake. It's a, uh, software program that connects you to other dimensions. I used it to contact a spirit in the Underworld. It's not exactly…legal."

Tabitha stared at me. "Why would you do that?"

"To find out what Melanie was talking about with the *alpha lyrae*. I know she's up to something, but I can't prove it. Also, I was, um, slightly misinformed about the program. I thought it would get me to a prophetess. It got me a tour guide."

"And a demon." Lenti leaped onto the couch and pawed at Tabitha's arm. "A demon with three heads. It was horrid."

Tabitha cradled Lenti in her arms. The two of them looked at me—Lenti self-satisfied, Tabitha accusing. My best friend narrowed her eyes. "I suppose you don't want to tell me how you got this…what is it? Wake?"

"Nope."

She sighed. "Oh, why the hell not. Show me what it does."

I grabbed my laptop and we moved to the dining room table.

Lenti, in Tabitha's lap, adopted a sort of penguin pose, sitting straight up with her front paws on the table.

I angled the laptop so they could both see, and logged into Wake.

The screen loaded, as it had before. Instead of the view from beneath the River Styx, the screen was pitch black. I tried hitting a few keys and clicking with my mouse, but nothing.

"Weird. Susan?" I tapped the side of the screen. "I swear it worked before." Was this a onetime use software? If so, I was going to duct-tape Dave's hands to his feet as punishment for overcharging me.

Tabitha frowned. "Do you hear snoring?"

I leaned forward and cranked the volume on the laptop.

She was right.

Soft snores emitted from the speakers. Susan was asleep.

"Susan," I hissed. "Wake up. Susan!"

The screen jumped, and then a scene faded into

view. It was the interior of a cozy, cave-like bedroom. The walls were composed of some type of mud or clay, and tiny white lights sparkled near the ceiling.

"Hmm, what? Hello?" said Susan's voice. "Oh, Rowan? And who was the other one—Lenti?"

The arms in front of the "camera" view suggested Susan was stretching. Apparently, she wore hot-pink pajamas.

"I'm bloody wrecked. I've only just fallen asleep. We were out dancing until I don't know when."

"Yes, it's us." I hesitated. "Um, my friend Tabitha is here too."

"Oh, is there another one? I thought it felt a bit crowded in my head. I'm Susan; nice to meet you. Yes, well, anyway, I was out last night with friends. Elysium has quite a club. Diamond Daze, it's called. Open twenty-four hours a day, three hundred sixty-five days a year. I mean, if there was time here. There isn't exactly. Or it doesn't work the same way as it does in the mortal world. Feels like I danced for a year. Oh, and they have the best drinks, and they're all free."

I blinked, trying to keep up with Susan's rapid stream of information. "Is this your house?"

"My flat, dear. It's a treehouse. Isn't it charming?" The view panned around the circular room, allowing me to take in a large window with lacy, white curtains; a white vanity with an opal-framed mirror; a dresser painted bright blue; and a mural, about three feet up and a foot and a half high. It wrapped all the way around the room and featured a scene of men and women in flowing white tunics, dancing and riding horses through a dreamy forest, all done in the impressionist style.

I almost asked Susan to get closer so I could study

it, but suddenly three fuzzy dog heads popped into frame.

Lenti yowled and shot out of Tabitha's lap. "The demon!"

"Honey, no." I started to get up, then sat. It was useless to chase a cat who moved like a tornado.

With a thump, Lenti landed on her cat tower and stuffed herself into the hidey-hole.

I guessed she wasn't coming out anytime soon.

"Wait." Tabitha squinted at the screen. "That's not Cerberus, is it?"

"Cerberella," I said. "A descendant of the original."

"Well, hello, baby," cooed Susan.

The picture sort of tipped backward and Cerberella's floofy faces suddenly filled up most of my screen. The flopping tongue at close range suggested one of the heads was licking Susan's face.

Tabitha made a strangled cooing noise.

I gathered that not being able to pet the dog was slowly killing her.

"So, are you back for the tour?" Susan yawned. "I know you're on the mortal plane, but it's quite enjoyable. I could probably take you in a minute. Just need a bit of coffee, you know."

"Actually, we wanted to ask about a phrase, *alpha lyrae*. Do you know what it might mean?" I'd asked her about it the last time, but she'd been in such a rush I wasn't sure she'd even remember.

"Oh, yes, you mentioned it before. I'm sorry, I have no idea what it means. It sounds lovely, though, doesn't it? *Alpha lyrae*."

The dog heads veered out of frame, and the angle of view shifted again.

Susan must be sitting up.

We had to keep her attention before she got distracted with something else. "Is there someone you could ask? I know it's a huge favor, but it's pretty important."

"Actually, we do have a library, and I live quite close to it. I've got to check my calendar, though, because I have several tours today."

A planner the size of an atlas appeared mid-air and the pages flipped of their own accord.

Unlike any planner I'd seen, the page was marked with runes and other figures. Several wisps of fog or smoke floated out of different spots on the page.

"First tour's not for an hour." The planner clapped shut and disappeared. "Plenty of time to check the library. Come along, Cerberella, there's a good girl."

Susan gathered the triple-headed dog into her arms and exited the treehouse, which involved sliding down a gold-plated chute into a forest clearing. She pointed out other large trees, also with little houses nestled in their tops, and chutes leading down from each one. Rickety rope ladders led back up.

How did Cerberella manage the climb?

Next we had to wait for the dog to relieve herself.

Two of the heads strained to sniff different bushes, and they ended up barking at each other while the third head whined. Finally the dog did her business.

Susan produced a hot-pink harness and leash, which magically attached itself to the dog. "Come on, girl, let's go," she cooed.

We hiked through the forest. Gentle light streamed through the evergreens.

Susan pointed ahead to a clearing. "This is Elysium District Two—sort of on the border between Elysium and the Summerlands. There's a District Three closer to the River Styx, and of course Elysium District One is where all the fun is." She laughed.

My head spun trying to sync this depiction of a breezy afterlife with my worst-case image of Megan alone in a dank basement. Did she have a cute treehouse, too? Did she go clubbing? Was she, in some weird way…happy?

I could only pray.

Susan was waving expansively at the forest. "Now, the library isn't strictly in any of those locations, but it's accessible from all of them. It's the hub, you see."

"Makes sense," said Tabitha. "What kinds of books do you have?"

"Oh, all kinds. All books in all the worlds eventually find their way here."

Soon we reached a clearing.

A round globe at least five stories high rose in front of us. It resembled a giant fishing float, made of aqua blue glass. Shapes and shadows drifted inside, but their forms were indistinguishable.

I blinked. "What is this?"

"The library, of course." Susan walked over to the globe and placed her hand against the glass.

An opening shimmered into being, as if an arched entrance had been laser carved out of the glass and simply fallen away.

Susan bent and told Cerberella to be a good girl, then stepped through the opening.

The inside was like a glass cathedral.

Susan tipped her head up and pointed out the painted mural on the immense circular ceiling, full of so many figures and animals I couldn't begin to figure out what stories they had come from.

Light streamed through openings in the ceiling and played over the white marble floor, and rippling light, tinted blue by the glass walls, danced across the room like ocean waves.

The interior was comprised of circular bookcases spiraling around themselves and up toward the ceiling like giant nautilus shells.

Other people—spirits, I supposed—browsed the shelves. It seemed like everyone had bodies here, despite it being the afterlife. Most people had a human form, but I spotted some faeries and one werewolf.

No one spoke, but flute music floated through the air.

Susan approached a circulation desk, an industrial-steel behemoth that clashed oddly with the rest of the library.

Behind the desk sat a woman with long black hair, red lips, large tortoiseshell glasses, and—incongruously—a black, strapless bathing-suit top. She looked up, but apparently there was no speaking in the library, not even to a librarian. She passed Susan a marble tablet, accompanied by a huge quill pen.

Susan dipped the pen in a bottle of ink and wrote on the tablet, *Alpha lyrae.*

The librarian slid the tablet back toward herself, spun it around, and frowned. She snapped her fingers and a gold coin suddenly sparkled into being. She passed the coin to Susan.

Susan didn't thank her or even respond; apparently this was how it was done.

As Susan passed the desk, my mouth dropped open. The lower half of the woman's body was a long iridescent green fish tail.

I had so many questions. For starters, how did she get to work every day?

But Susan's point of view veered away, toward the massive banks of spiraling shelves.

"What's the coin for?" I kept my voice to a whisper, even though we were in Susan's head, and no one should be able to hear us.

"The token locates the book." She was whispering, too. "You'll see. We just have to find the section…" Her voice trailed off and she paused. "Now, have they moved it again? Oh, dear…"

She sidestepped to the left and stopped in front of a bronze…slot machine? Out of the corner of "her" eye, it seemed like there might be more slot machines by other bookcases.

She inserted the coin into an empty slot, then she pulled a lever.

The bookcase rotated, spinning the shelves around and then stopping.

The section of bookcase nearest Susan creaked, and a book tilted itself out of the shelf.

"Here we are." She lifted the book off the shelf.

The large, heavy-looking book had a green cloth cover embroidered with intricate images of bones and skulls. The title splayed across in gold letters. *The Book of Ares.*

The title didn't strike any familiar notes for me. It sure didn't look like any grimoires I'd seen in college. "Is this a spell book?"

"I'm not certain, dear, I've never seen it before." Susan pried at the cover. "Oh, bother. It's one of those."

"One of what?"

"A locked book. You need a key to get into these."

"Doesn't the librarian have it?" It seemed pretty rude that she hadn't given Susan the key in the first place.

"No, it's not a literal key. A spoken key. Usually only higher-ups have access to those. I'm afraid as a tour guide I only have the lowest level of security clearance." She heaved a sigh. "Well, I'm sorry, dears."

I frowned. Melanie had been thinking about a phrase from a top-secret book in the Underworld library? Not sketchy at all. "You've actually been really helpful, Susan. Thanks."

"No problem, dears, come back and visit me anytime. It does get lonely sometimes, living the single life, you know?"

I promised I'd come back, then signed off. "I don't trust Melanie further than Lenti can bite her."

"Me neither." Tabitha drummed her long nails together. "A locked book? And Ares is the god of war, you know, so I'm not liking the book's title."

"Alex said Melanie was helping him find an alternate way out of his contract with Hades, and she was working on a spell. Maybe it's in the book."

"Maybe." She frowned at her phone. "Let me see if the Association has any information about the Book of Ares."

They didn't. The Association catalogued only books relevant to witches.

Tabitha and I found list upon list of witch grimoires, herb and plant field guides, and spell-casting primers. We found nada on the Book of Ares.

We tried Olympus, Inc. next, thinking a supernatural hotline would surely have information. I rolled my eyes impatiently through the pre-recorded message, then pressed Two. Just like the last time I'd tried calling, the elevator music lasted an interminable amount of time. I put it on speaker phone and made a snack, chatting with Tabitha and Lenti while we waited.

After almost an hour, I gave up and ended the call with a groan. "What's the point of a supernatural hotline if you can't even get through?"

Tabitha's eyes brightened. "Why don't you just ask Alex about it? I'm sure he's been to that library a hundred times."

"Because…how would I explain where I heard of either the book or the phrase?"

She stared at me. "You'd just tell him you read Melanie's mind."

"Oh, he still doesn't know she can do that," said Lenti airily.

"So you're just going to keep your powers a secret from him…what…forever?"

"I don't think we have a forever." I swallowed. "We agreed we should keep our thing casual, especially since we're openly violating Firm policy."

Tabitha rubbed the sides of her nose, like she might have a headache. "Then what about Noel? He's a walking dictionary of magical lore."

She was right. Noel was the first person anyone in the Firm called when they had a question about magical law. Lawyers from other firms even called him for advice. "Sure. I'll ask him."

"Ro." She waited for me to meet her gaze. "Do you have feelings for Alex?"

"I don't know."

"Yes," said Lenti.

When I glared at her, she innocently returned to

licking the half-slice of pizza on my plate.

Tabitha frowned. "You were a terrible liar before you had a mind-reading familiar. I don't know how you can keep any of this a secret long-term."

"Well, I can try," I snapped. I picked up my wine, and Tabitha sipped hers in silence.

Chapter Sixteen

I hurried off the elevator and booked it through the doors onto the eighth floor.

I had fifteen minutes to get in and out of Noel's office. It was the only opening in his schedule this entire week, and I'd had to bribe Elizabeth with donuts in order to claim it.

Lenti and I hurried past attorneys hunched over pages of notes, past legal assistants typing at their cubicles.

"Exactly fifteen minutes," said Elizabeth sharply as I hurried past her desk.

I shot her a look, then I knocked on Noel's door.

The senior partner sat at his desk, bent over a pad of paper, drawing a quill pen across the page. He was the only attorney who still used a quill. He glanced up and motioned me inside.

Unlike the other partners' offices, Noel's office had no windows.

The older vampires were more sensitive to the sun, and where a brief exposure might give someone like Arjun only sun poisoning, Noel could actually die from the sunlight. Instead of sterile corporate fluorescent lights, he lit his office with several banker's lamps.

I'd heard he'd wanted to install gas lamps, but the building management wouldn't allow it.

"Rowan." He adjusted the lapels of his frock coat.

"What can I do for you?"

I took the brocade armchair on the opposite side of his desk.

Delicate leaf-like patterns etched the surface.

"I need to ask you about something kind of unorthodox."

"I'm so sorry, I don't mean to be rude." Noel glanced at the grandfather clock in the corner, which showed it was nearly ten a.m. "But it's time for my morning snack, and if I don't monitor my levels, I get very weak. Will it offend you if I drink while we talk?"

"Be my guest." I was used to the mini fridges every vampire kept in his or her office, plastered with biohazard symbols.

Noel's mini fridge was his one concession to modernity other than his computer.

Instead of retrieving a pre-portioned blood bag from the fridge, though, he opened a small vintage vanity and removed a garnet-red bottle with no label. Uncorking it, he poured the blood into a black mug embossed with the Ainsley Barfield logo.

I nodded toward the bottle. "Breaking out the good stuff early?"

"Gift from a client." He replaced the bottle in the vanity. Sitting, he took a discreet sip from his mug. "Please go on."

I'd considered different ways to approach this, including honesty, but I wasn't sure if the Firm could discipline me for using illegal software on my own time, so I'd decided to play it safe. "Do you know what the Book of Ares is?"

He set his mug down. "Where did you hear that name?" His lip curled up, as if he'd just tasted something disagreeable, revealing a thin coating of blood on his fangs.

My stomach churned. The blood was fine in theory, but seeing it like that was a little too visceral. It reminded me too much of the one time when I was a child, and my mom had yanked my stubborn loose tooth free. My mouth had filled with blood. I licked my lips now, trying to get rid of the memory of the rusty taste. "I went to a coven meetup with Tabitha, and some of the witches were talking about it." It seemed like the safest explanation, and it was one he couldn't easily challenge.

Noel strode over to the bookshelves lining one wall of his office.

Many of the books were hardbacked and leather-bound, mixed in with frayed journals with yellowed pages. A gilt-stamped maroon Bible peeked out from one of the top shelves.

I'd always wondered why Noel kept it when he couldn't even enter a church, but I'd never been brave enough to ask.

He bent and ran his long, thin fingers over the spines of a complete set of the North American Pan-Magical Codes. Sliding a volume off the shelf, he paged through it.

"Noel?"

He held up a finger, his gaze still fixed on the book. I sat back and waited.

"Ah. Here we are." Striding toward me, he flipped the book around and dropped it into my hands. With one long thin finger, he tapped the title on the page. *North American Pan-Magical Code, Otherworld Grimoires Act, Title 27. Part F, Offenses and Penalties.*

My stomach dropped out of my body and landed

somewhere in the basement as I read the legalese.

It shall be unlawful for any person to knowingly or intentionally acquire, read, or otherwise access an otherworld grimoire; copy, reproduce, or distribute, in whole or in part, an otherworld grimoire; or perform any spells or parts of spells from an otherworld grimoire. Such action constitutes Intent to Wield and is a Class Ten felony.

I swallowed back nausea and slid the book away. "The Book of Ares is an otherworld grimoire?"

Noel sat and adjusted the cuff of one sleeve. "One of the most dangerous. Do you know who Ares was?"

"The Greek god of war."

He nodded. "For many generations, there was a cohort of magicians in England who worshipped Ares."

Ah. That explained why the title of the book was in English.

"They developed a number of spells designed to help them wield power at any cost, and eventually codified them into the Book of Ares in 1591. The Book was responsible for several wars until finally, in 1718, a group of vampires, werewolves, and witches banished it to the Underworld."

Now I knew why the book was magically locked. Spells to wield power at any cost... "Do you know if these spells can break magical bonds?"

"I don't have an exhaustive list. Most of the spells involve blood magic. Sacrifices. The Book is supposed to be bound to the Underworld for eternity, but some of the binding magic was improperly done, and pieces of the book have surfaced here and there." He drummed his long fingers against the desk. "And you're absolutely certain you heard this matter being discussed over wine and cheese?"

Lenti and I both held our breaths and released them at the same time. I set the law book down on the desk and gently closed it. Once again, I thought about telling him the truth. If he didn't believe me, I could show him the crystal and read his mind on the spot. *Perhaps you don't want to lose your personal power.* Dr. Marks's words floated back to me.

I cleared my throat. "What do you know about Melanie Harper?"

"Our client? Sharp. Innovative businesswoman. What are you asking?"

I'd have to be blunt. "Did you know she's a Stygian?"

"Of course. We scan every client as part of the intake process. Her identity isn't widely known, though, so how did *you* know?" His eyes narrowed.

Shit. "She's friends with Alex. It wasn't hard to figure out."

"That's true. He referred her."

"Well, do you think she's trustworthy?"

"Rowan." He took another sip from his mug. "The Firm has a rigorous risk assessment process with multiple checkpoints. When we decide to take on a client, we do so only after that client has passed our assessment. We don't take on clients if the representation would harm the Firm. The entire partnership signs off on it. Now, what does this have to do with the Book of Ares?"

Tell him, said Lenti.

I heaved a breath. "One day when she was here, I

read Melanie's mind. She thought a phrase—*alpha lyrae*—and I don't know what it means exactly, but I know it has something to do with the Book of Ares."

He stared at me. "I don't understand. Haven't you told me you struggle with spell casting?"

"I do, with normal stuff. It's a long story, but I just recently got unblocked and found out I have some power. Here, I'll show you." I closed my eyes and stretched toward Noel's mind. I slipped inside, and a wave of quiet fury washed over me. Then he booted me out. Definitively. Like a slap.

I opened my eyes.

"I see." His voice was cold velvet. "Eldritch magic. Powerful stuff, if you can learn to wield it properly."

"What do you mean?"

"You're weak." He stood abruptly. "I threw you out of my mind just now. A real eldritch witch could have resisted me."

I didn't like the power differential created by him standing while I sat. I got to my feet, my heart racing.

Lenti shoved her face next to mine and clung to my shoulder, shivering.

"Why are you upset at me?"

"You're required to disclose your magic to HR. I suppose you don't remember that from your hiring process, or perhaps it didn't register at the time because you didn't have any powers to speak of then. Some powers are restricted within the four walls of the Firm. Mind reading is certainly one of them."

Icy sickness washed over me. "I didn't realize."

"Now you do. Once you leave my office, I suggest you go straight to HR. Do you see the problem with reading minds in a law firm, Rowan? Client confidentiality is paramount. That's why we sound-spell our offices during client calls. It's why we keep case files in locked cabinets. Clients have an expectation of privacy when they discuss matters with us, and in fact it's a violation of PMBA ethics to allow unauthorized access to those conversations. If you persist in reading the minds of clients, the Firm is at risk of liability. Sanctions. You could easily be terminated for this."

"All right. I didn't know. I'll go talk to HR." Shit. Was the Firm going to magically hobble me at work? "But what about Melanie thinking about the Book of Ares? Doesn't that concern you at all?"

"*Thinking* is not prohibited under the magical codes." Sarcasm tinged his voice. "So unless you witnessed her violating one of these specific rules, she would have done nothing wrong. As I've already explained, the Firm makes decisions about client representation according to a set of standards. I trust you'll respect the choices of the partnership, which has been doing this for a very long time."

His cold, pale-gray eyes bored into me, and the message was clear. *Stay in your lane.*

I stared at the sharp white points poking down over his bottom lip, his thin-but-strong shoulders, his long fingers with those large knuckles. For the first time, I didn't feel safe in his presence.

At the same time, my blood boiled. I'd come to him in good faith because I truly believed Melanie was a threat. I'd worked with him for three years, but apparently my word meant nothing.

The crystal burned against my skin.

"Thanks for the advice." My voice came out soft and shaky, which it only did when I was furious. Really intimidating. If you piss me off, I'll *whisper* at you.

Noel glanced at the grandfather clock. "I have to prepare for a client call." He didn't make eye contact as he sat back down, slid his mug aside, and scribbled something on his notepad.

I backed away and opened his office door with unsteady hands. Pausing in the doorway, I glanced over my shoulder. The Ainsley Barfield mug sat several inches from the edge of the desk. Narrowing my eyes, I nudged it with my mind. It inched toward the edge. Again. It slid farther, tottered a little, and then—

"Good heavens!" said Noel.

Pieces of the mug scattered across the floor in a small pool of blood.

I breezed out of his office.

Behind me, he hollered, "Elizabeth! Can you get one of the staff to clean this up, please?"

My lips twitched. *A real eldritch witch could have resisted me*, he'd said.

Am I real witch now, Noel?

****

"Just tell them you can only read vampires' minds," Lenti said, as she cleaned her face. We'd gone back down to my office to regroup. "Then they can't stop you from listening to Melanie."

"I don't think that's how it works. If they do a spell or whatever it is to restrict my power, it'll probably restrict it across the board."

"Then only tell them about the telekinesis. You're not very good at it anyway." One side of her face fur now stuck straight out, damp and stringy from her wet paw.

"What about me breaking Noel's mug?"

"It wasn't bad." She switched to wiping down the

other side of her face. "I'd have gone for something more dramatic, like making all the books fly off the shelves."

I fiddled with the crystal around my neck. "I wonder if I can stop them from blocking me." Would a psychic shield hold up against whatever spell HR would put on me?

"When do you have to go see them? What's HR, anyway? Are they like a disciplinary council?"

"Human Resources. They do the hiring and firing." The crystal's tiny heartbeat fluttered against my chest. "Melanie knows I can read her mind, too. Even if I could stall on reporting to HR, how am I supposed to get into her head again?"

Lenti flopped over and stretched into a small sun patch. The black splotches on her fur lit up with edges of deep red. Her eyes closed. "I thought *alpha lyrae* is the spell she's doing to help Alex, so why do you need to read her mind again?"

"That's just a guess. He didn't know what it was called." There was something about Melanie I didn't like or trust. Those predatory eyes, that too-perfect smile. And what CEO dressed like she was walking a runway?

Or was I just jealous?

I sighed and stood up. "I guess I should get the HR visit over with." Noel would check to see if I'd kept my word. "Are you coming?"

One eye popped open. "I'm sleeping."

"You don't want to come with me?"

She let out a small huff, sort of a cat-sigh. "Rowan, I require a minimum of twelve hours of sleep per day. It's important that I get adequate rest."

Okay, then. "I'll try not to be gone long."

"Our contract's been finalized, by the way." She

yawned. "They just need your signature."

Thump.

I stared at my desk. A sheaf of legal-size pages had just landed next to my keyboard. I hurried over and scanned the first page. *Permanent Witch-Familiar Bonding Agreement.* Startled, I checked the date. Had Lenti already inhabited my life for a month? Sure enough, she had. It was time to make things permanent, unless either of us wanted out. But we didn't.

No wonder she wasn't freaking out about coming with me to HR. She knew now I wasn't going to leave her.

I picked up a pen, and the pages curled themselves over, magically opening to each signature line. I grinned as I signed the final page. Below my signature, another line glowed. "Hey, gremlin? You have to sign too."

Not moving from her spot, she lifted one paw in the air. The image of her pawprint appeared on the signature line, as clear and bold as if she'd dipped her paw in ink. Her full name filled in below the paw print. *Altocumulus Lenticularis, Spirit of the Air, of the Seventh Realm of the Troposphere.*

The contract duplicated itself, and the original evaporated, leaving the copy on my desk. I flipped through it again and smiled. "Well, that's it. You're stuck with me now."

A soft snore met my declaration. My permanent best friend stretched out on the carpet, her eyes closed.

****

"All right, sign here, please." Kate, the HR director, flipped a form around and slid it across her desk. A sheaf of Ainsley Barfield-branded pens sat in an Ainsley Barfield mug like a quiver of tiny arrows.

I plucked one from the batch and scrawled my name across the bottom of the form.

"So, a copy of this will go in your file, and we'll also send a copy to your direct supervisor." She opened a folder and paged through the documents within it. "You report to Alexander Kouris, yes?"

My heart dropped out of my body. "Alex has to see this? Why?"

"It's standard policy to share these disclosures with your supervisor, as a matter of transparency. Because you can't use your powers at work, you might require accommodations to your job, and your supervisor would provide those. Why? Is there a problem?" She blinked, her expression completely blank.

"No. I just…didn't know how it worked."

She flipped the folder closed and set it aside. "Do you have any other questions before I perform the block?"

"Nope."

Kate nodded. "Please stand."

I stood and dusted cat hair off my pants. Maybe I could turn and run? Maybe it wasn't too late to move to Canada?

Kate approached me and placed one hand on my forehead. "Close your eyes and take a deep breath."

I inhaled and exhaled, as instructed, and imagined my shield going up. A steel wall, no doors, no windows. Rising foot by foot into an endless sky. I braced for the impact of whatever spell she was about to cast.

When nothing happened but silence, I slit my eyes open to peek at her.

The HR director stood still as a mannequin, her eyes closed, lips moving softly. There was a halo of multicolored light around her mouth, like a tiny complete rainbow.

I shut my eyes and held onto my shield with every ounce of my will. Damn it, how long was this spell going to take?

A jolt of energy hit the crystal and it buzzed against my skin like strong static electricity. The sensation startled me into opening my eyes, and the image of my shield fled my mind. The crystal shot tiny blue sparks, which fizzed out as they rained toward the carpet.

"Was that supposed to happen?" I crossed my fingers, hoping she'd say no.

Kate frowned. "Well, I don't know what's 'supposed' to happen. I've never blocked an eldritch witch before, but in theory it should work the same as it would for any other magic."

In theory? Ha. This lady didn't even know what she was doing.

"The block only holds within the Firm and a ten-foot-or-so radius around the building, so once you leave work you should be able to cast as normal."

"Okay." It seemed like I should say something else, but I certainly wasn't going to thank her for taking away my powers. I eyed the closed file on her desk, but now I couldn't even use my powers to sweep it under a filing cabinet when her back was turned. Shit, how was I going to keep this from Alex? "Um, see you, then."

When I got back to my office, Lenti leaped out from behind the filing cabinet. "Did it work? Did you block her?"

"I don't know. Let me check." I tried to read her mind but got nothing. I frowned. "Think about something specific. Your favorite meal."

"Cheating. You already know that one. I'll think of my favorite *Unseelie* cast member."

I'd have laughed, but nothing was funny right now. "Sure, okay." Once again, I sought her thoughts. I didn't hit any barriers, but I couldn't feel anything, either.

"Lenti? Can you read my mind? What am I thinking about right now?" I held the image of a huge, savory bowl of mac and cheese topped with a dash of hot sauce.

"Cheese stuff," she scoffed. I'd told her the real name of the dish a dozen times, but she wouldn't call it anything else. "With something disgusting on it."

Okay, at least Lenti's powers were still intact. I tried again but sensed a big fat wad of nothing. It was like turning on a radio to complete silence. Not even static. Only then did I think to touch the crystal around my neck. It was cold and lifeless.

Kate's spell had worked.

"Language, Rowan, language."

I glared at Lenti. "I didn't even say anything."

She blinked. "I heard what you were thinking."

With a groan, I strode to the window and put one hand on the cold glass.

At this height, I could sometimes hear the wind as it whipped around the building. It moaned softly now.

I leaned my forehead against the glass. Kate's spell was either un-blockable, or my psychic shield had a massive weakness. I was rattled when I spoke to her, which probably didn't help. "Alex is going to kill me."

Lenti pawed at my leg. "I can still become invisible, you know. You make an excuse to talk to him, and I'll steal the paper off his desk while he's distracted. If you like, I could also teleport into that HR lady's office and poop under her desk."

"That's sweet. And disgusting. But she'll probably just email it." My eyes widened. "Oh, no."

I raced to my desk and pounded my password on the keyboard.

Lenti hopped into my lap, placing her front paws on the desk where she could see what I was doing but also stay relatively hidden behind my desk and monitors.

When I opened my email, my ears started ringing. There, right at the top of my inbox, was a new message from Kate, with an evil little paperclip next to the message signifying an attachment. Sure enough, she'd addressed the email to Alex and copied me, explaining what she was sending and why.

"That's the form." I tapped the screen. "She just sent it to Alex. I'm dead." I should've been honest with him from the start, but it was too late to go back and do things the right way. Maybe I could explain myself to Alex, but he'd still be upset. I already pictured the disappointment in his eyes.

Unless…

"Do you know any spells to make things disappear?"

Lenti lifted her head and yawned. "Such as?"

"I don't know what spells, gremlin. I don't do normal magic."

"No, I meant what kinds of things do you need to disappear?"

"This email. From Alex's inbox."

"Oh!" She sat up, her peridot eyes bright. "I can do that."

"You can? Can you do it now?"

"Will you let me lick a bowl of the cheese stuff?"

"I'll let you lick ten bowls if you do this for me. I

think he had a meeting this morning, so you might have half an hour before he gets back. Shit, how are you going to get his password, though?"

"Silly Rowan. I can do the spell from here."

"You can?"

"Certainly." She hopped up onto my desk and sat in front of my monitor. "I simply need to see the email. Where is it?"

I double-clicked the message and it popped up in a new window. "There."

"Stand back, please."

I scooted my chair back from the desk and clasped my hands to my chest, barely breathing.

Lenti meowed, then let out a chattering noise. It almost sounded as if she were warming up for a performance.

As she started to sing in a garbled cat-yowl, I realized that's exactly what she was doing.

"La, la, la, la…"

I cleared my throat.

She glanced back at me. "Just preparing." Facing the monitor again, she let out an unholy sound. It resembled a low growl, but it was accompanied by hissing and meowing all at once, as if a chorus of stray cats had joined the party.

Unnerved, I put an extra foot of space between us.

As the sound continued, a halo of neon green light appeared over Lenti's head.

The email message from Kate floated out of my computer monitor and hovered in the air, like a holograph.

Lenti swatted the message with her right paw.

The image disintegrated into thousands of

individual pixels, and then evaporated into thin air.

The halo over her head vanished.

Then she vanished, too. A moment later her familiar weight settled on my right shoulder.

"Your wish is fulfilled."

Her whiskers tickled my face.

"Holy shit." I sat and stared at my screen. The email was gone. Not in the deleted items, not in the trash, not in any subfolders. I wished I could see Alex's computer screen to be a hundred percent sure the spell had worked, but it's not like I could log into his computer.

Could I?

No! No, I had to stop here. The email was gone. Unless Alex had checked his email on his phone during his meeting…but, no, he'd told me he was presenting his proposal for revised data-retention policies to the partnership. He wouldn't check his phone while he was in a room with a bunch of attorneys.

Lenti hopped into my lap and kneaded her paws on my left thigh. "You're welcome."

I winced and petted her head. "Sorry. Thank you, gremlin. You saved me."

"Ten bowls," she reminded me.

"You've got it."

She made painful biscuits on my thigh for another thirty seconds, then settled down into a black-and-white ball on my lap and went to sleep.

I stared at the little yellow "idle" circle next to Alex's name in Muse. The second it changed to green, I sent him a message. *How did your presentation go?*

He responded within seconds. *Great! Check your texts.* He added a big smiley face.

I picked my phone off the desk and read his message

with a racing heart.

—I can't stop thinking about you. Have dinner with me on Saturday night? I'll cook for you. Lenti can come too. You two can spend the night.—

My insides melted. He'd picked a night that wouldn't conflict with girls' night. He'd offered to make dinner. He was including Lenti.

And if we could convince her to give us a little private time, there might also be a repeat of that night at Broadway Pearl. Maybe I could bribe her to leave us alone for a few hours with episodes of my favorite reality show and a slice of cheddar cheese…

This text must mean he hadn't seen Kate's email. Lenti's spell had worked.

I texted him back.

—We'd love to.—

I laid my phone on the desk and touched the lifeless crystal around my neck. Nausea rolled my stomach, and a chill washed over me. I shivered and zipped up my cardigan.

That moment in a movie or TV show where the criminal makes a fateful decision that starts them down the path of a life of crime? I suspected I'd just done the equivalent. Kate's email was the dead body I buried in the desert. I'd cleaned up the evidence, covered my tracks, and no one would ever know.

That's what they all think, isn't it? No one will ever know.

Chapter Seventeen

I stopped on Alex's front porch and tugged my maroon blouse a bit lower. The V-neck drew attention to my boobs. The push-up bra helped, too. I'd worn my favorite jeans and ankle boots, and my only jewelry was the crystal, which conveniently dangled just above my cleavage, practically pointing to it.

I set down my duffel bag. I hoped he wouldn't be alarmed by the overstuffed bag, but a sleepover with a cat required extra supplies, like a litter box. "Should I knock or ring the doorbell, do you think?"

No response. I looked down at the spot Lenti had been standing moments ago. She was gone, clearly having teleported inside.

It's unlocked, she said in my head.

I twisted the handle open and rapped on the door, just to be safe.

Lenti was already trotting through the living room. "YOLO, Alex, we have arrived."

"In the kitchen."

I hauled my duffel bag inside and shut the door.

By the time I'd gotten my shoes off, set up Lenti's litter box in the downstairs powder room, and made it into the kitchen, the little cat was already perched on the kitchen island.

Her head bobbed up and down, tracking Alex's hands as he diced onions on a cutting board.

"Hi." I smiled and held up a bottle of cabernet. "Thanks for having us."

"Hey, beautiful." His eyes lit up as he stepped out from around the island and tugged me close for a kiss. "Oh, you didn't have to bring anything, but that's sweet." He took the wine and gestured toward the barstools at the island. "Sit, I'll pour you a glass. Lenti, are you hungry?" He glanced at me. "I got a few different kinds of cat food. I'm not sure what she eats."

"I eat the same food you do." She stretched her paw toward the cutting board.

I nudged her paw out of the way. "No, you don't. Onions and garlic are poisonous to cats, remember?"

"I could heal myself." Lenti licked her paw and mashed it against her left ear.

"The cat food is just a snack." Alex rummaged around in a cupboard and came back with five different brands of canned cat food. "I've got fresh salmon for your dinner."

She perked up. "Much better. I'll accept a snack, then."

We both laughed.

Alex already knew Lenti well.

It was cute, the way he spread out the cans in front of Lenti and let her pick. While he spooned chunks of tuna onto a small plate, I poured us glasses of wine.

I sipped my wine and studied the ingredients spread across the counter. Ground beef, butter, and various spices. My stomach growled. "What are you making?"

"Moussaka." He sampled the wine, gave an approving nod, then returned to chopping onions. "Kind of a Greek lasagna with bechamel sauce. Traditionally it's made with lamb, but I wasn't sure how you felt about lamb, so I'm using beef." He picked a three-by-five recipe card off the counter and handed it to me.

I studied the ingredient list, packed onto the card in lines of neat cursive. "Is this your mother's recipe?"

"She learned it from her mother, but yes. When I went off to college, moussaka was the only thing I could cook. It was a hit with my roommates."

I passed him the card. "And the ladies, I bet."

He shrugged and smiled, his eyes twinkling.

Lenti scarfed her food and Alex let her out into his yard to explore.

I relaxed with my elbows on the island, taking lazy sips of wine while we chatted and Alex cooked. The rich scents of oregano, tomatoes, and cinnamon mingled with the faint smell of saltwater—Alex's scent.

He turned the heat down and slid a lid onto the pot of meat sauce. As he placed another pan on the stove, he said, "So have you heard anything from that PI the healer recommended?"

"Not yet." I sighed. "He asked for a copy of my birth certificate, and I sent that a week ago. Nothing since."

He glanced at me over his shoulder. "Your birth certificate? Why does he need that?"

"So he can find my out who my dad is. Dr. Marks thinks Megan and I got our powers from our dad. I didn't even know him, so it's possible. The Association's genealogy records have nothing, but maybe the PI can find something."

"Interesting." He sliced off half a stick of butter and placed it in the pan. "How do you feel about all this? It must be strange not to know the origins of your magic."

"It is. I'm skeptical, but it would be nice to know more."

He nodded, flipping the burner to a higher setting. "If I can do anything to help, let me know."

"Thanks." I took a long slow drink while he chased the butter around the pan with a spatula. There was something about his muscular body poised over a stove. Endearing and sexy at the same time. "So what about your arbitration? Did Hades's lawyers ever agree to anything?"

"Um, not yet." He sounded distracted, his attention focused on the pan in front of him, but something in his tone caught my attention. His mind swam with anxiety.

"Nothing's happened? They're still stalling?"

"Still stalling." He whistled as he slid the butter back and forth. The image of Noel's disappointed face filled his mind. *I don't know how long we can keep pushing back the date. The lawyers are getting impatient.*

Alex was the one delaying the arbitration? Why?

I started to ask him. Then I remembered I couldn't. I slipped away from his mind, fighting uncertainty. I didn't want anything to spoil this night. Couldn't I put away the girl detective act for one evening and just enjoy being here? "Well, putting up a psychic shield is getting easier. Lenti and I have been practicing every night. Wait until you and I practice again. You'll be proud of me."

"What about the telekinesis? Are you still breaking things?" He winked at me over his shoulder.

I made sure to hold eye contact for a beat before answering. "Only when I come."

Desire flashed in his eyes. He crossed to the island, leaned across, and kissed me long and slow, sliding his tongue into my mouth.

He tasted like the deep plum and cherry of the wine. I nipped and sucked on his lower lip.

Behind him, the butter sizzled in the pan, and he hurried to stir it. "I'm not going to make it until dinner. How do you feel about pre-meal sex?"

I laughed. "Dessert first? No objection."

We talked and joked our way through the rest of his meal preparation as he layered the eggplant, meat filling, and bechamel sauce into a dish.

He slid the pan into the oven and set a timer, then looked around the kitchen and laughed. "Well, it looks like my cupboards exploded in here, but I promise it'll be worth it."

"Let me help you clean up." I hopped up and hurried around to the other side of the island, reaching for the cutting board.

He gently pushed away my hands. "We can do this later." He glanced out the window and burst out laughing. "What's she doing?"

I peered through the window.

Lenti stalked through the yard. She wriggled her butt, then pounced on something. A moment later, she crouched low again and slunk along the ground.

"Hunting bugs, I think." I shrugged. "Or maybe she's just hunting grass."

"Will she be occupied for a bit?"

"Oh, yeah. We don't have a yard, so she's in heaven right now."

"Good." He backed me up against the island and slid one hand to my waist, the other up my side to cup my left breast. As he kissed me, he slid his warm fingers inside my shirt and bra to fondle my nipple.

That simple touch sent a wave of pleasure through my body. I sighed against his mouth and leaned back, relishing his sure and gentle touch.

Still kissing me, he tugged on the waistband of my jeans. He teased me, sliding one finger inside the fabric and running it along my stomach.

Pleasurable and almost unbearable. I decided to help him out by unbuttoning my jeans.

Grabbing the zipper on my jeans, he slid it down. "Let's warm you up, darling."

The endearment left me a puddle of emotions in his arms. I held onto his arms, sliding my hands over his biceps, savoring the feeling of his muscles bunching. He tugged my jeans down, then my black lace underwear, just low enough to expose my bare center, essentially locking my legs together. He dragged his mouth down my chest and used his lips to nudge aside my bra, taking my breast into his mouth. His sure strong fingers slipped between my legs, rubbing the outer folds until I was slick and hot.

He slid two fingers inside me, and I gasped and dug my hands into his back. My legs were clamped together around his hand, held in place by my own halfway-discarded clothing.

The man knew exactly what he was doing.

He took my nipple between his teeth, tugging gently. His mouth shot sensation to my center

With his fingers making slow circles inside me, I was already on fire, and now my body burned with need. I moaned softly, anxious for more of him. He thrust his fingers in and out, reminding me what else he could do with other parts of his body. Vibrations built and heat bloomed inside me.

He kissed up my chest and the side of my neck, then paused with his lips on my earlobe. "You feel so good on my fingers. So wet for me."

I squirmed and rocked against him. Even his words could zap pleasure into my veins.

"I want you inside me," I gasped. "Now." I didn't care anymore that we were in the kitchen. Or if his neighbors saw. Nothing seemed important right now except for Alex and his hands and his mouth and his body merging with mine.

A sound rumbled from his throat, sort of a chuckle and growl combined, a raw and primally amused noise. He scooped me into his arms and took me up the stairs to his bedroom.

The walls were a calming tan, the blinds a pale cream.

Alex tossed me onto the king-sized bed, and I landed on the caramel-covered duvet.

It smelled like him, wild and briny.

Alex stripped his clothes off, and naked, crawled toward me.

The crystal. I tugged the chain over my head and dropped the necklace onto the nightstand. Rolling toward him, I slid up my shirt hem, anticipating his warm skin against mine.

He smiled and shook his head. "Let me undress you."

I sat back, and he lifted the bottom of my shirt, kissing my ribs. Painfully slowly, he peeled back the fabric, exposing my skin one inch at a time, kissing a slow trail up my body.

He nudged my shirt up over my head, but instead of slipping it completely off my arms, he wrapped the fabric around my arms to gently bind them.

Oh. We were going there, were we? I flexed my wrists and grinned at him.

"Not too tight, is it?"

I laughed. "It's great. I don't mind you tying me up."

He exhaled huskily and kissed me on the mouth, then slid his lips down to my breasts. Once again, he kissed and tugged at my nipples until I was breathless under him. Lifting his mouth, he kept one hand on my left breast, caressing it while he slid his other hand down my stomach and between my legs.

A flick of his finger, a hint that poured heat into my center again, and then he slid my jeans all the way off.

He took his sweet time removing my underwear, pausing to touch, then lowering his head to lick my sensitive folds.

I sighed and slid my legs wider, running one hand through his soft black curls. The sight of his head between my legs almost made me come on the spot.

Finally both of us were naked, and he rolled on a condom. He straddled me, rubbing himself against me.

I bucked and shifted, but he tilted his hips back, just out of reach. I laughed. "You're definitely torturing me tonight."

"Good things come to those who wait." He slid the tip of his erection in, just barely, then drew back again.

I groaned. He went on like that, teasing me, locking gazes with me in between long kisses, his eyes full of passion and intensity. His quick breaths told me he was getting off on this slow progression as much as I was.

Finally, he braced himself over me with one hand, the other hand gently pinning my wrists in place on the bed. With a long sigh, he slid himself all the way inside me, deep, and held himself there.

The stillness was more than I could bear. I gasped and lifted toward him. "Alex."

He smiled. "Darling." He kissed me again, his tongue seeking mine as he thrust in and out, slow at first, then faster.

I locked my ankles around his back, trying to draw him in farther, relishing the feeling of fullness. My center spiraled with vibrations, the world narrowing to nothing but Alex and me, his voice, his breath, his touch. The orgasm shot through me with ferocity, my entire torso tingling.

Alex rocked back and forth, murmuring my name. "Ro…" he groaned and thrust a final time. He collapsed against me, and we lay there panting.

When we'd recovered our breath and I'd extracted myself from my shirt sleeves, he rolled against my back and wrapped his arms around me. He smelled like sweat and musk and the ocean. I twisted toward him and curled against his chest, drawing in his warmth.

Then something occurred to me.

"Oh my gods." I shot up. "The moussaka."

He laughed and pulled me back down against his chest. "We'll hear the timer, love. Don't worry."

I relaxed against him. Wait, he'd called me "love." Another slip? I glanced at the crystal on the nightstand, but it would be weird if I suddenly got up to put on a piece of jewelry. I heaved out a breath and ran a hand over the flock of ravens tattooed on his side. This was supposed to be a casual thing. We'd both agreed, but our agreement hadn't changed my feelings.

Or his.

"That's a big sigh."

"Just thinking."

He tucked a finger under my chin, nudging my head up until I met his gaze. "What's going on in there?"

Oh, boy. How did I begin to explain? I didn't want to emotion-vomit, especially if he wasn't feeling anything close to the same. I traced my fingers along the line of his jaw. "I guess I'm just wondering if we're still on the same page about…us."

He smoothed my hair back from my forehead. "Which page, exactly?"

"We said we would keep it low-key."

He nodded. "We did."

I took a slow breath. "But it feels like we're lying to ourselves."

A smile tugged one side of his mouth up. "All right, I confess. I don't see this as a casual fling. I know it's complicated, especially with our work relationship, but Ro…" He kissed me softly. "I have feelings for you. Surely that's obvious by now. I mean, I don't make moussaka for just anyone." He grinned.

I chuckled and ran my hands through his soft curls. "I like you too, Alex. A lot." More than I was willing to tell him right now.

He drew my hand down and kissed the back of it. "Does this make you my girlfriend?"

My heart sang at hearing the word *girlfriend* in his smooth baritone. "I'm okay with that."

"Good." He kissed me again. "You'll be happy to know I'm a very good boyfriend."

A sliver of ice worked its way into my warm happiness. Melanie. I managed a smile and sank back against the pillow. "I hope I can measure up to your past girlfriends."

"Darling, there's nothing to measure up to." He kissed my cheek, then my forehead. "You're intelligent, funny, and beautiful, and you're perfect just the way you are."

"Thanks. Sorry." I sighed. "It's just that Melanie's sort of intimidating."

He lifted his head. "How did you know Melanie and I dated?"

Shit.

"I mean, she's helping you with your case. And you said your ex-girlfriend was the one who helped falsify your reaping records. Two plus two?" The lies tasted bitter on my tongue.

"Okay." A frown flickered across his face.

Silence stretched over us like a fog.

As I fiddled with the edge of the blanket, he said, "What's wrong? There's something you're not telling me."

Oh no.

"Um…" I sat up, gripping a fistful of the blanket as if the downy fabric could somehow give me strength. "I read your mind."

"What?" He, too, sat up.

"I read your mind. I saw Melanie in your memories, and…it was obvious."

His lips parted, a confused frown lining his forehead. "You're a telekinetic."

"I am. Not a very good one, yet." I pointed at the crystal necklace. "But when I wear that, I'm a pretty decent telepath."

"I never even sensed you." His quiet, flat tone sliced through my gut. "My magic doesn't extend to mind reading. I told you that before."

"You did."

"And you read my mind anyway. Just intruded on my thoughts, like it was nothing."

"It wasn't like that. Listen, Alex, I had a good reason." The words spilled out like blood from a wound. "When I found out Melanie was a Stygian, I was worried about whether she was dangerous, so I sat in on a meeting between her and some of the attorneys. When I read her mind, she was thinking this phrase. *Alpha lyrae*. It's from the Book of Ares, which is—"

"I know what it is," he snapped. "It's where she's getting the spell to free me from my contract with Hades. Did you know that?"

"I wondered if that's what it was, but I didn't know for sure—"

"You could've asked me."

"I just…She seemed…I don't know, you should have seen the way she looked at me." Calculating. Cruel. I told him what Melanie said at lunch about me being nothing more than a plaything. That alone should have gotten Alex on my side. Instead he was looking at me like…like I had betrayed him.

He rolled out of bed and grabbed his boxers off the floor. "You only saw what you wanted to, which is that Melanie is automatically untrustworthy because she's my ex."

"Maybe so." I picked at the blanket. Had I misjudged her? Was she really just a protective but friendly ex, trying to do Alex a favor? I plucked my necklace off the nightstand and slid it over my head. "I was trying to protect you."

"And what about when you read my mind and didn't tell me? How was that protecting me?" He snatched his T-shirt and yanked it on.

"It wasn't." Apparently we were getting dressed angrily, so I scrambled out of bed and picked up my shirt while he tugged on his jeans. "I was protecting myself. I've had some shitty relationships. I've been cheated on. When we started spending time together, I wasn't sure how you felt about me, and I wanted to know I wasn't wasting my time."

"You could've *told* me." He spread his arms wide, palms up. "You could've asked me what I wanted. I'd have told you in a heartbeat this wasn't just a fling. You're the one who said we should keep things casual. Did I ever say I wanted a one-night stand?"

I snorted and tugged my underwear over my hips. "You didn't want to hear my petty insecurities. You would have run screaming the other direction."

He marched over to me. "I'm not Dave, Ro. You could've trusted me with your feelings. Gods."

"I didn't know." My voice broke, and tears gathered in the back of my throat. "I'm sorry. I know I should have told you, but I was so scared."

"What else do you know about me that you haven't told me? What have you read?" Horror washed through his gaze. "Did you read me while we were having sex?"

"No. No." I held up my hands. "I swear. I can't do it without the crystal. Without it, I'm just a witch who can't even do an email-organization spell."

He crossed his arms. "Then how the hell did you break a champagne glass that night at Broadway Pearl?"

"I was wearing the crystal while you...you know. Went down on me. I took it off before we had sex because I didn't want to read your mind then, okay?" I placed a pleading hand on his chest, but he kept his arms tightly locked together. "I swear I'm telling you the truth. It's not like I've been scouring your mind for every single thought for weeks. I've checked a few times to see if you were really into me or not. And when you told me about the San Juans, I saw the image of you canoeing with your mother. She…she was beautiful."

"She was." He ran his hands through his hair and groaned. "Shit, Ro, this is killing me. I care about you, but to find out you've been lying to me since almost day one?" He threw his hands up and paced across the room.

"I don't know what to tell you." I sniffed back tears and stepped into my jeans. "I screwed up. I know. But I really like you. I…I just hope you can forgive me."

He paused and his broad shoulders slumped. "Trust is really important to me. Number one in a relationship. This is going to be difficult for me to get past."

The sight of his immobile posture ignited a sudden flame. The crystal pulsed against my chest, feeding the fury. "Why is it okay for you, but not for me?"

He whipped around. Finally. "I'm sorry?"

I crossed toward him. "Why is it okay for you to lie but not for me? You kissed me the first day we met and didn't tell me you were a Stygian. That's lying by omission, and I forgave you. And you never told me about your history with Melanie, either, which is weird."

"I didn't want to make you feel bad, I guess." He shrugged. "There's nothing between us anymore, at all. I'm sorry."

"I forgive you." I put my hands on his shoulders, wincing at the bunched muscles, the way he didn't reach for me. "I can understand why you didn't tell me. Why can't you do the same for me?"

He shook his head. "This is a pattern with you, isn't it?"

I just stared at him. I met his gaze, waiting for him to soften, for the regret at what he'd said. I saw nothing but steel there, and I pushed away from him, my whole heart aching. That's what Alex really thought of me. That I was a dishonest person, a manipulator. Rich, coming from a Stygian.

"You're such a hypocrite. Your entire power is built on a foundation of lies and manipulation. You told me yourself it's like plate tectonics, that you can't turn it off. Everywhere you go, everyone will want to be your best friend and do favors for you and give you free hotel upgrades. You want me to be honest, but you don't want to give up a power that makes life all rainbows and ponies for you." My hands shook, and the crystal seared my sternum. "*You're* putting off the arbitration, not Hades's lawyers. I read your mind."

"I'm buying time so Melanie can prep her spell," he snapped. "She has another way."

"You're buying time so you won't have to give up your power. We're the same, Alex. We're exactly the same, except I don't kill people."

We stared at each other, our chests heaving, taking shallow breaths. Fury blazed from his eyes, and I knew it burned in mine.

He said nothing.

He wasn't going to, I realized, because he didn't think he'd done anything wrong. My heart folded in two. "I should go."

"You probably should."

Neither of us moved. I sought his mind, wickedly pleased with how easy it was to read his thoughts. I expected blazing anger, but found a deep pain, a weight like a hundred-pound stone, dragging him down.

Part of him wanted me to stay, and I waited for him to ask. I wasn't going to throw myself on the train tracks for a man anymore. I'd done that too much in the past.

When he said nothing else, I spun around and stomped down the stairs. Hauling open the sliding-glass door, I hollered, "Lenti! Change of plans. We're going home."

"But I'm hunting."

"Now," I barked.

She teleported to my shoulder. "Ro, what…" Her voice trailed off. "Oh."

"I'll tell you everything later." I gathered my purse and re-packed the duffel bag, then shoved my feet into my shoes. All that time, Alex remained upstairs. Wasn't even going to come say an angry goodbye. What an asshole.

I whipped around and glared at his bookshelf. Several books shot off the top shelf and fell to the ground with satisfying thumps.

"I'm leaving," I shouted up the stairs, just in case he cared to know.

The only response was a muffled sob.

My anger cooled, leaving behind a sharp wound, like someone had excised my heart. Lenti and I drove home in silence.

Chapter Eighteen

"Tabitha's here, Tabitha's here!" Lenti raced to the door, letting out a series of high-pitched meows.

I trudged after her. I'd changed into my pajamas as soon as I got home and had texted Tabitha while I was scarfing nacho chips out of the bag. Goddess bless my best friend. The second I told her what happened, she'd said she was on her way.

When I answered the door, Tabitha was holding a bouquet of flowers and a cloth grocery bag. "Sorry it took me a few. I made a stop." She handed me the flowers and the bag, then bent to pick up Lenti. "Hi, cutie."

"Aww." I choked back fresh tears and invited her in. In the kitchen, I put the flowers into a large, blue mason jar. The bag contained four pints of ice cream, a bottle of white wine, and a bag of white-cheddar popcorn. My favorites.

We settled onto the couch with our treats and poured glasses of wine.

Lenti snuggled on the cushion between us.

Tabitha squeezed my hand. "Tell me everything."

I swallowed back tears and told her about my talk with Noel, Kate blocking my powers, and Lenti deleting the email. I recounted the argument with Alex almost word for word, as it was seared into my brain.

Lenti, normally attached at the hip to Tabitha, kept

one paw on my leg.

When I'd finished the part where I slammed books off the shelf and stormed out of the house, Tabitha sighed. I waited for her to say she *I told you so.*

Instead, she gave me a quick hug. "I'm sorry, Ro. Love sucks."

"Is that what this is?" I peered into the bag of white-cheddar popcorn, already half gone. I stuffed another handful into my mouth, then dusted off my fingers. "I thought it was the doomed infatuation of a hopelessly naive witch."

"Oh, sweetie. What are you going to do?"

"Do?" I snorted. "I'm going to become a spinster. Lenti and I will move to Canada together and raise sheep. Or alpacas."

"Ooh, *can* we move to the country?" Lenti's eyes widened. "My fifth cousin became a barn cat, and she got to kill mice every day."

"Maybe after I pay off my student loans." I rubbed her ear, and she flopped onto her side, purring. "The whole argument sucked, but the thing that's killing me the most right now is Alex thinks this all happened because I was jealous of Melanie. I mean, yes, I was a little, but I honestly don't trust her, and no one cares. Even Noel is up her ass."

"I care." Tabitha set her glass on the coffee table and pursed her lips. "I don't trust her either. Why the hell does she need an otherworld grimoire to get Alex out of his contract? I wish we could get into the book to look up that spell. Why are there laws against everything interesting?"

My hand stilled on Lenti's side. "We *could* get the book."

"But Susan told us it was locked."

Lenti rolled into a sitting position. "Oh, I see! We'll do the same thing as last time."

Tabitha frowned. "What are you talking about?"

"Remember how you two got the City Elysium Group case file?"

"No." She put her hands up. "No way. Has the wine scrambled your brain? You just told me that Noel showed you a magical code stating that it's illegal to own a copy of the Book, much less open and read it."

"He did." I stood. "But I don't think I care anymore."

"You could go to prison."

I hurried down the hall, grabbed my laptop out of my room, and returned. I set the laptop on the coffee table and logged in. "Yeah? Who's going to know? This isn't like Wake, where the Association can monitor network traffic. This is a physical book, Tabs. Unless I invite the Witches Council over for dinner, they're never going to see it."

Tabitha shook her head. "Absolutely not. I'm not breaking a law. I draw the line at criminal activity."

"Then teach me the spell." I grabbed her hand.

Lenti wriggled her back end and leaped onto the coffee table. "The perception spell was used to envision the case file when we couldn't see it. We'll see the Book through Susan's eyes. All you need is the mirror spell, which I can perform."

Of course. A smile spread across my face. Leaning down, I kissed Lenti on the head. "You brilliant, marvelous troublemaker."

"You guys." Tabitha was now curled into a ball at the end of the couch, hands clapped over her nose and mouth, like she thought our penchant for rule breaking was airborne. "This is a very bad idea."

"I think it's a great idea." I fired up Wake.

Tabitha slid down in her seat, whimpering.

Adrenaline rising, I checked the text file and plugged in the dimension code. The kaleidoscope of blue twisted and swirled over the screen. Screw Noel and the pan-magical codes. Screw Alex and his double standards for honesty. Screw Melanie. I was going to get the book of Ares, unlock the damn thing, and find out what the *alpha lyrae* spell did. Maybe the spell would break Alex's contract, but that didn't mean it was safe.

The image resolved into blue water and a stalactite-laden cave ceiling. Susan was swimming in the Styx again, turning lazy circles. There was no sign of Cerberella.

"Susan?"

She shrieked. "Oh! Rowan."

"And Lenti."

"You snuck up on me. I was just having a swim after my last tour of the day. Large group. Mostly senior citizens, and they're lovely, but they do tend to ask a lot of questions."

"I'm sure. Listen, can you get us back into the library? It's kind of an emergency."

"Some of the girls and I are supposed to go to Diamond Daze tonight, and I need time to get ready, but let me see." An hourglass appeared in the air, golden sand falling gently from the top globe to the bottom. "I suppose we've time for a quick trip, since we'll pass it on my way home."

"Thank you, thank you, thank you," I gasped. "We owe you."

"No problem, dearie, now let me just climb out…"

She clambered onto the shore, inexplicably clothed. Did she magically re-dress after swimming, or was her clothing waterproof?

We started off through the passage, following the River Styx as it wound through the cavern. As the ceiling lowered, the stalactites gave way to frost-like crystalline structures. Everything glowed with that same ethereal blue light.

"Where does the light come from?" I asked.

"Oh, Hades added it a long time ago, with magic. He got too many complaints from arrivals that the River was hard to see. That's what made him think of adding a tour guide to the Underworld, actually. I've only been doing this for a bit, but most tour guides stay on for quite a while. It's good work, and you get to know so many people."

The cushion next to me shifted, and I glanced over.

Tabitha had crept over. She smiled sheepishly.

I nudged her and then turned back to the screen. "How long have you been in the Underworld?"

"Goodness, I don't know. Time sort of is and isn't here. I'd guess somewhere around twenty years on the mortal plane? Maybe twenty-five?"

"I see." I wondered how she'd died, but it seemed rude to ask. "And you're…happy here?"

"Yes, I have everything I could ask for. An adorable flat, friends, all the food and drink I could ever want. And I never gain any weight." She laughed, a bell-like sound. "As I said, it does get a bit lonely at times living the single life, but I just need to get out there more."

The concept of afterlife dating had never occurred to me, but I supposed it made sense—all these souls apparently occupied physical forms, and you wouldn't stop being human just because you were dead. Hopefully Megan had a place to herself. Had she made friends? What did she do all day? Did she ever think of me?

"Anyway, we're coming to one of the exits now, but you can see the intake area for new souls over that way."

She swiveled around so we could see through her viewpoint.

Off to the left, the passage opened up into another cavern. Neon signs ran the perimeter of the cavern, labeled *First Name A through C, First Name D through F*, etc. Dozens of people lined up behind them, waiting to be called forward to a row of desks.

At each desk stood a centaur. The centaur closest to us stared at his computer screen, a glaze of boredom on his face. "Next."

I shuddered at the thought of waiting in a line to be processed when I died. Hopefully I'd arrive on a slow day. Had Megan stood in these lines, too?

Susan took us through a short side passageway, up a set of steps, and emerged into the light.

There was no sun, but overhead a flock of clouds reflected pink-and-gold light.

We took a path through a field and into a forest, and a short while later, we emerged into the clearing where the library sat.

Inside the dome, the magical blue light danced across the floor.

Susan strolled over to the circulation desk, where the same fish-tailed woman sat, glaring as she stamped the inside of a book.

She rolled her eyes and slid over the marble tablet and pen.

Susan's gaze swung around, facing away from the desk. "Dears, I forgot to ask what to write? What are you looking for?"

"Same thing as last time," I said. "*Alpha lyrae.*"

"But that book was locked."

"It's okay. We just need to see the cover."

"Well, all right then." She turned toward the librarian again.

"Who are you talking to?" The woman's glare burned like a laser.

"No one, Elora, just myself. Trying to remember my guest list for a party I'm having in a couple of days, you know how it is." Susan scrawled on the tablet.

Elora narrowed her eyes, flipped the tablet around, and snapped her fingers. As before, a gold coin appeared in her hand. She passed it over.

Susan took the coin without comment and approached the nearest slot machine.

I spotted only one other person out of the corner of Susan's eyes; the library was nearly empty right now.

Susan slid the coin into its slot, tugged the lever, and the bookcase spiraled around.

Finally, the shelf ground to a stop, and the Book of Ares tipped itself off the shelf into Susan's waiting hands. "What should I do now?" she whispered.

"Just look at the cover. Keep staring." I nodded at Lenti. "Go ahead."

"The thoughts of your mind become visible to your eyes." A purple flame burst into life over each of her ears. "So shall it be."

Tabitha's soft voice joined hers.

Something thumped in the kitchen.

"What are you doing up there? Is that a spell? Ooh,

how exciting, what's just happened?"

"I'll explain later," I said. "We have to go, but thank you so, so much."

The three of us leaped up and ran into the kitchen.

Where was the book? It was at least the size of a dictionary. Where could it be? I yanked open a cupboard and bent to check. "Nothing."

"It must be here somewhere. Maybe the spell dropped it in the fridge?" Tabitha opened the door to check. "Nope."

"It's here," said Lenti. She sat on the small kitchen island, staring down at a small object.

I hurried over to examine it, and my heart sank.

There on the island sat a miniature copy of the Book of Ares. It was no more than three inches high and maybe a couple of inches wide. Every detail was replicated in miniature, even the embroidered bones and skulls.

"What happened?" I picked up the tiny book. "Even if I can get this open, I'm going to need a magnifying glass to read it."

Tabitha shut the fridge door and came over to examine the book. "The mirror spell reproduces the object in proportion to how it appears to the spell caster. When we copied the City Elysium Group case file, I was the one who envisioned it, and I know what size case files are. But I suppose to a small cat, looking through a computer screen, the book would've appeared…small." She scratched Lenti's chin. "It's okay, sweetie, you did a good job."

"Of course I did. You're welcome, Rowan." Lenti shoved her head into Tabitha's hand, demanding further pets.

I stared at the miniscule tome. "Do you think

possession of a book this size would be considered a small crime?" Hysterical giggles frothed from my lips, and I collapsed against the kitchen island.

Tabitha and Lenti stared at me.

When I'd regained control of myself, Tabitha said, "How are you going to get it open?"

"Yeah, that's the part of this plan that—wait." I stared at her and Lenti. "What if the *alpha lyrae* is the key? Remember Susan said it required a spoken key?" Holding the book in one palm, I fixed my gaze on the tiny gold letters in the title. With my other hand I touched the crystal at my chest. Couldn't hurt to have a little extra power. Directing all my will at the book, I said, "*Alpha lyrae.*"

The cover lifted a couple millimeters, and then clapped shut.

"Maybe you have to say it a few times." Tabitha patted my shoulder. "Try again."

I nodded. "*Alpha—*"

"That's not why it moved." Lenti stretched her front legs out and sank down, her butt rising into the air, in a cat version of downward dog.

I frowned. "What do you mean?"

"You're a telekinetic." She yawned. "You were using your magic."

"Of course," murmured Tabitha.

I clapped a hand to my forehead. I'd been so rattled by my fight with Alex, I hadn't even considered that telekinesis might work on a locked book. I widened my stance.

"Wait." Tabitha placed a hand on my back. "Lenti, get on Rowan's shoulder. We should be able to pour a little bit of energy into you while you cast. Kind of like extra batteries. It might help."

"Couldn't hurt."

Lenti leaped into position, and I placed one hand on the crystal again so I could feel its warmth and stay connected to my power. I concentrated again, taking my time, allowing the energy to flow through me. My eyes grew wide as heat jolted down my spine and shoulder, emanating from Tabitha and Lenti. Extra batteries, indeed. I imagined the book opening, sending all my will into the cover.

It lifted a couple millimeters.

Open, I told it.

The gap between cover and pages widened. Beneath my fingers, the crystal burned.

Open. Open. Open.

The cover wobbled, then fell open.

Tabitha, Lenti, and I cheered.

I leaned down, squinting at the inscription on the first page.

In the lower right corner sat an illustration of a bird. It wriggled and loosened itself from the page, fluttering into the kitchen.

I shrieked.

Lenti leaped off my shoulder and darted after it, chattering a sort of agitated "eck, eck, eck."

"Oh. Good," I said. "There'd better not be any plague rats in this thing." I placed the book on the counter and went to dig through my storage closet for a magnifying glass.

****

I didn't own a magnifying glass, but Tabitha had one from a few Halloweens ago when she'd dressed up as a famous detective. I spent the rest of the weekend ruining my eyesight by squinting through the magnifying glass at the Book of Ares. It didn't help that the book was written in Early Modern English, and many of the S's looked like the letter F, which slowed my comprehension. By Monday, I was only a handful of pages in, and so far, there was no sign of the phrase *alpha lyrae*.

I'd encountered no more living illustrations—so far—but the miniature bird was still loose in the apartment. It had taken up residence on the string of white lights I'd tacked over the front window and started building a nest from stray pieces of Lenti's fur.

Lenti had already nearly taken out the lights trying to teleport to the nest, and I'd had to bribe her with cheese so she wouldn't murder the little creature.

I didn't dare take the book to work, but it seemed dangerous to leave it alone in the apartment. After some discussion, Lenti and I agreed she would stay home and guard it. At lunch, I'd drive home to check on her. If something went horribly wrong, she could teleport to the office and track me down.

She was surprisingly calm about the whole thing, but fear hollowed my stomach as I triple-checked the lock on my door. What if something happened to her? What if the book sprang to life and attacked her while I was gone?

Now who had abandonment issues?

The sixth floor felt strange today. Alex was physically present, but a massive invisible wall separated us now. I couldn't help myself; I sneaked past his office, hoping for a glimpse, at least to see if he was okay. As I neared, though, my heart dropped.

His office was empty, the lights off.

Maybe he just wasn't in yet. Or maybe he had a meeting this morning.

Blowing out a breath, I continued. My route took me right past the tech-support cubicles, and I pretended to be busy scrolling through my phone. I wasn't in the mood for Dave right then.

"Good morning, sunshine," he called.

I glanced at him and hurried on. Behind me, a chair squeaked, and then rapid footsteps pounded toward me. Oh, gods. I didn't need this.

"Hey." Dave caught up to me in moments.

Sadly, one of the advantages of vampirism was speed.

"What's wrong?"

"I'm fine." I continued toward the break room, desperate for a cup of coffee, but he kept pace with me. "Just tired."

"Are you sure? We're friends. You can talk to me if something's wrong."

I held back a snort. We most certainly were not friends, but there was no point in correcting Dave's delusions right now. I remained silent as he trailed me into the break room, chatting about another concert he'd been to, as if we were the best of buds.

I slid a mug into the coffee maker, then tapped the button for French roast. A stream of java shot into the cup. "Hey, you haven't seen Alex, have you?"

"Not yet, why?"

I shrugged. "Just curious. He's usually in by now."

"It's only eight-thirty, give the guy a break. He's probably getting fancy real coffee somewhere, not like this crap they serve us. Did you know these beans are overroasted? You can taste how acidic they are."

Goddess save me, was he really going to hold forth on coffee quality at this hour? I gritted my teeth and willed my beverage to finish. The second the last drop hit the mug, I snatched it away and hurried out of the break room.

"Come on, what's wrong?" Dave strode next to me, clinging like a barnacle. "You're in a weird mood. I'm worried about you."

"I'm fine," I snapped. "If you see Alex, will you let me know?"

"Oh, holy shit." He grabbed my arm, spinning me toward him.

Coffee sloshed from my mug onto the carpet and dripped onto my shirt. "Dude—"

"You and Kouris." His pale blue eyes were wide. "Something's going on with you two, isn't it?"

"Shut up." I glanced down the hall. We stood only a few feet from other offices, and anyone could overhear us.

"You're not even denying it!"

As I stalked away, he followed. "What happened? Did you have a fight? Is he married?"

I spun around. "Dave?"

"Yeah?"

"Mind. Your own. Damn. Business."

A sly grin spread his lips, and his fangs slipped out. "Whoa. Sassy this morning, are we? Must've been a bad one. Or the sex was really good."

"Go to hell, Dave." I almost threw my remaining coffee at him, but I needed it too much. I whirled around and stomped toward my office.

This time he didn't follow.

I slammed my door shut, chest heaving. The crystal

was cool and comatose on its chain, tucked under my shirt. Too bad, because I'd love to telekinetically hurl Dave's monitor to the floor. If this is what I had to deal with today at work, maybe I should tell everyone I was sick and just go home. I'd much rather stare at tiny script in a deadly grimoire than endure any more of Dave's smug nosiness.

Or sit here moping over Alex.

"Get it together, girl," I mumbled. This was exactly what I hadn't wanted to happen—to fall under the thrall of some guy, then to spin out of orbit if the relationship didn't work out, sitting around mourning until I was physically sick. So, if I didn't want that to happen? It didn't have to. Things might be shit between Alex and me, they might even be irreparably broken, but I still had a job here at the Firm. I could either swoon or get to work.

I drained my coffee in a few gulps—Dave was right, it did taste a little bitter—and logged into my computer. Every few minutes I choked back a wave of stomach-wrenching anxiety. Alex was fine. Lenti was fine too, probably sitting on the back of the couch watching the tiny bird.

I finally lost myself in the easy rhythm of taking screenshots and pasting them into documentation. An hour or so later, someone knocked on my door.

Alex.

I motioned for him to come in. He slipped inside, shutting the door quietly behind him. A cautious distance veiled his expression.

"Hi." I picked at a hangnail. "Um, how…how are you?"

"All right. I've got another presentation to the

partnership in a few minutes."

That explained the full suit. It was light gray, the same one he'd worn his first day on the job, and he looked achingly good in it, his light-brown skin glowing. His face still carried a slight flush, his curls a hint of dampness from his morning workout and shower. The memory of his body against mine flooded back, and my chest stung.

"Dave said you needed to talk to me."

Fricking Dave. "Oh. Not exactly, I mean—you just weren't in your office when I got in, and I asked if he'd seen you, that's all. It wasn't, um…" I shrugged. I was doing this all wrong. "But I do want to apologize for Saturday. I wasn't trying to…anyway, I'm sorry, Alex, I'm so sorry."

His expression iced over. "I can't talk about this right now, If you don't need anything work-related, then I have to get ready for my meeting."

"Right. Of course. We'll…we'll talk later." Would we, though? The wall between us was a mile high.

"Okay." He cleared his throat and turned to go.

There was a sudden high-pitched yowl, and Lenti sprang past him. "Watch it, buddy, you almost stepped on my tail. Rowan!" She leaped into my arms. "You have to come home right now. We have a huge problem."

Oh, no. Something to do with the Book of Ares. "Uh…Can I work from home the rest of the day?"

"I suppose." He eyed us warily. "My meeting's over about nine-thirty. Call me, I guess, if you need something."

He sidled out the door.

I packed up my stuff as fast as I could, and Lenti and I ran for my car.

Chapter Nineteen

When we entered my apartment, I almost fell over.

Plopped onto my living room floor, chewing on one of my fancy gold sandals with two of her three heads, was Cerberella. She hopped up, yipped several times, and raced over. Her tail wagged frantically.

"How did you get here?" With a sigh, I knelt to pet her middle head. I glanced at the sandal and cringed.

Lenti hopped onto the coffee table and began giving herself a bath.

Only then did I register her reaction.

She wasn't hiding, screaming, or running away.

"I thought you were scared of dogs."

Lenti stretched. "I was. When I first saw her, I thought she'd come for my soul. I prepared for battle. I cursed her in every language I know, and *nothing happened*. She just sat there, drooling." She glanced up. "It turns out she doesn't speak English, feline, Stygian, tropospheric, or even basic demonic. She's just an *animal.*"

I pursed my lips. "Yes, well, that's what dogs are."

Cerberella rolled onto her back, all of her tongues hanging out.

"Not a very smart animal, either. She did that." With one paw, she indicated a yellow puddle on the hardwood.

"Delightful." I stood and checked the front door, then the sliding glass door that led to the balcony. Both

285

were closed. "How did she get in here, anyway?"

"I have no idea. She just appeared out of nowhere."

What in the world? Could Susan have sent her? But no, that didn't make sense. "Did anything happen with the Book of Ares? Any more birds? Anything?"

"No. Until this bundle of bones appeared, I was guarding the book as you instructed. It's right here." She nodded at the little book, which sat next to a stack of coasters on the coffee table.

I picked it up and slid out the bookmark that I'd used to mark my place. With the magnifying glass, I inspected the page I'd left off at—*An Incantation for Crossing Borders*. The words of the spell were so tightly packed onto the page I could barely read them even with the magnifying glass. One line caught my attention, though—*Then call forth Queen Mab, and let her tangle the worlds into a knot so vexing it cannot be untied.*

Tangled worlds? That might explain Cerberella's presence in my living room. *Some of the spells are too dangerous to even mention,* Noel had said. Was the Book of Ares that powerful? Could a spell be enacted simply by reading it?

I tried not to panic while I picked up the wreckage of my sandal and cleaned up the mess on the floor. At least this wasn't a plague rat or a bunch of bats or something. I could deal with a small, friendly hellhound. I'd just use Wake to let Susan know what had happened, and she could help me find a way to get Cerberella home. Simple.

"Stop!" Lenti hissed. "Hey! Cut it out!"

I whipped around, the cleaning spray still in my hand.

Cerberella snapped at the air near the couch. Her

middle head snapped merrily at a small, jagged opening in the air.

It was about three inches off the ground and an inch wide, completely dark, almost like a section of dead pixels on a computer screen.

I walked around behind it, and it disappeared. As I came back around to the front, it re-emerged, a dark amorphous blob in my apartment.

She gnawed away.

The hole widened.

Lenti hopped from the coffee table and charged Cerberella, herding her away from the hole.

The dog wagged her whole behind, apparently thinking this was a new game.

I bent and placed my ear to the opening. Cold air brushed my cheek, and there was a faint howling noise, like wind.

Don't panic, don't panic. A three-headed dog had just eaten a hole into the fabric of space-time, no big deal.

I examined the broken strap and pockmarked sole of my sandal, sighed, and fetched the other one from the hall closet. I passed it over to Cerberella.

She plopped down and gnawed happily away.

I pointed at Lenti. "Watch her. Don't let her make the hole any bigger."

"Listen, you evil little imp." Lenti sat down directly across from Cerberella and stared her down. "If you so much as twitch, I will claw your face to shreds. Got it?"

The dog tipped one of her heads up and panted. The other two heads kept eating my sandal.

"See? You can say anything to her. She doesn't understand." Lenti sounded way too thrilled by this fact.

"Be nice." I grabbed my phone and sent two urgent

text messages in all caps. It was time to call in reinforcements.

****

"Oh, dear." Tabitha stared at the opening. She beamed a flashlight into it, frowned, then shook her head. "I can't see anything."

Both Tabitha and Alex had shot over to my place in record time. Tabitha had arrived first, with Alex on her heels. Lenti and I briefed them on what had happened as best we could, and now all of us were gathered around the air-gash, with the exception of Cerberella, who'd made a solid dent in the sole of my sandal and was now working on disassembling the foot strap.

Alex crouched on the floor.

I allowed myself one second of indulgence to check out his ass in those pants.

He stared through the opening with one eye, then the other. He sniffed it a few times, coughed, and passed his hand across it. He stood up. "Nothing definite. Could lead anywhere."

"What do you mean?" I squinted at the opening. "I thought it was just a void of some sort."

"Hellhounds' teeth have magical properties. She's opened a portal. We just don't know into what world. And if it gets bigger, something could get through, something you don't want loose in this world." Alex pinched the bridge of his nose and shut his eyes. "I can patch it, but I'll need to do a ritual to close it completely, and that'll take time. Whatever you do, don't let her chew on it again. And for gods' sake get her a dog bone." He nodded at Cerberella. "Someone hold her, please. Give me a little room here."

Tabitha scooped the dog into her arms, and all three

heads whined and licked her.

Lenti hopped onto my shoulder, and we stepped back.

Alex passed his hands across the tiny opening, speaking in the guttural tone of some foreign language, perhaps Stygian. Chills streamed down the back of my neck.

A clear film slid across the hole, like taut plastic wrap. Alex blew on it a few times, inspected it from all sides, and stood. "It'll hold."

"What did you do that for?" Lenti hopped to the floor and went to inspect the patch. "Open it wider and shove the dog through."

"No, we need to get her back to Susan." I touched Alex's arm, then remembered I wasn't supposed to be doing things like that anymore. "You can get to the Underworld, right? Can you take her home?"

"It depends. The next new moon is tomorrow, but Melanie and I are meeting to do her ritual. If we get done early, I can open a portal, but…"

"Right." My voice rasped.

He crossed his arms. "I assume you agree that breaking my contract with Hades is slightly more important than getting rid of a Pomeranian."

"Obviously," I snapped. "But the next new moon won't be for a month. What am I supposed to do with a hellhound for a month? Tabs, can you take her?"

"I wish." Her face fell. "Paul's allergic to dogs as well as cats."

I threw a pleading look at Alex. "Can I at least work from home? Or do you want me to haul this thing to the office? Because I can't leave her here all day."

"No, I agree she needs to be supervised." He rubbed

his eyes. "I suppose you'll have to work remotely for the time being."

"Can I stay here with Ro?" Tabitha's eyes sparkled. "Are you making remote work an official policy?"

"It's on my list." Alex gave her a wry half-smile. "Let me get past severing my contract with the god of the Underworld first, okay?"

I pursed my lips. The idea of him spending any time with Melanie filled me with agony. She would be his personal hero, getting him out of his contract. I could already imagine a scene in which Alex threw his arms around Melanie in utter gratitude, and she planted a huge kiss on him. The image of Melanie in his bed flashed through my mind again. Now that I knew what Alex could do to a woman in bed, the thought of him having sex with Melanie made me want to hurl. Would he call her darling, too? Would they get back together?

"I have to get back to the office." Alex waved his hand in the general direction of the supernatural hazard zone that was now my apartment. "Tabitha, if you want to work from home the rest of the day too, go for it. I…really don't care. Call me if you need me." He started for the door.

Tabitha crouched next to Cerberella. "I'll stay with her so she doesn't run out the door." She raised her eyebrows at me.

Right. This was my chance to talk to Alex. As I followed him to the door, Lenti whined, "We're *keeping* it?"

In the hallway, I shut the door and leaned against it, as if it could give me strength to face Alex. "Thank you for coming. I appreciate it."

"Sure." His jaw tightened as he adjusted one of his

sleeves.

"You're still mad at me."

He heaved a sigh. "I'm astounded you would mess with something like the Book of Ares after Noel told you it was illegal. You have no idea how deadly this book is."

"Then why does Melanie need it to break your contract?"

He threw his hands up. "Because it's virtually the only book with spells strong enough to nullify blood magic! A contract signed in blood has real power, it's not just a piece of paper with a bunch of legalese. It's either this or the arbitration, and you know how I feel about that. It's a last resort. I don't understand what you're trying to accomplish here."

"Something doesn't feel right." I slid my hand into his. He didn't grasp my fingers, but he allowed me to hold onto him, at least. "Whatever Melanie's doing, it's dangerous. What if there are consequences you didn't foresee?"

"There won't be. We know what we're doing, Rowan. You don't understand Stygian magic, and I don't expect you to, but try to have a little faith."

"Faith?" I barked a laugh. "You won't even listen to me when I tell you that all my instincts are screaming that something is wrong. You won't believe me when I say I didn't mean to hurt you, that I was only trying to protect myself."

"I do believe you, Ro." His voice dropped low, cracking with emotion or exhaustion or both. "I just don't know if we would work, long-term."

The wound on my heart, which had just begun to scab over, broke open again. I tugged my hand away, walked inside, and slammed the door.

****

Tabitha, bless her, called Paul and told him she was staying at my place for a couple days due to a "witchy emergency." She didn't have any classes to teach, so the two of us set up shop at my small dining room table with our laptops. In between checking our work emails, we distracted Cerberella with toys and playing fetch, hoping to keep her from eating more holes in my apartment.

She kept licking the patch, but to Alex's credit, the edges held.

The stress of dealing with Cerberella, combined with the excitement of having her favorite aunt Tabitha over for a slumber party, proved too much for Lenti. She insisted on moving her cat bed to the dining room table, and fell asleep there, snoozing much of the day and night.

By early evening the next day, all of us were ragged.

Tabitha and I had taken turns most of the past night and the current day with the eyeball-bleeding task of examining the Book of Ares.

Cerberella had had two more accidents in the kitchen and decimated the smaller dog toys I'd picked up from the pet store.

I'd had more caffeine than could possibly be FDA recommended, and Tabitha and I had consumed nothing but fast-food tacos, including for breakfast.

The miniscule bird, meanwhile, had finished its nest and was now cheeping happily from above the front window, which drove Lenti out of her mind.

"We don't kill our bird friends," I yelled at Lenti for the fiftieth time as she yet again attempted a teleportation to the string of lights.

This time she dragged several feet of cord down as

she dropped to the floor. She let out a yowl. "I just want to get closer to it."

"Cerberella!" snapped Tabitha. "Stop that! Damn it, she's doing it again!" She dashed over to the dog and hauled her away from the couch.

The filmy edges of Alex's patch curled away from the ragged hole. Wind whistled through, accompanied by an eerie high-pitched howl.

Tabitha hefted Cerberella into her arms and sighed as two of the heads began licking her arms. "Have you heard from Alex today? How long is it going to take him to do this ritual?"

"I don't know." I cleared my throat. "I'll, uh, I'll follow up." I'd pinged him this morning on Muse, and he was clearly online, but he wasn't answering.

Cradling Cerberella, Tabitha sat down and shook her head at my personal laptop. We'd tried using Wake several times to contact Susan, but we kept getting a blank screen. "I don't know why this isn't working." She pounded several keys.

Drip. Drip. Drip. I flinched and hurried to the kitchen sink, but just like the last time I'd checked, the tap was off. The faucet was leaking for no reason.

I blamed the Book of Ares. The sooner I could find the *alpha lyrae* and then destroy the book, the better.

I scooped out a fresh can of cat food for Lenti. After watching to make sure she was eating, and not chasing the bird, I settled back down at the table. I searched the number for Olympus, Inc. and dialed.

"Thank you for calling Olympus, Inc. Healers and healers' assistants should press One now. To speak to a member of our customer service team, press Two. For spell repair, press Three. For a *deus ex machina*, press

Four. For all other inquiries, press Zero."

"What are you doing?" Tabitha yawned and leaned back in her chair.

I punched Four. "Getting desperate."

"Thank you for calling our *deus ex machina* department," said a different pre-recorded voice. "Please leave your message at the beep, including details of your request and your contact information, and we will get back to you as soon as possible."

Of course.

A long beep blared. I rolled my eyes. "Yeah, hi, this is Rowan Baird. I'm trying to find out about something called *alpha lyrae*. It has something to do with the Book of Ares, and Melanie Harper is using it to try and help my, uh, friend Alex Kouris out of his reaping contract. I can't find any information about this *alpha lyrae* thing, and it would really help if you guys could call me back instead of making me talk to robot voices all the time." I added my number and hung up.

"Do you think they'll call you back?" said Tabitha.

"Probably not." I picked up the magnifying glass and flipped to a new page in the Book of Ares.

My mouth dropped open. I put my nose two inches from the page and read it again. "You guys, I found it."

Tabitha gasped. "What? Let me see." She dragged her chair next to mine and leaned close.

One of Cerberella's heads licked my hand.

Lenti teleported over to the table and peered down at the book.

The Alpha Lyrae, the page was titled. *To Open a Passage Between Worlds.*

We read through the spell together. At first, I was afraid to summarize it for Lenti in case it activated the apocalypse. As I studied the incantation, though, it became clear that this was a blood-magic spell that would only work if you murdered some people. The spell called for a series of symbols to be drawn on the ground in the "place of opening," and for an object from each of the two worlds to be placed in the center of the circle, along with a golden goblet. You were then supposed to sacrifice three victims, spilling their blood into the goblet and on the ground. This would fix the portal "for all time."

A permanent portal between the Underworld and this one? It sounded like exactly the kind of thing Hades would be after.

And exactly the kind of thing Melanie would help him with.

My hands shook as I set down the magnifying glass. "Melanie's not going to break Alex's contract. She's going to kill him."

"And two other people." Tabitha picked up the glass and peered at the middle of the page again. "It says to fill the goblet with the blood of the deep, blood of the night, and blood of the gray."

"In the realms of the air, we refer to the magic of vampires and werewolves as night magic," said Lenti. "Blood of the night could be either."

"Shit." We worked with plenty of vampires and werewolves, some of whom worked on Melanie's case. She had easy access to victims, although I couldn't imagine how she planned to lure someone as strong as a vampire or werewolf to their death. "So, Alex is either blood of the deep or blood of the gray." Melanie would need a third victim, but she probably had that under control.

Tabitha set down the magnifying glass. "Didn't you say he's meeting with Melanie tonight so she can supposedly help him? Where would they go?"

"I don't know." I grabbed my phone and frantically dialed Alex's number. It rang three times, then switched to voicemail. I texted him to ask where he was. Pacing the kitchen, I checked my phone every few seconds.

"He's not answering." Tears clogged my throat. Panic rose like a riptide, ready to carry me away.

"Okay, take a breath. It's only five o'clock now. You said he works late a lot, right? He might still be at the office." Tabitha hopped up. "Come on. We'll go find him. If he's not at work, we'll try his house."

We grabbed our purses and, since I couldn't leave the Book of Ares by itself in my apartment, I threw it into my purse. We bundled Cerberella into the backseat of Tabitha's car.

Lenti rode on my shoulder, her face tucked against mine.

The soft purrs coming from her throat seemed soothing, but when I petted her, she was shivering.

We got to Ainsley Barfield a little after five-fifteen, and since it was the end of the day, we easily found parking in the garage.

Lenti dematerialized, but Cerberella had no such talents, and we couldn't leave her in the car.

Tabitha found an oversized sweatshirt in the back seat of her car and stuffed Cerberella into the garment. No humans worked in our building, but we didn't need security asking questions about a fluffy hellhound trotting through the lobby.

One of the heads poked out of the hood, while the other two wriggled around in the shoulders.

Fortunately, we didn't see anyone else on our way to the lobby, and from there it was a straight shot to the sixth floor.

Tabitha badged us in, and we rounded the corner toward Alex's office.

It was empty, the lights off, door locked.

"Damn it," I muttered. I sent him another text.

—Melanie's trying to kill you. Get away from her.—

Voices drifted down the hall.

Odd, since most people cut out right at five p.m. We headed toward the source.

Les and Dave were frantically hacking away at their keyboards while Marin spoke on the phone to someone in a low, worried voice.

Tabitha and I traded glances. This didn't look good. I waved to catch Dave's attention. "What's going on?"

Cerberella yipped and strained in the sweatshirt, squirming in Tabitha's arms. A second head poked its nose through the hood.

"Is that a hellhound?" Dave blinked and then shook his head. "Never mind. Noel's missing."

I grabbed Tabitha's hand and squeezed the life out of it. Were we too late?

Les looked up. "Yeah, he disappeared this morning after a break. It was clear and sunny today, so everyone's worried he might have gone outside, maybe gotten sick somewhere. He missed a deposition prep and two client calls." He stared at something on his screen. "We're trying to track his cell phone right now. We've been going through his email, but there's nothing."

"Do you have access to his calendar?" I came around to the other side of the cubicles and peered over Dave's shoulder. "Did he have any meetings scheduled with The City Elysium Group?"

"I can check." Dave squinted at his monitor and clicked his mouse a few times. An electronic calendar popped up. He scanned it, then pointed to a slot. "Uh, yeah, he had a phone call with them this morning at ten. He told Elizabeth he was stepping out shortly after that, maybe ten-thirty? She thought he was just taking a break. But like Les said, he never came back."

I clapped a hand over my mouth. "He's the blood of the night."

"Sorry?" said Dave.

"One of Noel's clients is planning to do a blood ritual to open a permanent portal between this world and the Underworld. She's going to kill Noel and Alex."

Marin, another tech, spun around. "Alex? He just left a few minutes ago."

My heart caught in my throat. "Alone or with someone?"

"With someone. A woman."

"A six-foot-tall redhead?" When Marin nodded, I swore and kicked the side of Dave's cubicle. "He's with her already. Where would they go?"

Lenti rematerialized with a pop. "She needs open space."

Marin, Les, and Dave flinched.

"What the hell, now you have a cat, too?" said Dave.

"I am a familiar, foolish man, a spirit of the air in cat form," said Lenti haughtily. In a more normal tone, she added, "Blood rituals must be conducted on solid ground. She'll go outside."

"The construction site," gasped Tabitha. "The City Elysium Group is planning to break ground soon. Elizabeth told me."

Dave held up a hand. "Who's going to do a blood ritual in the middle of Portland? Too many ordinaries around."

"Not at the construction site." I remembered the notes from the case file, my skin growing cold. "It's magically cloaked. To the outside world, it's a park."

"That would work, then." Dave ran a hand through his floppy hair. "Any idea how long the ritual takes? If it's complicated, that might buy you some time."

"No, but once Melanie has what she needs…" My heart dropped. It wouldn't take her long to slash Noel and Alex's throats. And whoever the third victim was. For all I knew, she had that person already. "Can you guys get everyone who's still here to meet us at the site for The City Elysium Group's condo? The address will be in the case file. It's on the waterfront."

"Elizabeth's still here. I'll call her." Marin clicked on her headset again and murmured, nodding as she wrote something down. "It's 304 South Passerine Street."

I opened my maps app and punched in the address. It wasn't far. "Get everyone you can and meet us there." We couldn't wait for everyone to rally. We had to get there now, before Melanie killed the man I loved.

Unless she'd already done it.

No. I couldn't think that way. Alex was alive. I felt it in my gut.

Tabitha and I ran for the elevator, Lenti on my shoulder, Cerberella racing along and barking. The security guard in the lobby called something after us, but we ignored him and darted into the parking garage elevator.

The distance from the elevator to our parking spot

felt like a hundred miles. Fortunately, our building was only blocks from the east waterfront.

We hopped into the car and Tabitha took Sparrow Street south, then drove west on Garden, seemingly hitting every light on the way. Traffic was heavier than I'd hoped, but we made it to the construction site on Passerine in fewer than ten minutes.

Tabitha pulled into a two-hour parking spot and slammed on the brakes.

We leaped out.

Twin signs for The City Elysium Group and a construction company guarded the site entrance. A chain link fence surrounded the area.

The gate was locked, but with Tabitha and Lenti boosting my power, I broke the lock

We darted through the gate.

As soon as we passed through the perimeter, the air changed. All outside sound switched off, as if we'd entered a recording booth.

In the distance, traffic flowed along the bridges in total silence. A filmy substance clouded the air, and the late evening sun streamed through it, throwing hazy golden light across the excavator and the piles of dirt and gravel.

The cloaking magic.

Cerberella flopped onto the ground and rolled around in the mud.

"So where the hell are they?" My voice broke.

Tabitha squeezed my arm. "They've got to be here. Where else would they go?"

"They're here." Lenti stood alert, her ears flicking different directions. "I can smell them."

I slid my cell out of my purse. What do you do when

you can't find your phone? You have someone call it. I pointed to my phone, catching Tabitha's gaze, and then dialed Alex. She nodded.

We listened.

A faint answering ring sounded to our right.

I crept in the direction of the noise, listening as the ring grew louder. When it went to voicemail, I hung up and redialed.

Tabitha and Lenti followed.

Closer…closer…

"Really?" said Melanie's voice.

The ringing cut out abruptly.

And suddenly, there they were. Melanie, in black athletic gear, held a cell phone with two fingers, disgust curling her lips.

Six men flanked her, three on either side.

Given their wide shoulders and thick necks, they were probably guards.

The group stood next to a large circle inscribed in the mud.

In the center of the circle, Noel and Alex, their arms and legs bound in silver chains, sat back-to-back.

A golden goblet perched at Noel's feet, along with a quill pen and a bright-blue stone.

One goblet. One object from each world. Two victims. They needed one more, which meant it had to be one of us. Shit.

This was definitely a trap.

I didn't care.

"Alex." I dashed toward him.

Melanie lifted a hand, and the next second, I froze in place, limbs locked.

"Sorry, pumpkin." Melanie's smooth voice crawled

over my skin. She glared at Alex. "You keep your ringer on? What's wrong with you?" With a huff, she tossed his phone to the ground. "Thanks for ruining my dramatic reveal."

I flicked my gaze to the side.

Tabitha, Lenti, and Cerberella were all frozen as well. Lenti hissed furiously as she yowled either spells or curses. Maybe both.

I glared at Melanie, anger hot in my blood. "You bitch. Let them go."

"*Oooh, scary.*" She smirked. "Now that you've said that, I'll definitely let them go. Oh wait, I won't, actually. Boys?" She nodded at her companions.

Four of the guards blazed over to us. One of them scooped Lenti into his arms, one picked up Cerberella, and the other two grabbed Tabitha and me.

Tabitha let out a string of Latin, Lenti hissed, and Cerberella barked.

I screamed, the crystal burning against my skin as I channeled my blood-boiling anger into my power. If ever there was a time for telekinesis, this was it. *Come on.* I willed my limbs to activate.

One of my arms twitched.

Well, that would show them.

As the guards carted us over to Melanie, Tabitha, Lenti, and Cerberella slumped in the arms of their captors. Their eyes slid closed.

I gritted my teeth. It was all I could do since I couldn't punch Melanie in the face. "What did you do to them?"

"Relax." She rolled her eyes. "They're just sleeping. Hades will probably have some use for them. He doesn't appreciate when I murder potential employees."

"She's so cute," cooed the guard who held Lenti. "Maybe I could—"

"You're not keeping the cat," snapped Melanie.

"But—"

"Later. Bind her."

The "her" turned out to be me. Before I could blink, two more of the guards had wrapped my arms and legs in silver chains. One of them deposited me in the circle, leaning me next to Alex.

The heaviness in my limbs dissipated, but the chains now immobilized me.

Ah. Me. I was the third victim.

Well, shit.

"Ro." Alex's voice was raspy. His left eye had swollen shut and bruises purpled his cheek. "I'm sorry."

"Don't be." I choked back tears. I couldn't lose it now. Somehow, I had to get us out of this. I struggled to sit upright.

I strained at the chains. The crystal pulsated against my chest, and I threw all my will and energy into the metal. Nothing. Not a snap. Not a crack.

Noel was gray as a corpse, as if he hadn't drunk blood for days. He blinked at me and shook his head. "No use," he mumbled. "The silver."

Oh, right. Silver nullified magic. Mine included.

We were beyond screwed.

Melanie glanced at one of the guards. "Hank, page him again, would you?" Strolling over to us, she smiled cruelly. "Sorry for the delay in your deaths. The god of the Underworld isn't used to being on a schedule."

So, Hades was on his way. My heart sank, but I glared up at her. "Yeah, well, everyone from the Firm knows we're here. They're coming to help, so you might want to—"

"Let you go?" Melanie burst out laughing. She pointed across the construction site. "Are those your reinforcements?"

Several figures stood outside the gate. With a leap of hope, I recognized Dave's floppy hair. But the group wasn't trying to break in or rush toward us. They just stood there, talking.

"I *allowed* you to see the entrance to this place. Everyone else sees it as a park. Including your little co-workers. Nice try, though."

I glared at her. "Am I the blood of the deep or blood of the gray?"

"The gray. Eldritch magic." She pointed at Alex. "His magic is of the deep. And I'm sure you've figured out Noel is supplying the blood of the night."

Noel lifted his head with some effort. "Even if you succeed in opening this portal, you'll have an army of vampires, werewolves, and witches to contend with on this side. Have you thought this through, Melanie?"

"Have I thought this through? Let me see." She tapped a finger on her chin in a mock show of considering his point. "Are you asking me if I think the armies of the Underworld are a suitable match for a motley collection of blood-drinkers, dogs, and humans? Yeah, I think we'll do all right, but I appreciate the concern."

I tipped my head back against Alex's shoulder. "Are you okay? Who hit you? I'll kill them."

"I'm all right." He turned and kissed my cheek with dry, cracked lips. "I'm so sorry. I never wanted you to come after me."

"So I should've just let you die?"

"Better than both of us dying."

My heart wrenched. "I'm not giving up. But in case we don't make it out of this, I love you."

His eyes glinted with tears. "I love you too."

Melanie made retching noises. "Gods, that's disgusting. Alex, really, a witch? She's such a joke."

"He didn't seem to think so when I was in his bed," I snapped.

"Please." She snorted. "You're so far beneath him."

"Careful," said Alex. "You're talking about the woman I love."

She smirked. "Enjoy it while it lasts, then, which is about, oh, thirty more seconds. He's here."

A deep shadow fell across the circle.

Mere feet in front of us, an opening yawned into existence. Wind howled through it and blasted across our faces. The temperature plummeted.

I inhaled on a gasp, and cold air knifed into my lungs. My breath puffed out in tiny clouds.

A beam of blue light pierced the void, illuminating cave walls on either side.

A tall, broad figure strolled out of the opening and into this world. Hades carried a spear with a multifaceted obsidian tip. Leather cuffs encircled both his wrists. Long, curly hair flowed down his back, but unlike in classical drawings of the god, he was clean-shaven. Bare-chested, he wore black leather pants.

Leather pants?

Oh, right. His heavy-metal phase. Apparently, it was back.

He smiled, revealing pointed teeth. Frostbite blackened his lips. His bright-green eyes with their slitted black pupils resembled a crocodile's.

"Well, well." He strolled through the ritual circle. "Welcome home, Alex."

"Go to hell," spat Alex.

Hades threw his head back and laughed. "That's your job. You'll be in Tartarus soon enough." He nodded at Noel. "I believe this cancels our planned arbitration. Sorry." Turning to me, he leaned down and ran the point of his spear beneath my chin and along my jaw. "Rowan. I understand you're one in a million, as witches go. When I first set out to open a portal, I didn't know if I could find anyone with the blood of the gray, but conveniently, my little minion Alex stepped right into your path."

This asshole. Standing here, posturing as a metal artist from the eighties and waving his spear around. And now he had the audacity to stand here and gloat. "Please. You're not going to do that thing, are you?"

He frowned. "What thing?"

"You know, the thing all villains do, where they wax eloquent about their evil plans for five to ten minutes, giving me just enough time to find a rock to bash you over the head with?"

He leaned down and leered at me, his teeth inches from my face, his breath stinking of decay. "No. I'm not."

And then he stood and thrust the spear through my heart.

Chapter Twenty

My soul drifted several feet above my slumped and bloodied body.

Alex screamed, struggling against his chains.

Apparently, I'd just died. *Huh.* I should probably feel something about that, but it elicited about as much emotion as brushing my teeth did. It was just a thing. I was dead now.

I was also bodiless. That did concern me. Susan and all the other souls we'd seen in the Underworld had bodies. How did this work? Would I be reunited with my body soon? Maybe someone had to come clean it up first, since Hades had done significant damage to the torso region. From what I could see, there was a lot of blood. I didn't know it was possible to emit that much blood.

A sudden blast of electric guitars, drums, and piano filled the cavern, the sounds ricocheting off the walls. Fog billowed across the site, and beams of multicolored light chased each other through the fog.

Everyone's heads snapped to look toward the spectacle.

I gathered from the alarm on Hades's face that this wasn't the start of his heavy metal concert.

A deep voice echoed, "And now… Introducing… The one. The only. Eunomia!"

The music swelled, and the applause of an invisible audience erupted.

A bright-yellow construction crane materialized, mounted on a truck.

The fog dissipated, revealing a woman in a safety harness suspended from the top of the crane about fifty feet up. The woman nodded and waved, her long white hair swishing side to side.

The music and applause cut out abruptly.

"Go ahead, George," called the woman.

In the truck cab, a man in a hard hat and neon-yellow vest yanked a lever. Orange safety lights flashed around the truck cab and a piercing *BEEP BEEP BEEP* accompanied it. The crane jerked and began lowering the woman.

There was a gentle whisper in what would have been my ear if I'd still had a body. "You may return."

A sucking sensation grabbed at me, like a vacuum, and then I was lying on the ground in something sticky.

My blood. It was a pool of my own blood. That was fine, no problem. Right?

I rolled over and sat up. The silver chains that had bound Alex and Noel disintegrated to silver dust.

"Welcome back." Noel stood, and then he examined the burn marks on his wrists.

"Goddess curse you!" sputtered Tabitha as she struggled out of the guard's arms.

Cerberella let out a series of yaps.

Alex scrambled toward me, crushing me against his chest. "You're alive. You're really alive."

"Yeah, well, I died first." I tugged my sticky shirt up and ran a hand over my chest and stomach, but there didn't seem to be a gaping spear wound, so that was good. "I'm so sorry, Alex, about everything."

"I'm sorry, too. Gods, I love you." He helped me to

my feet.

I leaned up to kiss him.

Tabitha barreled toward us and bear-hugged us with the force of a semi-truck. "I couldn't stop it. I couldn't do anything." She stepped back, her face going gray. "By the goddess. Your chest!"

"I'm fine." There really was a *lot* of blood on my shirt. I hiccupped and clapped a hand over my mouth. Nope, not going to vomit.

Alex wrapped me in a hug and kissed the top of my head. "What's with the crane?"

The woman was still making slow progress toward the ground, accompanied by the steady warning beep.

Melanie, Hades, and the guards stared motionless at the spectacle.

I shrugged. "I was dead. How should I know?" I glanced around for Lenti but didn't see her. Was she hiding?

The woman made it about halfway to the ground. The crane hitched and froze, and she swung gently on the wires.

The operator yelled something.

"Ro…" Tabitha's voice was faint. "Didn't you call for a *deus ex machina*?"

"Oh, shit." I looked up at Alex. "I called Olympus, Inc. You know, the god hotline?"

He raised his eyebrows. "How did you get through?"

"Really?" Noel brushed off his jacket. "I've tried them a dozen times and I always get stuck in a phone tree."

"I guess someone got my message."

The crane shuddered, and the woman swung back and forth like a pendulum.

There was a thunk. The operator fiddled with the lever, wrenched it back, and threw it forward again.

The crane lowered with speed.

The woman plummeted down, then jerked to a stop a few inches above the ground. She sighed heavily and unhooked herself from the safety harness. Struggling out of it, she dropped unceremoniously onto the dirt. "Thanks, George." She waved at the crane operator, righted herself, and strolled toward us. "Sorry. He's new."

We stared at her.

"I'm Eunomia." She gave a quick bow. "Goddess of law and legislation. You're Rowan, right? And you're Tabitha? I'm the *deus ex machina* you requested."

"That's not possible," spat Hades. "Those hotlines are backed up for weeks. *I've* never even gotten through." His body remained still.

Oh…he, Melanie, and the guards were now frozen in place. *How does it feel?*

"We're under new management." Eunomia smiled. She wore a sleeveless black jumpsuit and carried a thick black book. "Now. Let's see if we can rectify this situation." She snapped open the book and flipped to a page in the middle. "Ah. Okay, I see." She clapped the book shut.

"Wait." Panic hollowed my chest. "Where's Lenti? Is she hiding?"

Eunomia frowned. "I don't know who that is."

"My familiar. Where is she?"

The goddess shook her head. "I only know what's in the request. Your ticket doesn't include details about companions."

Tabitha squeezed my hand. "Ro, I'm so sorry."

My newly revived heart screeched to a standstill. Shaking my head, I backed away. "No, she's just hiding. Do you see a body? She's probably gone invisible."

"Sweetheart." Alex reached for my hand. "When you died, her body just sort of…"

"Faded," said Tabitha.

No. No, no, no. Her life force, bound to mine. When I died, she died.

I doubled over as a sob burst out of my throat. My heart ached in a way I never knew was possible. Lenti, a massive attitude packaged in a tiny body, who had scratched and purred her way into my soul. Lenti, who had finally trusted me. Who had protected me from Alex, from Melanie, from myself. Lenti, Fluffball of Doom.

I couldn't live without her.

"I'm back, bitches!" crowed a chipmunk voice. "What did I miss?"

An enormous black-and-white wildcat stood before us.

It was Lenti, but not. It looked like someone had taken a picture of a bobcat and a picture of Lenti and mashed them together.

I gasped and hurtled toward her. "Lenti?"

"Of course it's me."

Collapsing to my knees, I threw my arms around her neck. "I died. I thought you were dead."

"Air spirits don't *die*." Her tiny voice seemed even more ridiculous in her ferocious new form. "When you died, my animal form disappeared and only my soul remained. When you were revived, I selected a new form. It simply took a few minutes to finalize."

"You're a—what are you now?"

"A bobcat with cooler markings."

I laughed and kissed the top of her head. As I stood, Cerberella bounded toward us, all three heads barking.

"Oh, no, this thing is still here?" Lenti bared her fangs at Cerberella.

The three-headed dog jumped at Lenti's face, tongues wagging, determined to get a lick in.

"Ack. Okay. Argh." Lenti made garbled noises as she backed away from Cerberella's slimy greeting.

Alex pulled me into his arms and kissed me longer than was work-appropriate.

Noel grumbled something, and Melanie made more gagging noises.

I sniffled happily and turned back to Eunomia. "Can you get us out of here?"

"Soon. We have one item to take care of." She snapped her fingers.

A scroll dropped out of thin air onto the ground and unfurled itself.

The writing appeared to be in Greek, which I had never studied in college, but I did recognize Alex's signature at the bottom. It was written in a streaky rust-colored ink. Blood?

"Rowan, could you do the honors, please?" Eunomia pointed at the scroll. "Alex's contract can only be broken by the death of the one who loves him. That's you, I believe."

I smiled up at him. "Yeah, it is."

"She can't love him." Hades, his body unable to move, was doing some kind of face-twitch. "His magic is too powerful to allow that."

Eunomia's dark-brown eyes gleamed. "Normally, yes. But Rowan's psychic magic has allowed her to resist Alex's influence, especially as she's grown stronger.

Love is a funny thing."

"I don't believe this," muttered Melanie.

"Hmm, we'll have to…well, never mind HR." Noel chuckled. "Cancel the arbitration, I suppose."

Eunomia nodded at me. "Just dab a little blood on your finger and then place it over Alex's signature, please."

I swiped my thumb across my T-shirt, coating it in blood. Bending down, I stamped my thumb over Alex's name.

The scroll disappeared in a puff of dust.

Hades, Melanie, and the guards unfroze, groaning as they clutched their heads.

Alex keeled over and vomited. Not the reaction I was expecting after I personally freed him from his contract. I bent and rubbed his back as he dry-heaved. "What's wrong with him?"

"An unfortunate side effect," said Eunomia. "From the disintegrating magical bonds caused by Alex's contract being broken. Everyone in the vicinity who shares the same type of magic, in this case Stygian, is affected. I'm afraid I can't do anything to help him, but he'll be all right in a bit."

"Of course." Noel's face lit up. "I've heard of the phenomenon, of course, but I've never witnessed it. It's known as the Martin-Welsh Effect." His lips parted, pure joy on his face. If he'd had paper and a quill pen, he probably would've started taking notes.

Stumbling forward, Hades grasped at his spear. He hefted it slowly and painfully, as if it weighed a thousand pounds. "The effects of the magic—" He gasped. "—will wear off soon. Leave now, or I'll kill you all. Including you," he snarled at Cerberella.

The dog whined and darted behind my legs.

"You're a lucky bastard," said Melanie to Alex. "Ow." To Hades, she said, "Don't you have anything I can take for this?"

She took his arm, and the two of them stumbled toward the portal into the Underworld. The guards followed, moaning.

Moments later, the opening zipped itself shut, leaving us bathed in waning evening light.

"If there's nothing else I can do for you"—Eunomia looked around at everyone—"I'd suggest you all go home and get some rest."

Home. The word had never sounded so good.

"Wait." I dug into my purse and took out the Book of Ares. "Can you take this with you?"

"Certainly. Oh, this must be a first edition. I've never seen a sprite-sized one before." She tucked it into her pocket. "By the way, in about a week, you'll receive a survey about the service you received today. It would mean a lot if you could answer a few questions."

Of course there was a survey. "No problem." I'd fill out a hundred surveys. Alex was free, Lenti and I had come back from the dead, Tabitha and Noel were alive, and I was in love.

Alex retched again.

Did I have any club soda at home?

Eunomia smiled at us and snapped her fingers. She, her crane, and George disappeared.

Alex took a deep shaky breath, and I helped him up.

Lenti nudged my hand. It was much easier for her to do that from her new bobcat height.

I scratched her huge, fluffy ears.

Cerberella bounded toward us, her three heads

yapping joyously. She flopped over at my feet, panting. One of her heads tilted toward me, while another gazed adoringly at Lenti.

"We're not keeping it," said Lenti.

Tabitha held up her hands. "Paul's allergic."

"The thing is, I have nice hardwoods." Alex shook his head.

I put my hands on my hips and gave them the stink-eye. "So, I'm supposed to keep a hellhound and a bobcat in my apartment?"

"We'll figure it out." Alex nuzzled his nose against my hair. "Let's get out of here."

Epilogue

Tabitha took the barstool next to me and clinked her wineglass against mine. "Cheers to a normal week."

"I'll drink to that anytime." I took a long sip of my wine before setting my glass on the kitchen island.

Alex stood at the sink, washing off the cutting board, and Paul was just putting a large pan of moussaka in the oven.

"Well, almost normal," I added.

"No luck with the portal, then?"

"Not yet." Alex had been trying to close the portal in my apartment for the past week, but it had resisted all of his efforts. He'd re-patched the hole, at least, and I was keeping Cerberella distracted with dog bones, but at some point, the pet store was going to run out. "Noel's coming over this weekend to see what he can do."

Tabitha nodded. "I saw him this morning. He's a lot better."

Noel, it turned out, had been poisoned by a bottle of blood that Melanie had given him as a gift. The poison had weakened his magic as well as his physical strength, and for the past week he'd been out while a healer tended to him.

"Did you see the email from HR? The Firm is now quarantining all client gifts before they go to the attorneys."

"Not surprised." Alex set the cutting board in the

drying rack and turned around, wiping his hands on a dish towel. "They're also beefing up their scanning spells for new clients."

"Gods, I'd hope so." I glanced out the window toward the yard.

Lenti slunk along the ground, eyes wide, stalking something.

Nearby, Cerberella rolled in the grass, her tongues lolling out of each of her heads.

Good thing Alex had done a cloaking spell over his yard. One of his neighbors was an ordinary, and the other was a warlock.

I didn't think either would take kindly to the presence of a bobcat and a three-headed dog.

"She seems pretty happy," I said to Alex, as Cerberella popped up and chased after Lenti. I'd been worried she would miss Susan, but when we contacted Susan through Wake she explained that Cerberella wasn't her dog—she just kept company with the current Underworld tour guide.

Susan offered to take her back, but Cerberella wouldn't let Lenti out of her sight and even slept on her at night.

And as much as Lenti grumbled about Cerberella's excessive licking, I'd caught her using Cerberella's butt as a pillow. So, after much discussion and a lot of groaning on my part, we agreed that Cerberella would stay with me.

Paul set the oven timer and picked up his wineglass. "All set." He walked over to Tabitha and kissed her.

Alex picked up his own glass and slipped his arm around me. "I'd like to propose a toast." He gazed down at me, his dark eyes warm and kind. "You told me once that there must be a loophole in my contract with Hades, and you were right. It was you. So, to you, my love."

We cheered and drank.

Paul whispered something to Tabitha that made her blush.

I stood and folded myself into the comforting circle of Alex's arms. He held me close, and the crystal beat steadily against my chest, matching the rhythm of my heart.

A loud chime sounded from the other room. I slipped out of Alex's arms. "Let me just turn off my ringer."

He kissed my hand. "Come back soon or I'll miss you."

I grinned at him and hurried into the living room. Sliding my phone out of my purse, I silenced the ringer.

A notification filled the top of my screen. I had a new email from Tomás González, the PI that Dr. Marks had referred me to.

Opening the email, I read his short explanation for the attachment, then read it again. My mouth dropped open.

I ran back into the kitchen, phone in hand. "You guys." I thrust the phone at Alex. "That PI just emailed. He—I—"

Alex frowned and zoomed in on the image. "What is this?"

"It's my birth certificate." I braced my hands against the kitchen island. "My real one. The original was forged. And my dad—"

Tabitha and Paul crowded in to read over Alex's shoulder.

Alex stared at me. "Well. I wasn't expecting that."

A word about the author…

Alexa Sullivan writes humorous, contemporary paranormal romance. Inspired by her previous career in IT, she imagines a world where the mundane meets magic, and where vampires and werewolves are lawyers. Oh, and there are cats, too. She lives and works in the beautiful state of Oregon, where she sets all of her stories. When not writing, she can be found hanging out with her husband, walking her cats on a leash, and watching far too much Bravo reality TV.

https://www.alexasullivan.com